Antiques & Avarice

A White Mountains Romantic Mystery

224 319 3251

Jane Firebaugh

Cover designed by Jane Firebaugh
Cover background picture courtesy of
https://www.flickr.com/photos/49024304@N00/4502782
296/in/photolist-7RTWiw-663w6u-8CaXgk-bBUR7T-
iFfitf-ncm3C-bDqBfX-979oyx
       https://www.flickr.com/photos/49024304@N00/
       Used Under:
https://creativecommons.org/licenses/by/2.0/

ISBN-13:
978-1519516077

ISBN-10:
151951607X

DEDICATION

To Michael and Nora.

ACKNOWLEDGMENTS

I would like to thank my Beta Readers for their generous donation of time and energy, and all my friends (offline and online) who encouraged me.

Table of Contents

CHAPTER ONE

Olivia McKenna grimaced as she straightened her back. It seemed as though people always put the smallest items on the bottom shelf, and the farthest to the back, so you had to twist yourself into a pretzel getting to them.

But it was worth the effort this time, she chortled to herself, carefully placing the hand-painted, 24K gold-trimmed antique Japanese sugar shaker into her basket with glee. Not a scratch on it and a perfect maker's mark on the bottom. Maybe it wasn't worth a fortune, but it would make a perfect addition to her small collection and at a ridiculously low price too.

She could hear the faint sound of raised voices from what sounded like a TV in the back somewhere. It made a comfortable backdrop for her thoughts as she meandered slowly down the crowded aisles.

There were a few things on her clients' wish lists she was hoping she might find in this cluttered little shop since it was in a charmingly remote rural area, mostly surrounded by old farm houses. Visions of butter churns had been dancing in her head during most of the drive out there. She had one client who would pay top dollar for a decent antique glass Dazey butter churn, enough to cover her mortgage for the month and her sugar shaker, and would even allow her to buy quite a few more antique chandelier crystals, if she were lucky enough to find some. "Please let there be just one really nice old Dazey churn here," she whispered, as she continued down the crowded, dusty aisle.

She heard quick moving footsteps, an odd shriek then the faint tinkling of the bells on the front door of the store, and she started searching the shelves a little more hurriedly, now that it seemed she wasn't the only customer anymore.

She had been happy not to see anyone else in the shop, as it always gave her more pleasure to examine and touch all of the beautiful, old items without distractions. Well, now she had just better get on with looking for what was on her list; no more touching everything she passed.

On the center shelf, to her right she spotted an old cast iron mechanical piggy bank depicting a cute little pig in a high chair. She took a penny from her purse, placed it on the tiny tray and pushed the lever. The pig grabbed the penny, tossed it into his grinning mouth and swallowed it. Olivia beamed, as she placed the bank into her basket. *That's one off the list, and a fairly lucrative one at that.* The other plus was she could keep it for a few days to enjoy before delivering it to her client, who was also a friend.

She glanced around as she started to consult her list again. It was odd that she hadn't seen or heard anyone else in the shop since she'd come in, except for hearing whoever came in a few minutes ago; she still hadn't seen them and it wasn't a large shop. *Well, at least I don't have to worry about fighting over the items I want to buy,* she thought, dismissing the little niggle of concern.

Olivia slowly made her way through the rest of the aisles, picking up a couple of small things for people on her list, but not finding any more of the pricier items. She found a few little things for herself that she couldn't resist, though where she was going to put them, she had no idea. Finally she placed her basket on the counter and opened her purse.

"Hello?" she called, as she pulled money out of her wallet. "I'm ready to checkout."

The store was completely silent.

"Is anyone here? Hello!" she called louder, looking around in mild annoyance.

It had been lovely being alone while she searched through the gorgeous old things in the shop, but not nearly as nice to be kept waiting once she was ready to leave.

"Well, I don't have all day, and I really do want these things, so I will just leave the money here on the counter for you under this large bowl," she said half to herself, checking the price tags on the items she'd chosen, and placing the appropriate amount of money under the bowl. "It's a good thing New Hampshire doesn't have sales tax," she murmured.

As she turned to go, she was struck with the realization that the bells she'd heard earlier might have been the owner leaving, not knowing that she was inside. *Was she now locked in?* "Oh please, give me a break!" she muttered in consternation, hurrying to the front door.

The knob turned easily and she stepped outside in relief. She quickly opened the passenger side door to her Suburban and placed her finds on the floor, carefully wrapping the sugar shaker in one of the old towels she kept aboard for that purpose.

As she started to walk around the vehicle, she heard a rustle and a long-haired calico cat jumped up onto the hood of the SUV with a thump and meowed loudly. The fur on her tail was bristled up like she was upset. Olivia was owned by a dog, but she was a sucker for animals of all types.

"Hi gorgeous, do you live here?" she asked, stroking the long fur after letting the cat sniff her hand. "You're a beauty, aren't you?"

The cat purred and rubbed against her chin, settling down quickly.

"Oh my, look at your gorgeous sparkly collar; it's almost as stunning as your eyes," she cooed scratching behind the cat's ears.

"Okay, I have to get going sweetie," she said after a moment, taking the cat and placing her up onto the porch of the shop. "Hopefully your people will come and take care of you soon."

Olivia walked back and climbed into the suburban, but before she could start the engine, the cat jumped back onto the hood again. She stared at Olivia through the windshield, blinking her pretty amber colored eyes.

"Oh boy," Olivia laughed, getting out of the car, "You sure are a very persistent little girl. What am I going to do with you?" She picked up the fluffy little cat and climbed the porch steps again. She hesitated for a moment, trying to decide whether to go back inside the shop to see if the owner was somewhere in the back, but the cat meowed plaintively, so she made up her mind and opened the door.

The cat shot from her arms and ran toward the back of the store, meowing loudly. Olivia rushed after the cat, narrowly avoiding a pair of old skis that were leaning a bit too close to the aisle.

"Kitty," she called, "come back here, little one. Oh man! I hope you do live here, or the owner is going to kill me for letting you in." she muttered apprehensively, pushing a strand of dark auburn hair out of her face.

The cat was silent now, and had disappeared somewhere in the back room behind the counter.

"Hello!" Olivia tried again to get someone to answer. "Kitty, kitty, kitty!" Feeling a bit desperate now, she reflexively looked over her shoulder to see if anyone was watching, then tiptoed around the counter and into the room behind it.

"Kitty, you are going to get me into so much trouble," she whispered, creeping farther into the dimly lit room.

As her eyes gradually adjusted to the gloom, she froze in horror at sight of a large pool of blood, spreading out from the head of the old man who lay sprawled on the wooden floor in front of her.

A slight movement from beside the old man broke the spell and she screamed, startling the cat who she quickly realized she'd seen sniffing the man's arm. She knelt to check his pulse, but was not able to feel anything from the veins in his neck or wrists.

Olivia grabbed her cell phone from her purse and called 911, explaining the situation as best she could, then picked up the cat and sat shakily in a chair near the old man's body, stroking the cat, not sure if she was trying to comfort the cat or herself.

~~~

It seemed like a very long time before she heard the sirens from the ambulance and state police car, as they

ANTIQUES & AVARICE

screeched to a stop outside, but was in reality only a few minutes.

She hurried to open the door, still carrying the cat in her arms.

"Where is the patient?" a young paramedic asked as he rushed up the steps carrying his medical kit.

"He's in the back room," Olivia responded quickly, leading the way. "I found him lying there, and I couldn't feel a pulse," her eyes were moist, as she remembered the stillness in his neck and wrists. "He must have fallen and hit his head. I'm pretty sure he is dead."

A State Trooper hurried in on the heels of the paramedic, and a second paramedic gently pushed Olivia aside to make way for the stretcher he was bringing into the room. As she stepped back out of the way, a young and rather excited looking police officer took her arm.

"Ma'am, My name is Trooper Fallon. I'm going to need to ask you a few questions," he said leading her into the main part of the shop away from the back rooms. He found an antique high-backed chair and gestured politely for her to sit.

"First, I'll need to see some ID and get your name and address for the record please," he said, pulling out a small notebook and pen.

"Olivia McKenna, 44 East Watchtower Road, Birchwood, New Hampshire 03738," Olivia said quietly, showing him her Driver License. The cat mewed softly, and she resumed rubbing between her ears.

"Ms. McKenna, how did you happen to be here today? Do you know the shop owner, uh, Mr. Lewis Ketterer personally?" the officer consulted his notes for the owner's name.

"No, I just came to see what kind of stuff the shop had. I love old things, and when I heard about this place, it sounded interesting," she looked up as the other police officer walked over and motioned to his partner to follow him into the back room.

"I'll be right back ma'am, please wait out here and we'll continue in a moment," he said as he got up.

Olivia agreed to do so, wondering if the elderly man was really dead or if she'd possibly just been too freaked out to feel a very weak pulse. "Poor kitty," she murmured, "I hope your dad is okay after all." The cat kneaded her lap and purred.

Slamming car doors and the tinkling of the bells on the front door announced the arrival of two detectives, the Medical Examiner, and one of his assistants. Peering out the window at the coroner's van, Olivia's heart sank. She had really started hoping that she'd been wrong and that the guy was alive after all. *Hopefully he had some family that would take care of the cat.*

Abandoned by the state trooper for a while, Olivia wandered around the shop again, her gaze shifting aimlessly between a huge jar of old marbles on the counter, a fairly decrepit pair of wooden snowshoes hanging on the wall and finally landing on a pair of antique sheep shears that were lying directly under the snowshoes atop a pile of similarly old, rusted tools.

The sheep shears stood out because of the slick, wet look to the seven inch long blades, and because when she'd looked at the pile of tools earlier, the shears hadn't been there. Olivia stepped closer and knelt to get a better look at the shears. Then she jumped up and yelled to Trooper Fallon.

The young cop walked over looking slightly annoyed

at being disturbed.

"Ma'am, is everything okay? What happened?" he asked.

Olivia pointed to the sheep shears and said "I think they have blood on them." She immediately felt a wave of nausea. "Oh my stars, he was murdered, wasn't he?" she cried in horror, as the significance of the bloody shears sank in.

"I was in here shopping and someone was in the back room killing him!" Olivia's knees gave way and she sank to the floor in shock, the cat shooting from her arms and running under a shelf in panic mode.

The trooper rushed to help her up, but she waved him away.

"Just give me a second," she said, holding her hand up, breathing deeply to try to calm herself. "I'll be okay in a minute."

Slowly, her nausea abated, and she allowed the officer to give her a hand up. Once she was steady, she knelt again and peeked under the shelf, calling softly to the frightened cat. "Come on kitty," she said quietly. "It's okay now." The little cat bravely crept back out and let Olivia pick her up.

"Ma'am, why don't you sit back down over here and I'll have one of the detectives come and talk to you, Okay?" He led her to the high-backed chair and after watching to make sure she was sitting, he walked into the back room and spoke to the taller of the two detectives.

Olivia couldn't hear what was said, but the detective turned and started toward her immediately.

He was one of the most attractive men she'd ever seen. *Tall, broad shouldered, and oh my, he even had a sexy little dimple in his chin.*

How can I possibly be thinking about sexy chins with that poor old man lying dead in the next room? Olivia gave herself a mental smack.

"Good Afternoon Ms. McKenna, I'm Detective Lieutenant Josh Abrams, from the State Police Major Crimes Unit of the Investigative Services Division, I understand you're the one who found Mr. Ketterer's body and that now you've also managed to possibly find the murder weapon," his deep well modulated voice held a touch of incredulity.

His subordinate came into the room carrying a camera and knelt in front of the pile of tools, taking shots from various angles.

"Yes, I did," Olivia answered, briefly distracted by the photography going on nearby. "So he really was murdered?" she asked sadly.

"It looks that way right now, Ms. McKenna," his voice was gentle. "Trooper Fallon said that you told him you came here just to shop, and that you didn't know the owner personally. Is that correct?"

"Yes, I'd never met him," Olivia stated. "A friend had told me about passing by this shop recently and thinking it looked like a great place to find some of the things on my clients' lists, so I decided to give it a shot," she felt her eyes tear up again. "I'd just spoken to him on the phone this morning when I called to ask the shop hours, at least I guess it was him, he sounded elderly."

"You say you spoke to the victim this morning? What time was this?" His tone was hopeful. "This could give us a better idea of when he was killed."

Olivia's hazel eyes opened wide, "I guess I haven't had a chance to tell anyone yet, but I think he might have been killed while I was looking around the shop for the things on my list."

"What makes you think that?" the detective asked sharply.

"A few minutes after I arrived, I heard the bells ring on the front door, and assumed another shopper had come in. But now that I've thought about it, I never heard the bells again, so it must have been the killer leaving," she said pensively.

"How long was it from when you heard the bells until you found the body," he asked.

"Whew," Olivia sighed in frustration. "I never even glanced at my watch until I was trying to pay for my purchases and not finding anyone. That was at 11:30 AM," she paused to think. "It was probably close to half an hour to forty-five minutes since I'd heard the bells."

He looked at her closely. "You didn't call 911 until 11:52. What took you so long to call if you found the body at 11:30?"

"Oh no, I didn't find the body then, I just tried to yell toward the back, but when no one answered, I left the money for the purchases on the counter under the big blue and white bowl, and took my stuff out to the car." She was quick to explain.

"So how did you manage to find the body, if you left? Why did you come back?" he was looking at her rather suspiciously now.

"I'm sorry, I am not explaining the sequence very well," she smiled. "After I took my purchases out, this cat jumped up on my car," she motioned toward the cat in her lap, "so I was patting her for a while, then when I tried to leave, she jumped on my car again. I thought she probably belonged to the owner here, so I opened the door and went back in to try yelling for someone again, but she ran into the back room and I was afraid to leave her there in case she didn't belong here after all." Olivia explained as coherently as she could. "So I followed her and that's when I found the body."

"So this isn't your cat?" Josh asked, trying to follow her rambling account. "I just assumed it was yours. Yes, I do know not to assume anything," he grinned at her, displaying a set of gorgeous pearly white teeth.

Olivia smiled back, feeling an unexpected surge of pleasure at that grin. "Well, it was pretty easy to make that mistake, since I've been carrying her around the whole time you've been here. What else would you think?" She smiled again.

"Okay, so I need you to basically take me through all of your movements from the time you arrived until you found the probable murder weapon," he said becoming a little more formal again. "Let's start from the parking lot." He led her out of the shop.

When she had walked him through her whole visit, he told her that she was free to go, walking her out to her vehicle, but said that he might need to contact her again if he had any more questions.

To her mild disappointment, he was all business without even a hint of that gorgeous smile.

"Detective!" she called as he turned to go back inside, "What should I do about the cat? I can't just leave her here with no one to take care of her."

He thought for a moment, "If you can wait until the officers have canvassed the neighborhood, I will have them ask if there is someone to care for the cat while they're questioning the neighbors."

"Sure, I'll wait," Olivia walked over and sat down on the porch swing cuddling the sweet little calico. "I'd hate for her to end up in the pound or living as a stray."

"Okay then, I'll let you know what they say as soon as I hear back from my officers." He gave her a little half smile and walked back inside the shop.

The mild, autumn breeze felt nice on her skin, and Olivia leaned back and settled in for the wait.

CHAPTER TWO

A town police car pulled up and discharged two officers, one female and one male, who hurried into the shop, barely sparing a glance at Olivia.

It wasn't long before they were on their way back out, presumably to question the neighbors. The male cop was looking a bit rattled, and his partner seemed like she was trying to hide her amusement. They were followed out by Trooper Fallon and his partner.

Josh Abrams was not happy. He usually didn't mind working with local cops, but once in a while they just had to send him an idiot. How the heck Pike managed to step into some of the blood, he couldn't fathom. The guy'd been a cop for ten years; where was his head? Unfortunately, not on the platter Josh would've liked to put it on.

Alright, get over it, he told himself. *At least we already had all the pictures and measurements done, so he didn't cause too much damage. Hopefully he'd be better at talking to the neighbors than he was at being around a crime scene.*

Josh watched as the Medical Examiner and his assistant got the body into the bag and on the stretcher. *Poor old man never had a chance,* he thought. *The murderer knew just where to strike with those shears,*

right at the base of the skull. He must have died instantly.
Josh hated violent crimes that involved old people, kids
or animals.

"Hey Lieu, you 'bout ready to head back to
headquarters? I think we're all done here," Detective
Sergeant Bob O'Brian asked, walking up behind him.

"No, I'm going to wait for the locals to come back
and report what they found out from the neighbors first,"
Josh said. "The civilian who found the body wants to
make sure the cat is taken care of."

"Yeah, she's a looker, ain't she? Whoo!" O'Brian
smirked at his superior officer, "and I don't mean the
cat."

Josh rolled his eyes, but silently, he had to agree. She
was such a petite little thing, with her loose dark reddish
brown curls. He'd bet those curls were as soft as silk. *Get
a grip Josh,* he warned himself. *She is a suspect. It
doesn't matter that she's not a very likely suspect, a
suspect is always off limits.*

"So what do you think happened here? Someone
came in, stabbed the old guy then heard our cutie pie out
there, so he got scared and took off?" O'Brian was
obviously ready to brainstorm. "Maybe it was a relative,
hoping to inherit from the old guy."

"Right now, we don't have any fingerprints to speak
of, no suspicious hairs or fibers, and the only footprints
we have are from an idiot local cop, so until we've heard
back from the canvass, I'm not even trying to guess."
Josh was frustrated and getting a little irritated by his
subordinate's wild guesses. "You can take the car and go
back to the HQ to start writing up the report and I'll catch
a ride with Fallon and McNabb as soon as everything is

wrapped up here."

"Sounds good to me," Bob grinned, patting his stomach "The wife's making corned beef and cabbage tonight and I've been hungry all day just thinking about it." He hurried out the door before Josh could change his mind.

Josh shook his head, grinning at O'Brian's hasty retreat. Bob's wife Marie did make the best corned beef and cabbage he'd ever eaten, but then O'Brian was always hungry.

He wandered through the shop taking pictures of each section, and trying to be sure they hadn't missed anything relating to the murder. It was amazing that Olivia McKenna had found the murder weapon, or he figured it was the weapon, as it sure looked to him like a perfect match to the wound. The ME would have the last say on that.

If she weren't so small, he might consider Ms. McKenna a serious suspect, but it was hard to imagine her being able to even reach the base of the tall, thin old man's skull without standing on a chair, even harder to imagine the old man letting her do it. *Nah, she was technically a suspect, but unless she had help, it was physically impossible.* This train of thought cheered him up a little. She really was a looker, as O'Brian had said.

The door opened and Officers Pike and Davis came in talking to each other about their interviews.

"So, did anyone have any information for us?" Josh looked at Davis, ignoring Pike.

"We talked to the neighbors to the east on both sides of the road for about a mile up, and no one remembered seeing anyone unusual driving by, except for one man, who looks like a Hell's Angel, that said he saw someone on a bicycle, but didn't really pay any attention to him," Shannon Davis said, looking at her notebook. "He remembered the bike was one of the skinny racing type ones where you have to hunch over the handle bars, and the guy riding it was wearing the type of clothes you'd expect someone on a racing bike to be wearing. Unfortunately, he couldn't remember anything else about him. He thought the helmet was black. The people next door to the west of him didn't answer the door. She closed the notebook.

Josh sighed, "Did you remember to ask about the cat?" Hopefully he could at least solve that problem.

"Yes, the lady next door to the shop said the old man didn't have any relatives and that we should take the cat to the animal shelter, or that we could drown it for all she cared. She didn't seem to like animals very much." Shannon said, looking disgusted. "No one else could offer any information at all about the cat, though the others also agreed that the victim didn't seem to have anyone close to him."

"Okay, good job Officer Davis, you two can head on out now and I'll lock up once Fallon and McNabb are back," Josh was still pointedly ignoring Officer Pike.

Officer Pike turned and walked out shamefacedly, as Officer Davis said goodbye to Josh.

As soon as their car pulled out, McNabb and Fallon walked in looking depressed.

"Nobody home at the closest three houses to the west," Joe McNabb stated, pulling on his salt and pepper mustache. "None of the others saw anything at all today. What the heck do these people do all day, watch TV?"

"We asked about the cat too," Fallon spoke up, "but

no one knew anything and they weren't interested in taking it."

Josh's shoulders slumped, *so much for solving even that problem.* "Okay gentlemen, thanks for your help. Make sure to send your reports to us over at Headquarters when you've gotten them written up." He smiled and clapped them both on the back as they got ready to leave. "I'll close up here; you guys have a good one."

He heard the car pull out and sighed, thinking of how to tell the beautiful woman outside that he'd have to take the cat to the shelter. He couldn't take it home, his apartment didn't allow animals. He imagined Olivia's lovely hazel eyes filling with tears of disappointment, and he sighed again.

Josh took one last look around the crime scene, and walked out the front door, locking it behind him. He turned to see Olivia sitting on the swing looking at him expectantly.

"I don't have good news," he said grimly. "Apparently, there is no one who wants to take the cat, and I can't, so unfortunately, I will have to take her to the animal shelter."

Olivia sprang to her feet. "Would I be allowed to take her home with me, or are you legally obligated to take her to the shelter? She isn't evidence or anything, right?"

Josh smiled in relief, "You can most definitely take her home with you. I didn't realize that was an option." He grinned, "I thought she was your cat originally anyway."

Olivia cuddled the cat to her chest, eliciting a mew of complaint at the constriction. "Did anyone know what her name is?" she asked, "or her age or anything? She looks young, doesn't she?"

"Yes she does look young," Josh said, reaching to stroke her long fur. "To answer your other questions, no one knew anything about her, nor did they seem to care, so I think you and she can just choose whatever name works best for you. Do you have other pets?" he asked, finding that he wanted to know everything he could about her.

"Yes, I have a young Golden Retriever named Molly who I found at the shelter almost a year ago," she smiled. "Thankfully, she loves cats as well as other dogs, so unless this little kitty hates dogs, we'll be just fine."

"I'm glad that worked out so well," he said as they walked down the porch steps toward her Suburban. "I'll most likely be calling you to come in for a more formal interview over at Headquarters in the next few days."

"That'll be fine," she said as he opened the driver's side door for her. "Hmm, I hope she travels well." Olivia set the cat on the passenger seat carefully, and looked around as a thought struck her. "Where is your car?"

Josh was dumbstruck. *His brain wasn't working any better than Pike's.* He just stood staring at her in amazement until they both laughed.

"Come on, get in, and I'll drop you at your station house or barracks, as I think you guys call it." she offered grinning. "You can hold the cat until I see how good of a rider she is, otherwise she might end up sitting on top of my head or something."

"Actually, I work out of headquarters, rather than the barracks or station house, just to make it more confusing. I am so sorry to ask you to do this," he said, as he walked to the passenger side and got in, lifting the cat to his lap.

"I meant to ask the other troopers for a ride to Headquarters on their way to the barracks, but got distracted and forgot. I technically shouldn't even be riding with you."

"Why on earth not?" she exclaimed, then paused. "Oh, I'm a suspect, right?" Olivia looked sideways at him as she pulled into the street. "Which way is Headquarters?"

"Make a right at the next two stop signs, then just stay on 302 and it'll come up on your right in about five miles. Yes, you are technically a suspect," he stated frankly, "though to be honest, I really don't think you're the murderer."

"Why not?" she asked with a raised eyebrow. "Because I'm a woman? Not that I am the murderer," she was quick to add. "I just don't want you to think I am a helpless little thing because I'm female."

Josh grinned at her show of spirit. "I don't think I'll be making that mistake. Wasn't it Shakespeare who said '... and though she be but little, she is fierce.'? He was a smart man."

"Yes he was, and it seems you are too," she laughed. "The kitty has settled down nicely in your lap; I think she'll be a good traveler," her eyes couldn't help lingering on his long, slender fingers as they stroked the cat's ears. His eyes met hers for a second and she felt a jolt of electricity run through her body.

"Yes, she is a calm little kitty, especially for having just come from a murder scene," he said. "Headquarters is on your right just up ahead."

She turned into the almost empty parking lot and pulled to a stop. "Delivered safe and sound," she smiled. Olivia took the cat from his lap so he could get out.

"I really appreciate the ride," he said. "If you think of anything at all that you remember from earlier, or have any concerns, just give me a call, day or night," he handed her his card. "My cell number is on the back."

"Okay, thanks, I will definitely call if I remember anything that I missed telling you," she said lowering the window as he closed the door. "It was nice meeting you Detective Josh Abrams, though the circumstances weren't so nice," she laughed softly.

"It was nice meeting you too Ms. Olivia McKenna," he gave her a crooked grin. "I'll be talking to you again soon." He turned and walked into the Trooper Headquarters.

Olivia couldn't seem to stop smiling as she drove to the market near her house to pick up some supplies for her new cat. Luckily, the kitty acted like a seasoned traveler, or a well behaved dog, riding quietly in the passenger seat just as she had in Josh's lap, and waiting patiently while she quickly shopped.

"Okay little girl, time to meet your doggie sister," she said finally pulling into her driveway and turning off the engine shortly before dark. "You guys are going to love each other—I hope," she crossed her fingers for luck. "It's been a really long day."

After a lot of mutual sniffing, a few hissy snarls and one mildly scratched nose, the two animals seemed to decide that they liked each other.

Olivia set up the litter box in the downstairs bathroom, and after moving a couple of trinkets, she put two dishes for the cat on a tall, narrow, three foot long table that was stationed above the dog's dishes. *Perfect,* she thought, *the cat will be able to reach it, but Molly won't.*

"Okay, what are we going to call you?" she asked the little cat who was busily checking out her new home. "Hmmm, you're such a pretty little girl, you need a pretty name." Olivia thought for a while, as she put away her purchases of the day, "How about Sheyna?"

The cat looked at her and rubbed against her ankles.

"Sheyna it is." She smiled, scooping the kitty up and giving her a kiss on the head. "Okay then, Sheyna and Molly, I think it's time to fix us all some supper; does that sound like a plan?" she reached for the pots and pans.

Once everyone had been fed, Molly had gone out into the fenced back yard, come back in, and Olivia had cleaned up the kitchen, she turned on her computer and typed a quick email to her friend Andrew, who was the client who wanted the mechanical bank, reporting her success, and decided to go ahead and pack it up, so it would be ready to deliver the next time she was out. After finding the dead guy, her enthusiasm for the items she'd found in his shop had been dampened a little.

The sugar shaker she'd gotten for herself though, looked way too fabulous with her other antique sugar shakers for her to give it up. She locked up the house and headed for the shower. What a crazy, bizarre day it had been.

After her shower, she found Molly and Sheyna on her bed, each somehow managing to take up almost half the bed. She laughed, "So where am I supposed to sleep?" They just looked at her. Sheyna blinked. *How lucky I am,* she thought as she snuggled in between the two animals. They both cuddled up against her, and drifted off to sleep.

CHAPTER THREE

The next day dawned bright and beautiful, so Olivia decided to make the most of it by getting up early.

She'd checked Sheyna's collar last night and noticed that she had a current rabies tag, so this morning she called Coos County to ask who the vet was in their records, then called the vet to find out if Sheyna was up to date on all of her shots. Fortunately, she was, so an immediate vet trip was one thing off Olivia's list. She also found out that Sheyna's previous name had been Chloe and she had definitely been Ketterer's cat. Now that she'd named her Sheyna, and Sheyna seemed to like it, she was sticking with it.

While she drank her coffee she checked her email and found a reply from her friend Andrew, the piggy bank client, who would love it if Olivia could drop the bank off for him when she was in the neighborhood. The other little items she'd found for clients yesterday, were only a small part of what they were looking for, so she wouldn't bother to email them until their orders were more complete.

After breakfast Olivia gave the house a thorough vacuuming, letting her mind wander back to yesterday in the antique shop before she found the body. She had the feeling there was something she was forgetting, something that might be important, but she just couldn't bring it into focus.

Instead, after a while her mind roamed to the handsome detective and how she'd felt when he smiled at her, the tingle of electricity that seemed to pass between them in her car. She hadn't been so attracted to anyone in a long time, but then she hadn't met anyone as attractive as Josh Abrams before either. It wasn't only the physical good looks, of which he possessed more than enough, it was that crooked smile, his gorgeous green eyes, and something about him which seemed a little wounded.

Olivia snapped back to reality as Molly started barking and growling near the back door. Turning off the vacuum, Olivia hurried to see what Molly was so upset about. She heard the screen door slam shut and someone running across the wooden deck, and the slam of her wooden gate, but by the time she looked out the window, she didn't see anything amiss. Cautiously opening the door, so the animals couldn't get out, Olivia stepped out to check things over.

Once she was sure there was no one in the yard, she allowed Molly to join her. There was an overturned flower pot on her deck with the soil spilled out and the pretty, autumn mums broken and trampled. By the door she found a chisel, which didn't belong to her, and upon closer inspection it looked like someone had tried to use it to force open the door.

"Good Girl Molly!" she cried. "You scared them off before they could break in." She sank to the deck with her back against the door, thinking intensely. *She'd lived in this house for four years and had never heard of an attempted break-in anywhere in the neighborhood. Was it a coincidence that someone tried to break in to her house the day after she'd almost witnessed a murder?* She'd never really believed in coincidences.

But why? She hadn't actually seen anything, hadn't bought anything expensive enough to murder someone over. Olivia was perplexed. "I guess it's time to call the oh-so-handsome Detective Josh," she said to Molly, getting up and leading the way back inside. "I think this qualifies as a genuine concern."

Before she had a chance to call Josh, the phone rang. It was her best friend Abby McElhattan, who was an interior decorator, reminding her that they were supposed to go to an estate auction together on Thursday night. Olivia filled her in on the murder and her new cat, as well as she could over the phone, then she told her about the attempted break-in. Abby asked if she had called the police and when she said not yet, Olivia winced and held the phone away from her ear, as Abby yelled *"Why not; are you crazy?"*

After Olivia agreed to call the police immediately and to keep her posted on new developments, Abby let her off the phone, with a promise of meeting her at the estate auction. Sheyna jumped up onto the little table where her dish was and plaintively meowed.

"Well, I guess it is time for a little snack for you Sheyna girl," she said, pulling out a couple kitty treats and a larger doggie treat for Molly. "Here you go guys; now I'm going to call Josh, so behave yourselves, and no stealing from each other." Olivia dialed the number Josh gave her and started pacing as she waited for him to answer.

"Lieutenant Abrams," his voice gave her a jolt.

"Hi, Detective Lieutenant Abrams, it's Olivia McKenna. You said to call if I had any concerns. Someone tried to break into my house a few minutes ago, and Molly, my dog scared them away," she spoke in a rush. "They left a chisel behind and trampled one of my potted plants, as they ran off, so she must have startled them pretty badly."

"Are you and the animals alright?" he asked. *"They didn't make it into your house, did they?"*

"No, Molly went crazy growling and barking and they ran away before I could even get to the door to look out."

"Could you tell if there was more than one person, if they were male or female, anything at all?" he asked. *"Have there been any break-ins in your area recently?"*

"No, none in the last four years I have lived here," she said. "I couldn't tell if it was a man or a woman, but I think it was only one person, from the way it sounded when they ran across my deck. I didn't touch the chisel, so if they weren't wearing gloves, there might be fingerprints on it."

"Okay, stay inside and keep your doors and windows locked. I'll be there in half an hour to forty-five minutes."

Olivia put the phone down and ran to double check all the doors and windows. Molly and Sheyna followed her through the house, watching to see what she was going to do next. Once she was sure that all was secure, she rushed to change out of her old ratty sweat pants and into something nice. Several outfits later, she was finally dressed in a pair of white Capri pants, a sleeveless turquoise top and beaded sandals. Molly and Sheyna were lying on the bed surrounded by cast off clothes.

She spritzed a little perfume behind her ears, called the animals out of her room and closed the door on the chaos, then hurried downstairs to make sure the rest of the house looked presentable. *Thank goodness I vacuumed,* she thought, as she quickly dusted everything she could reach. She had just finished washing the breakfast dishes when she heard the knock at the front door.

"Okay, you two, best behavior," she laughed, as the dog and cat raced each other to the door. She peeked out the window and saw the detective standing on the porch looking around at the yard. She picked Sheyna up and told Molly to stay.

"Hi," she said opening the door with a rueful smile. "Welcome to the crime scene."

He gave her a sympathetic grin, as he walked in. "We've got to stop meeting like this."

Her stomach fluttered at his deep voice. The man was just way too sexy. "So, thank you for coming in person," she said, her voice a bit higher than she planned. "I wasn't sure if a little thing like this warranted a hot detective. Hot shot! I mean a hot shot detective!" she felt her face turning bright red.

"I kinda liked it better the other way," he said with a huge grin that made her feel weak in the knees.

She took a deep breath and set Sheyna on the floor, giving herself time to recover her wits. "Let me show you the chisel and the marks on the back door." She managed to avoid his eyes, as it seemed way too dangerous not to. *He's like a Basilisk,* she thought, *one look into those sexy green eyes and I'll end up being lunch.* She dropped that thought like a hot potato.

Olivia picked Sheyna back up so she couldn't run out, and opened the back door. Josh knelt to look at the marks on the door jamb, took a couple of pictures, and pulled on a pair of latex gloves. He took a plastic evidence bag from his kit and placed the chisel inside it.

"I'm guessing that you touched the door knob, right?"

Olivia nodded, "Yes, I didn't realize he had even touched the door then, I just instinctively shut it when I came out so Sheyna couldn't take off, though so far, she hasn't really tried."

"It's okay, he probably wore gloves anyway, but just in case we get lucky, I'm going to take your fingerprints, so I can tell if anyone else touched the knob." He dusted the door knob, door and jamb, with blackish powder.

Molly sniffed the powder and sneezed. Josh laughed and Olivia joined him when she realized he didn't mind Molly's sniffing.

"She didn't hurt anything," he smiled. "She's just curious about all this new activity. Aren't you girl?" he asked Molly.

She licked his face and wagged her tail like a semaphore. *Wow,* Olivia thought, *the man could definitely charm the ladies.* She supposed Sheyna would be eating out of his hand next.

"Well, there seems to be only one set of prints on the door, and I'd be willing to bet they'll match yours," he shook his head. "Figured it wouldn't be that easy."

"Would you like a cup of coffee or tea?" she asked as he finished packing up the fingerprinting kit. "I have some blueberry muffins that I made yesterday morning to go with it."

"That would be fantastic, coffee please," he said

appreciatively. "I never got a chance to eat anything yet today. I don't want to put you to too much trouble though."

"No, it's no trouble at all," she smiled, heading into the bright, sunny kitchen. "I could even fix you a real breakfast if you're hungry. How about eggs, sourdough pancakes and Vermont maple syrup?"

"I think I must have died and gone to heaven," he laughed. "Are you sure you don't mind? That seems like a lot of work to me."

"I don't mind at all," she smiled. "I love to cook, almost as much as I love to look for antiques."

She started brewing a fresh pot of coffee and put together a batter for the pancakes. She mixed it thoroughly, then lightly greased a cast iron skillet and waited for it to get hot. Meanwhile, she poured Josh and herself some of the fresh steaming coffee.

While she was cooking, Josh sat at her kitchen table and patted Sheyna and Molly, while watching Olivia out of the corner of his eye. *She was a gorgeous woman,* he thought. She loved animals; she loved to cook. He used to love cooking when he was married. He thought antiques were beautiful, though he didn't know much about them. He adored all animals. It was amazing how much they had in common. *She is still a suspect,* he told himself firmly. *Don't go there.*

Once the skillet was hot enough, Olivia dropped spoons of batter onto it and waited until they had nice popped bubbles, then flipped each pancake over and cooked them until they were golden brown. In another pan, she scrambled eggs in butter. When everything was ready, she put it on the table in front of Josh with a smile and set down a plate and silverware for each of them.

"Breakfast is served Detective," she handed him a napkin, then set the syrup pitcher and butter dish where he could easily reach them. "Would you like some orange juice?"

"No, this is just perfect," he gestured to the coffee and his already full plate. "You have gone way above and beyond. I honestly didn't think I was going to get a chance to eat anything today," he smiled in between bites. "Thank you so much for your generosity."

"Thank you for coming all the way over here for a simple attempted break-in, and for giving me an excuse to eat a second breakfast," she laughed. "Do you think this is related to yesterday?"

He nodded as he swallowed a bite of pancake. "Yes I do. It seems like too big a coincidence that someone would pick the day after you were present at a murder to try to break into your house."

"That's what I think," she said, before taking a bite of egg with syrup.

"Have you thought of anything else that you might have seen or heard yesterday, that didn't seem significant to you then?" he finished his plate and sat back watching her eat. He'd never noticed before how sensual a woman could look when she was eating.

"It's really strange," she said. "It's like there is something right there in the back of my mind, but I can't quite see it. Something I saw, heard, I'm not even sure, just something tickling there, wanting me to remember it." Olivia sighed in frustration, "It's absolutely maddening, especially now, when I'm being stalked or whatever this person is doing. I don't like it at all! I refuse to be a victim."

"Don't worry," Josh said quietly. "I'm not about to let you become a victim. Actually, I have a strong feeling you won't let yourself become one either," he smiled crookedly, as he saw her bristle slightly at the implication that she couldn't take care of herself.

"No, I won't," she said fiercely. She took a deep breath, "I will be very grateful for your help though. This is not something I am used to. I am also quite concerned that this person might hurt Molly and Sheyna, if he or she comes back when I'm not here. I think I'll be taking them with me everywhere I go until this is solved."

"I think that's a great idea," he said. "There's always more safety in numbers, better for you and them." Sheyna jumped into Josh's lap and rubbed against his broad chest. "I like her name; it fits her perfectly." He scratched her neck. "She definitely seems settled in and confident for being in a new place."

"Yes, she is adapting amazingly well. I honestly think she must believe she's a dog. She acts almost as much like one as Molly."

"Well, I'd better get back to Headquarters; I'm trying to get more information on the shop owner, Mr. Ketterer." Josh stretched and stood up, setting Sheyna on his vacated chair.

"Have you found out anything about why he was killed?" Olivia stood and started stacking the dirty plates. "If my attempted house-break is related to the murder, I'd really like to know *how* it's related, so I can make it stop."

"Unfortunately, I can't really discuss the case, with you, except for what you tell me," he apologized. "I did discover that there was more to Mr. Lewis Edmund

Ketterer than what met the eye," he said cryptically.

After reminding her to call him if anything strange happened or if she remembered what was bugging her about the day of the murder, he thanked her once more for the breakfast, and shook her hand, holding it perhaps a tiny bit longer than was customary.

The rest of the day passed uneventfully, except for one minor spit spat over who got to put their head on Olivia's pillow at bedtime. Sheyna got there first, but Molly was bigger, and once she sat on Sheyna, Sheyna decided she liked the other pillow just fine. Olivia climbed into bed and opened her book to read for a while. She was enthralled with the latest paranormal urban fantasy by Devin O'Branagan, and she stayed up reading later than she'd planned, not being able to put it down until she'd finished.

ANTIQUES & AVARICE

CHAPTER FOUR

Olivia woke to a kitty paw gently patting her nose. She looked up to see a pair of bright amber gold eyes peering into her own sleepy hazel ones. She turned to take a peek at the clock and groaned. She hadn't meant to sleep in so late. Molly's tail thumped the bed in excitement, sensing that Olivia was finally awake.

"Okay, okay, I'm up," she sighed laughing. "You two make quite a tag team."

After a quick shower, she donned a pair of blue jeans and a conservative tank top, then headed down to make breakfast. Both animals wolfed their food down and Molly asked to be let out in the back yard. So far Sheyna had been very good about being a strictly indoor cat; she hadn't tried to run out the door even once. Something tickled in the back of Olivia's mind again, but was gone before she could grasp it.

Olivia called her friend Abby, to ask her if her mom would mind watching the animals that night while they went to the estate auction. She could drop them off when she picked up Abby who lived only a couple of miles from her mom. Abby was sure her mom would be thrilled to do it, and she was happy to not have to drive there after

37

all.

"Thanks Abby. I'll pick you up first at about 4:30 then we can run by your mom's and still get to the auction on time." Olivia hung up and went to start a load of laundry.

After she put the clothes in the washer, she sat down at her computer and googled 'Lewis Edmund Ketterer, New Hampshire'. All the entries she found for Lewis Ketterer or Edmund Ketterer in New Hampshire were obituaries, there were no entries for Lewis Edmund Ketterer.

"Hmmm," she said to Molly and Sheyna. "This gets stranger and stranger. So does this mean that his real name wasn't Lewis Edmund Ketterer, or what? Maybe tomorrow we should take a little ride back over there to talk to some of the neighbors ourselves." She looked at Sheyna who was sitting next to the laptop, "How would you feel about that? I hope it won't make you homesick."

Sheyna purred and hit the delete button on Olivia's keyboard, erasing Lewis Edmund Ketterer's name from the screen.

The rest of the day went by quickly, and Olivia was soon rushing to get ready for the auction. As soon as she finished dressing, she packed some food for each of the animals in baggies, grabbed their bowls and pulled out the crates. Luckily she had an old puppy crate she could use for Sheyna. Molly was trying to help by carrying the bowls around the house.

Olivia quickly put the crates into the back of the Suburban and set them up for the animals to travel in. She went back in and picked up Sheyna, letting Molly follow her to the car. Molly excitedly jumped into her crate and lay down ready for a ride. Sheyna sniffed her crate, and cautiously crept into it when Olivia set her in front of it. Olivia fastened the crate latches and lowered the rear door.

She ran back up the steps to make sure the front door was locked, then hurriedly started the engine. She stopped quickly at the closest pet supply store and bought a new carry crate and a regular one to replace the old puppy crate for Sheyna, as well as dog food and a few other essentials. Olivia reached Abby's house ten minutes later and her pretty red haired friend came out carrying a bag of homemade cookies.

"Can't let us go hungry while we're bidding," she grinned, her green eyes twinkling mischievously. "So tell me all about the murder and the break-in."

Olivia filled her in on the details, as well as what she'd found when googling the victim's name. She didn't mention Josh, as she knew Abby would press for more information, and she really didn't want to get into that topic yet.

When they got to Abby's mom, Annie's house, Olivia introduced Sheyna to Annie; Molly already knew and loved her. Sheyna seemed content to stay with Annie. Olivia marveled yet again at how easily she adapted.

"Don't rush back," Annie said laughing. "I love having them here." The two animals followed her into the house and she closed the door.

"She really does, you know," Abby smiled, twisting the ring in her upper ear. "She misses Charlie too much still to think about getting another dog or cat. Hopefully one day she will though. In the meantime, never feel guilty asking her to babysit. The favor works both ways."

"I'm so glad she likes doing it, because right now, I

am way too nervous to leave them at home alone, and I would have hated missing this auction," Olivia grinned. "The estate belonged to a family who'd lived in the house for over a hundred years, so there should be some fabulous antiques. They may be mostly beyond my budget, but I have two clients with deep pockets and long wish lists."

Olivia loved going to auctions, though she had to keep strict control of herself, because it was all too easy to get caught up in the excitement of bidding and end up spending more than you should. *Regular estate sales were safer, where you took a number and when your group was called, you roamed through the house, swarmed actually; we're like a swarm of locusts descending on the house,* she thought in amusement.

They could feel the excitement in the air as they entered the auction house. They both registered and gave their credit cards in exchange for their bidder numbers. This auction house allowed credit cards, checks and cash for payment, unlike many, which took only cash.

It was five o'clock, so they had two hours to look at all the lots before the auction would actually start. Abby had gone to the earlier previewing the day before, so she already had a good idea of what she was interested in buying, and knew of a few things Olivia might want as well. She led her to those lots first, then they wandered through the house separately, taking notes so they could remember all the details of the lots they liked.

There was a great collection of items and the smaller, lumped-together lots of less pricy things were especially tempting to Olivia for her own house. She saw a gorgeous Tiger Oak chest of drawers that she knew one of her clients would kill for. Okay, bad choice of words, she inwardly rolled her eyes. She peeked at that client's list to see what her price range should be, and made a note about it for the bidding.

Abby walked over and motioned to her, "We'd better find good seats now, people are starting to sit down and we don't want to end up at the back."

Olivia waved to a portly middle aged man she knew from estate sales, as they found seats in the first row. Abby looked around, craning her neck to see who all was coming into the room.

"Oh no," she exclaimed. "There's Patricia Logan," the irritation in her voice was apparent. "I just know she's going to bid on that 18th century Country French armoire I want for the Fitzpatricks. It's precisely the type of piece she'll want."

"Maybe not," Olivia soothed her friend. "Hopefully, she'll bid on Lot Number 17, the Louis XVI Country French Armoire du Marriage," she consulted her notes. "That one is even more impressive and she's got the money for it. It comes first in the bidding too, so if she gets it, she won't bother with yours."

Abby still looked worried, "I hope you're right. It would be a fantastic sale for me if I can get it. It's exactly what we've been trying to find for their master bedroom."

A hush gradually settled over the noisy room, as the auctioneer and his assistants entered.

The auctioneer quickly introduced himself, explained the rules of the auction and started the bidding on the first piece. Olivia tuned out the auction, letting the chant of "I got seventeen thousand who'll give me seventeen-five," wash over her, as she studied her notes. All the items being auctioned in the first twenty lots were well over her price range, even for her top clients.

She looked around to see who else she might know, and had the oddest feeling that someone was watching her. Goose bumps broke out on her arms. She didn't see anything or anyone that looked unusual, but it was a while before she was able to shake the creepy feeling.

Olivia snapped out of her reverie when Abby's bidder's paddle shot up beside her.

"Twenty-four, gimme twenty-five," the auctioneer called. A paddle raised near the back. "I got twenty-five gimme twenty-six. Come on, it's twenty-five hundred, who'll gimme twenty-six?" Abby raised her paddle. The bidding went to twenty-seven hundred and fifty dollars, and Abby was beaming as the auctioneer called it sold.

"You were right Livvi!" she whispered in excitement. "Once Patricia won lots number twelve and seventeen, she didn't even stay for the rest of the bidding!"

Olivia smiled at her friend's happiness. "I just knew you'd get it."

Olivia won two of the larger 'client items', and lost out on a couple. She won the 1930's Tiger Oak chest of drawers for $650.00 and she knew her client would be happy to pay her a very generous finder's fee on top of that. It was a stunning piece.

She was quite pleased to have also won a small inexpensive lot that contained a bunch of old bottles, two of which were typical 'Cures All Diseases' bottles from the late eighteen-hundreds.

They went to pay for their purchases and Abby arranged to have the armoire delivered to her client's house tomorrow. Olivia asked them to load the chest of drawers and her other purchases into the back of the

Suburban. They were tired but happy as they drove to Abby's house.

"I'm going to drop you off first if you don't mind, so I can just go straight home with Molly and Sheyna," Olivia said when they were getting close to Abby's house.

"Sure, that is fine for me," Abby yawned. "I'm pretty wiped out myself."

"Call me soon!" Abby yelled as she walked up her driveway, her black leather boots shiny in the moonlight.

They waved to each other and Olivia headed to pick up the animals.

Molly and Sheyna were happy to see her and ran back and forth from her to Annie in excitement.

"They were so well behaved while you were gone," Annie chuckled. "You'd never know it from the way they're acting now, silly girls."

"I think animals are like kids, they always behave worse around their parents," Olivia laughed. "Thanks so much for watching them for me. Were there any problems at all?"

"No, not really. They were very good," she hesitated. "Molly got herself all in a ruckus at one point, barking and growling at the door, but she settled down after a while. Sheyna's fur poofed up like a Halloween kitty too. Must have been another dog out there that scared them."

Olivia didn't want to alarm Annie, so she kept her concern to herself, giving Annie a hug and loading Molly and Sheyna into the car. "See you soon and thanks again!" she called as she pulled out of the driveway.

Okay, that's two creepy things in one night, she thought to herself, *I know someone was watching me at the auction. I just couldn't see them.* "Girls, what scared you tonight? I so wish you could tell me. I guess I'm going to have to call Josh again tomorrow. Maybe he has some news."

~~~

Josh sighed heavily as he hung up the phone after talking to Olivia. He was starting to have a few ideas about the reason behind the murder, but why the killer would be stalking Olivia, he couldn't begin to figure out. Unless there was something she had seen or heard, but didn't remember . . . . It didn't make any sense.

He slammed his pen down on his desk. *Technicalities can hang,* he thought. *I know she is innocent and I'm not going to let anything happen to her, suspect or not.* He opened the case file again to reread his notes.

He hadn't felt interested in dating anyone since his wife had died. He'd thought he never would, but there was just something about Olivia that grabbed him and wouldn't let go. If he had to sit in front of her house all night to protect her, so be it. Meanwhile, he really needed to figure out why she was being targeted.

"Hendricks, can you come in here please?" he spoke into his phone.

"Yeah Boss!" Sergeant Earl Hendricks opened Josh's office door and stepped inside.

"Close it Earl," Josh said. "I need you to go over the Ketterer/Jamison files with me so we can make sure we're not missing anything."

"Lieu, so far about the only real information we've managed to be sure of, is that the victim's real name was Marvin Jamison, and that he was convicted of a couple of armed burglaries in Boston, served nine years in State prison in Massachusetts, and was released fourteen years ago," Hendricks replied. "I'm not sure how much help it'll be for me to go over it with you."

"Humor me Hendricks," Josh said looking slightly irritated, "We do know that during the next seven or eight years after his release, there were several burglaries in the Boston area, of which he was one of the primary suspects, but no one was ever convicted in those cases, except for the last one. Do you remember how he was caught?"

"Yeah, I think they caught him trying to fence a stolen antique Japanese sword collection from the last job," Hendricks thought back. "The cops working it knew someone else was involved in the burglaries, and were pretty sure it was Marvin Jamison, but they didn't have any way to prove it and he fell completely off the radar after that."

"You're right," Josh agreed. "There was simply no record of him existing from that point on, until now. Obviously he'd taken a new identity, moved to New Hampshire and had been lying low posing as an antique dealer."

"His partner's name was Henry Larsson, and I remember he claimed sole responsibility for the Olander job which is the one they caught him on. He denied any knowledge of the other burglaries, and said the only things he'd stolen from the house were the swords. I think he was convicted of Grand Theft as well as Burglary and some lesser associated crimes," Hendricks was on a roll with it now. "He spent four and a half years in the Penn, out of a seven year sentence."

"That's right. See, we know more than you think. I

believe this may be tied into the old burglary cases," Josh said. "Besides the antique Japanese sword collection, there were several very valuable paintings taken off the walls, a rare US gold coin collection that was worth a small fortune, and some priceless diamond jewelry stolen from Olander's safe." Josh paused for breath and a glance at the file, "The swords were the only items ever recovered. The homeowner, Olander had filed insurance claims and was paid well over eighteen million dollars for the combined value of the items that were never recovered."

"That's a lot moolah Lieu!" Hendricks whistled. "I'll bet the insurance people weren't real happy about it."

"That's the angle I want you to check on right now. See if you can find out if anyone involved in the insurance end of it has been around here lately or if there is anything suspicious about any of them."

"Right Boss, I'll get on it now," Hendricks sighed as he walked out the door.

Josh knew that Bob O'Brian was over at the antique shop now with an antiques expert and a couple of uniformed cops going through the place with a fine tooth comb to see if any of the missing loot was hidden there. So far, though they'd found some pretty pricey antiques amongst the junk, they had not located anything that they knew to be from the burglaries.

Josh decided to make some calls to see where Larsson was living now that he was out of prison. He'd definitely had a motive to murder Ketterer / Jamison if they'd been in on the burglaries together and Jamison had let him take the fall, then had run off with the loot and hidden from him.

Josh was able to discover that Larsson had been on

ANTIQUES & AVARICE

parole for a year and a half, plus another six months for a minor infraction after his release, and had finally finished that part of his sentence about three months ago. His former parole officer had no idea where he was now.

It took several more phone calls for Josh to find Derrick Lattimer, one of the cops who'd worked the case when Larsson was convicted. He arranged to meet him the following day at his station in Boston.

It was over a three hour drive each way, but Josh knew he had to get more information on both Jamison and Larsson. He also felt it would be helpful to get the cop's thoughts on whether they'd had any other possible suspects for the burglaries back then, in case he hadn't gotten everything in the files he'd asked for and received earlier.

A little before five o'clock, Bob O'Brian came into headquarters looking decidedly dusty and tired. Josh had to grin at his subordinate's disheveled appearance.

"Planning a new job as a chimney sweep, are you Bob? The look suits you," he smirked. "If you look like this, I can't even imagine what the poor uniforms look like," he referred to the local uniformed cops who'd been assisting O'Brian.

O'Brian looked disgusted, "Why on earth people pay good money for all that filthy, dusty old junk is beyond me! That antiques consultant we have working with us got all excited over some of the most ordinary looking old junk, like the stuff my ma used to have all over the house. It was ridiculous," Bob was on a roll. "After Dad and Ma died, my brother and I actually had to pay to dump most of that junk when we cleaned their house out to sell it."

47

Josh wisely kept his mouth shut, and made a mental note never to let O'Brian bring up that topic in front of Olivia, because he was pretty sure she wouldn't be able to keep her mouth shut.

"Did you guys find anything new at the shop?" he asked. "We've gone through the vic's computer and ledger books, and so far haven't come up with anything, but after you left this morning, I turned the computer over to the lab so we'll see if there is stuff hidden or erased that they can ferret out."

"Aside from tons of junk, the only thing of interest we found was a bunch of receipts for flights and hotels and such," O'Brian said. "Apparently Jamison got around . . . a lot. Europe, Asia, South America, Africa . . . especially Africa. He was smart enough not to buy an expensive house and car and draw attention to himself, but he definitely liked to travel. We even found a passport for the cat. Apparently her name was Chloe. He must have been taking her with him out of the country pretty often, ever since she was a kitten, since the passport was issued when she was ten weeks old according to what it shows."

"No wonder she is such a calm and relaxed cat; she's probably completely used to flying in planes, riding in cars, staying in hotels and who knows what all. I wonder if there was another reason for all of Jamison's traveling?" Josh mused. "I doubt his stripes had changed much since he got out of prison. Maybe he was up to no good, possibly using the cat as a cover somehow, maybe smuggling drugs? I know you're off tomorrow, but would you mind just quickly seeing if you can find out anything about his trips; I have to head into Boston to talk to a cop about Jamison's probable former partner, Larsson in the morning."

O'Brian agreed good-naturedly, happy not to have been asked to accompany his superior to Boston on a Saturday. He didn't mind a little bit of off duty work that he could do from his home computer, but he was looking forward to doing some serious fly fishing over the weekend.

"See you Monday Lieu," O'Brian said getting ready to go. "You can call me tomorrow evening for whatever I dig up; I'll be out fishing in the daytime and not answering the phone," he grinned and gave him a mock salute as he walked out the door.

CHAPTER FIVE

Olivia's weekend was relatively quiet and peaceful, though with Molly and now Sheyna, things were never that quiet. At least there had been no further scares or break-in attempts, so Olivia considered that to be peaceful enough.

She hadn't heard from Josh since Friday morning when she'd told him about the events from the auction night. While she figured he was off work on the weekends and she wasn't likely to hear from him, she found herself wishing he'd call. *Wow Liv,* she thought, *it's way too soon for that, if ever. Didn't you swear off relationships after Danny? Remember how much it hurts when they end,* she admonished herself sternly.

It may be over before it started anyway, she thought, *since nothing more had happened. She might not even hear from Josh again.* Her spirits drooped a little at this thought.

It was just after eight in the morning, probably still too early to go into town even on a Monday, so she poured herself another cup of coffee and sat at her computer to catch up on emails. The first three were spam, the next one was a statement from her bank and the last one was advertizing an estate sale the following weekend in Conway.

She quickly called Abby and asked if she wanted to go with her, and if her mom could please watch the animals again. Abby laughingly said yes to both questions and they agreed to meet at the sale, since it would open at seven AM and they would need to be there at the crack of dawn or earlier to get their numbers, if they wanted to be in one of the first groups allowed in, which they definitely did.

"Hello?" Olivia's cell phone rang. "Hi Mr. Trotter . . . yes, I do see old fishing gear sometimes." She listened for a minute then spoke loudly, "I said, yes, I do see it sometimes." She listened again, with a pensive look on her face, "Tackle? What kinds of tackle?" she yelled.

Molly flew into the room, knocked Olivia flat on the floor, sending her cell phone skittering across the tile then sat on her, looking proud of herself.

Olivia let out a yelp, "Molly, what on earth was that for?" she extricated herself from the dog and sat up. "What got into you?"

Olivia got up and retrieved her cell phone. "I'm sorry Mr. Trotter, I tripped over my dog," she fibbed, talking loudly. "I was asking you what kind of tackle."

Out of the corner of her eye, she saw Molly sailing toward her again and reached out to catch her before she could send her crashing to the floor again. She sat down and hugged Molly, "Mr. Trotter, I'm going to have to call you back in a few minutes, my phone is acting up," she yelled, hanging up.

Molly was sitting in her lap wagging her tail and looking like she was expecting praise. Olivia gently pushed her off and stood up. She thought for a minute, "Tackle!" she yelled, turning toward Molly expectantly.

Sure enough, Molly flew into her arms, almost knocking her down again, even though she was ready for her. Olivia sank to the floor, holding Molly and laughing.

"Well, I never expected you to know how to play football. I so wish I knew how you ever ended up at the shelter. You are a dog of so many surprises. I should arrange a football game with some friends sometime to show you off." She hugged her and scratched her belly, still chuckling.

At nine o'clock, she loaded Molly and Sheyna into the Suburban, grabbed the antique piggy bank for Andrew and drove into town. After leaving a very happy client with his new/old bank, Olivia headed to the home warehouse store to pick up a few hardware items. Molly walked on leash beside her in the store while Sheyna sat in her little soft carry crate in the shopping cart curiously checking things out from a safe distance.

The cashier gave Molly a treat, then offered one to Sheyna, who took it eagerly, but dropped it when she discovered it was a dog biscuit. The humans laughed and Sheyna looked at them with reproach.

"I'm sorry sweetie," the cashier said to Sheyna. ""We don't get many kitties coming in."

"It's okay," Olivia laughed. "She has some treats in the car; she's just a tiny bit spoiled. Thanks for trying."

Olivia got the animals loaded in the car, gave them each a treat for being so good and closed the back. She climbed into the driver's seat and was closing the door when it was jerked out of her hands and a man grabbed her by the arm and tried to yank her out of the car.

Olivia screamed and clung to the steering wheel with her free hand. Without even thinking she pivoted her body and kicked the man in the chest as hard as she could, using her full body weight. He fell back and she threw herself into the car, slammed it into gear and gunned the engine, spinning out of the parking spot, narrowly missing the car in front of her, and her attacker on the ground. The door swung wildly, as she sped away, until she was able to grab it and pull it closed.

Shaking hard, she dialed 911 on her cell phone, and quickly pulled into a busy parking lot a couple blocks from where she'd been accosted. The dispatcher said she'd have the police there soon. Olivia looked into the back to make sure Molly and Sheyna were okay. They didn't even look upset. She called Josh's cell phone and told him what had happened. He told her he wasn't too far away and that he'd be there within half an hour.

She soon saw the state police car coming down the street and found herself wobbling a little as she got out of the car. The adrenaline rush was slowly subsiding, leaving shaky nerves in its wake.

Olivia told the troopers what had happened and one of them immediately went back to where she'd been parked before to ask if anyone had seen the perpetrator or his vehicle, while the other cop stayed with her to get her account of the incident and the description of her assailant. She also informed him of her involvement in the ongoing murder investigation and gave him Josh's name and number just as he pulled up with a screech of brakes and strode over to where the Trooper was questioning Olivia.

"Are you okay?" he asked, looking at her intently, then peering into the back. "The girls okay?"

She nodded, still trembling a little from the fright and adrenaline combination. "We're fine, I'm just a bit shaken . . . they didn't even seem to notice." She attempted a wry grin.

"They knew you had it under control," he said with admiration in his voice. "Not many people would have been able to get away like you did. He turned to the Trooper, "I'm going to escort her to headquarters to see if she can find this guy in a mug shot book; I need you to check and see if the home super store has any cameras that could have caught this on tape. If you find anything, bring it by headquarters before you head back to your barracks."

Olivia followed Josh to his headquarters and he helped her get Molly and Sheyna out and take them for a brief walk. Sheyna was getting better at leash walking all the time. Pretty soon, she'd think she was a dog, Olivia mused—maybe she already did—she was way more affectionate and easy going than most cats Olivia had been around.

Josh led Molly up the stone walkway and inside the small headquarters building, which was shared with NHDMV. Olivia followed with Sheyna, and they were all buzzed into the inner door by a short, kind looking woman behind a glass window.

Josh led the way to his office. Once Olivia and the animals were all seated inside, he brought a bowl of water from the little kitchen in case Molly or Sheyna were thirsty. He offered Olivia water or soda, and she gladly accepted a bottle of cold water. Screaming had made her throat raw, and her mouth was dry from nerves. The water felt great.

"So, will you look through these pictures first and let me know if any of them is the man who attacked you?" he asked quietly. "Are you sure you're okay?" he rested his hand on hers for a moment. "That had to have been pretty frightening."

She took a deep breath and blew it out, nodding. "Yes, it was I think, but I'm okay now. It happened so fast that I didn't really have time to be scared until it was over. I'm still shaking from the adrenaline, but I'll be fine." She reached out her hand with a small sigh. "Let me see the pictures."

Josh spread six pictures in front of her on the table. Each was of a different man.

Olivia studied them intently for a few moments, then shook her head. "He was wearing a baseball cap pulled low over his face, and it just happened so fast!" her voice rose in frustration. "It's possible that it could be this one," she said pointing to the blonde man in the second picture from the left; "or maybe this one," pointing to another blonde man, "but I just don't know for sure. I only had such a brief look at him and his face was all snarled up like an angry dog's face."

Josh smiled at her. "You did a great job," he said. "You saved yourself and the girls too. I meant it when I said that most people couldn't have done that." He grinned, "I even know a couple of cops who couldn't have done it, and yes, they are men, before you ask." He laughed, anticipating her indignant question.

Olivia smiled, finally feeling herself starting to relax a little. It felt so good being around Josh. He made her laugh and he made her feel safe, not just because he was a cop or a big, strong man, but because he reinforced her belief in herself and her own strengths. *This man was a keeper,* she realized, and that thought scared her more than anything had in a long time.

~~~

Josh left Olivia sitting in his office with Molly and Sheyna and went to talk to his superior in the Major Crimes Unit. The first man she'd tentatively identified had been Henry Larsson. This whole thing was getting out of hand and he was afraid Olivia was going to get hurt if she didn't have police protection. He knew their budget wouldn't allow for much, but he had to try, otherwise, he was going to end up sitting in front of her house all night in his car, and that definitely wasn't the way he'd envisioned spending the night with her.

The captain's wife was sitting in his office when Josh entered, and maybe that helped Josh's case because to his relief, Captain Corwin agreed to provide an officer to stay outside Olivia's house at night, since this was the second time she'd been targeted since the murder. He'd only authorized it for three nights, and from six AM to ten PM she was on her own, but it was more than he'd expected.

Josh knew Olivia had had a traumatic experience today, even though she was handling it well. He decided to see if she would allow him to stay with her until the police officer arrived at ten pm.

"Well, I have good news and bad news," he grinned, walking back into his office. "Nothing that bad, actually, The Captain's wife Hilda, was there and I think that might have softened him up a little, because he did authorize protection, but . . . this is the bad news, not until ten pm, so I was wondering if I could possibly bring over a pizza or Chinese take-out and stay with you until your real protection arrives?" He saw her start to object and quickly said, "You'd be doing me a favor, because otherwise I'll be parked in front of your house starving until he comes."

Olivia shook her head laughing and agreed that sharing a pizza would be much better for everyone. Josh told her to be very careful until he got there, and if she could stay at a friend's house or in a safe public place where no one could get to her, until he got off work, he would feel happier about it.

She promised to be careful and said she'd go to a pet friendly book store to do some research on antique glass that she'd been meaning to get done. He could meet her there and escort her home.

Josh didn't know Olivia well yet, but one of the first things he'd noticed about her, besides her stunning looks, was her self-sufficiency and mental strength. To see how easily she agreed to all of his requests for her protection, told him more than any words could have, just how much the assault had shaken her. The fear still lurked behind her eyes. Josh wanted to see her easy confident smile come back.

O'Brian was leaving early for a dentist appointment, so Josh asked him to follow her to the bookstore, on his way, just to make sure she got there safely.

At a quarter past five, Josh headed to the bookstore. He parked and walked up to peer in the window. Olivia was sitting at a small table by a big stone fireplace with books and papers covering most of the table and Sheyna covering the rest. Molly was curled up on her feet. If there had been a fire in the fireplace and snow on the outside window sill, it would have made a perfect winter postcard. He just wanted to walk in and hold all three of them to keep them safe. Josh knew then that he was falling hard.

CHAPTER SIX

Olivia had a hard time keeping her mind on her research, and had found herself jumping at unexpected noises and being nervous when strange men came close to her. She really didn't know what her assailant looked like well enough to tell if he walked right up to her, so it was a little unnerving. She was ashamed of herself for being relieved when Josh arrived to follow her home.

The delicious smell of hot pizza wafted from the cartons Josh was carrying as she opened the door to let everyone inside the house. Olivia's stomach growled, and Josh laughed.

"Did you eat lunch today?" he asked. "I'll bet you didn't."

She smiled ruefully, "You'd be right. I never even thought about food until I smelled that lovely pizza."

She set plates and silverware on the table, then poured some kibble into Molly's bowl, mixed it with homemade vegetable soup, did the same with cat kibble for Sheyna, and set their dishes down for them. Both animals started eating immediately, though Molly gave a woeful glance toward the pizza first.

"I brought one with veggies and lots of cheese and the other one with all that plus pepperoni. I wasn't sure what you liked and I had a feeling you might be

ANTIQUES & AVARICE

vegetarian from what I've seen you eat. I forgot to ask earlier, so I thought I'd better be prepared." He opened the pizza boxes and chuckled, "I actually don't eat much meat but I do love pepperoni on my pizza."

"Wow, you're very observant," Olivia was impressed. "Yes I am vegetarian, not Vegan though. I eat everything except meat. It's been years since I ate meat. That was very thoughtful of you, especially when you weren't sure."

He smiled, looking both happy and mildly embarrassed. "Dig in while it's hot," he grabbed a large slice of pepperoni pizza and slid it onto his plate.

Olivia grinned broadly, feeling ridiculously happy all of a sudden. "Thanks for the pizza and the company, both are simply wonderful." She blushed and took a slice of vegetarian pizza.

"So, have you found out anything that you can share about the case?" she asked after a few moments. "I googled Lewis Edmund Ketterrer, and found only obituaries, so I am thinking maybe that was an alias?"

"Yes, it was," Josh laughed. "You are quite the detective yourself. His real name was Marvin Douglas Jamison. He was a professional cat burglar, and we think he got away with several large robberies at the end of his career."

Olivia thought for a minute, "So do you think one of the robbery victims killed him in revenge or did he maybe have a partner that he ripped off or something?"

Josh laughed again, "You seriously do have a detective's mind. He did have a partner, we think, who served time for the last robbery, and might have killed him over the loot, if he found him, and he refused to give

59

him his cut." He shook his head, "I haven't checked on the victims yet, but that is an excellent idea, and I will get started on it tomorrow. It seemed so likely that it was Henry Larsson, the partner, that I fixated on him and stopped checking for other possibles. Let me know if you are ever looking for a job." He laughed ruefully. "You might even get mine."

"I can't even remember what it is that keeps bugging me about the day of the murder; I'm definitely not next in line for your job."

The evening went by quickly, with a lot of playful banter, some definite electricity between them and a good bit of seriously fun flirtation. Sheyna and Molly joined in on the fun after dinner as they played catch with one of Molly's plush toys. Molly decided to forgive them for feeding her kibble instead of pizza.

At nine fifty-five Molly started barking and there was a knock at the door. A young Trooper informed them that he would be on duty outside until morning.

"I guess we should be wrapping it up," Josh said. "I'll help you clean up the kitchen, and then I'd better take off so you can get some rest."

Olivia didn't think he looked like he wanted to leave, but maybe she was projecting. "You don't have to help me," she said. "You also don't have to leave yet if you don't want to. I'm not tired at all." She put the ball back in his court.

"Well," he said, "If I stay, you'll have to let me help and you have to tell me a little more about what makes Olivia McKenna tick. All I really know is that you love antiques, cooking and animals, and that we have those things in common." He picked up their plates and carried them to the sink.

Olivia smiled as she started washing the dishes. "There really isn't much more to tell about me," she said. "I've never been married, Molly and Sheyna are my only kids, and I don't have any other family in the area. What about you?"

"I was married, but she died three years ago in a car wreck. I've pretty much been a workaholic since then."

"Josh, I am so sorry!" Olivia's eyes filled with tears of sympathy. She took his hands in her soapy ones, knocking the drying towel into the dish water.

They both looked down at their wet soapy hands, then at each other and suddenly he started laughing, and after a couple of seconds Olivia did too. They were still holding hands and looking at each other when he bent and kissed her.

The electricity was sudden and intense. They both pulled back in surprise.

"Wow!" Olivia and Josh stared at each other in amazement.

Josh took a deep breath and let it out in a rush. "I expected fireworks, but that was just pure fire," he said with a slow grin. "We'd better slow down or we might just ignite something we can't put out."

Olivia grinned a little shyly, "I think you're right. Wow!" She released his hands and stepped back awkwardly, smoothing her dress to give herself time to regroup.

Josh fished the dish towel out of the soapy water and wrung it out. He hung it over the dish drain to dry and Olivia took a new towel from a drawer and handed it to him. He took it very carefully, elaborately using both hands and they both started laughing, instantly banishing the awkwardness.

Once everything was dried and put away, Josh said goodbye to Molly and Sheyna, and Olivia walked him to the door. He took her hands in his and they just looked at each other for a long moment, then he lightly caressed her face with one hand, brushed his lips across her forehead and said goodnight, then he opened the door and they walked out.

Olivia waved to the officer in the car out front, then walked back inside and locked the door. She felt scared and giddy with delight simultaneously.

Molly asked to be let out the back, and Olivia walked out with her for a minute, breathing in the woodsy smell in the night air. When Molly was ready, they went back inside and Olivia made herself a cup of chamomile tea and they headed upstairs. She tried to read a mystery novel for a few minutes, but her mind kept wandering to Josh, and she might as well have held the book upside down. She finally gave up and turned off the light, embracing her thoughts, the way she wanted to embrace Josh.

~~~

The next three days were completely uneventful for Olivia. She and Josh spoke daily on the phone, but he was busy working the murder case, her case and a few minor ones as well, and she was busy with her own work, looking for estate sales and auctions where she might acquire some of the stuff on her lists, playing with Molly and Sheyna and refinishing some antique hand carved nesting tables she hoped to sell someday, though if they turned out just right she might not be able to resist keeping them.

Friday morning Josh called to ask her if she'd like

him to come over at four-thirty AM on Saturday to stay with Molly and Sheyna, so she could go early to the sale in Conway the following morning without having to worry about them. Olivia was stunned by his thoughtfulness and gratefully accepted, though she felt a little guilty, not leaving them with Abby's mom, who loved watching them.

She called Abby and explained that the State Trooper involved in her case was going to take care of the animals, as it might be dangerous for her mom, since the last time, someone had possibly been prowling around the house. Abby assured her that she hadn't even told her mom yet, so she wouldn't be disappointed. They arranged to meet at the sale at five AM and Olivia made a few more phone calls, updated her clients' lists, and made a breakfast casserole to put in the fridge for Josh, so he could just heat it up and have a nice homemade breakfast while he stayed with Molly and Sheyna.

After a quick lunch, she went out in the back yard to work on stripping the little Chinese nesting tables with citrus stripper. Once she got the stripper on using an old paintbrush, she had to wait for an hour to see if it was working well, or if she needed to add more and leave it for a longer time. The old finish was coming off, but she felt it was better to spritz the tables with a little denatured alcohol to keep the stripper moist, and leave it for another hour.

Meanwhile, she decided she might as well prep dinner for Saturday since it would be a hectic day so she chopped veggies, put them in a large zippered baggy and put it in the fridge. She could throw it in a pan with olive oil, spices, mushrooms, and a little seitan for a quick and easy dinner later, now that the veggies were chopped.

Back outside, she took a plastic putty knife and scraped the old stain and varnish off the first table. It was coming off beautifully now. The tables would be a rich reddish golden color, perfect to match her living room décor. So much for selling them, she laughed at herself. Well, maybe she would enjoy them for a while and sell them later if something she liked even better came along. That was one of her favorite things about her job.

Once all the tables were scraped, she used mineral spirits to wash the stripper off, working with paper towels first, and an old toothbrush for the carvings, then with mineral spirit soaked rags once the worst of the mess was off. The she dried them as thoroughly as she could. They would have to air dry overnight before she could apply Danish Oil.

Olivia cleaned up her work area, put all the nasty paper towels and rags into a plastic garbage bag, tied it up and took it out to the trash bin by the road. She carried the tables back inside to her storage room and set them out of the way to dry completely.

Sheyna decided she would dry the tables by rubbing up against the legs and Molly was helping by waving her long silky tail around the tables to circulate more air to dry them off. Olivia shooed Molly and Sheyna out of the storage room, laughing at their antics.

With her biggest chores for the day out of the way, she sat down at her laptop to catch up on emails and see if any of her facebook friends had posted new stuff. She had a good chuckle over a few funny posts, shared a couple funny memes she'd found somewhere else and replied to an old friend's email saying they might possibly be coming for a visit in the winter. Before she knew it, it was time to feed Molly and Sheyna and cook her own dinner.

She watched a video while she ate dinner then let Molly go out for a few minutes until she was done cleaning the kitchen. Once Molly came back in, Olivia was ready to go to bed. The alarm would be going off very early in the morning.

Olivia woke to the buzz of the alarm clock, and Molly licking her face at three-thirty AM. She groaned and yawned widely, as she rolled over and got out of bed.

The shower helped wake her up a little bit, and the coffee helped a lot more. She was dressed and on her second cup when Josh knocked on the door. She opened it quickly and let him in with a smile.

"Good morning Josh," she said. "You have no idea how much I appreciate this". She poured him a steaming cup of coffee, and put the breakfast casserole in the oven to get warm. "All you need to do is give it about half an hour to heat through, then put it on your plate."

"Wow, that's wonderful! I love your breakfasts," he smiled. "As far as looking after Molly and Sheyna it's no trouble and I will feel a lot better knowing they are safe, besides it gives me a chance to hang out with them," he grinned. "I really miss having pets; it's the only bad thing about my apartment. One of these days, I guess I'll have to move somewhere that allows them. Molly and Sheyna could come visit me then; they are total sweethearts."

"Well, believe me, the feeling is mutual," she grinned. "They positively adore you already and you are welcome to come visit anytime you want."

He gave her a long measured look, "I may just take you up on that sometime."

She blushed and smiled at him, "I think we'd like that." Slightly flustered, she picked up her purse, her lists, a thermos with hot coffee, and a small cooler with water bottles inside, and headed toward the door.

"I was thinking of taking Molly and Sheyna to the park later, if that is okay with you," Josh said. "It'll be good leash practice for Sheyna, and Molly'll love playing with the Frisbee."

"Wow. That would be awesome for them!" Olivia said happily. "They will definitely be your friends forever. I've been a little afraid to take them since the incident with that man. Thanks Josh."

"Have fun, and I hope you find lots of the stuff you're looking for," Josh smiled as he opened the door for her.

"See you around noon," she waved as she backed out of the driveway.

Abby was just pulling in, when she arrived at the sale site. There was only one other car so far, so they should get numbers in the first group of people allowed in. Of course, there may be some cronies of the people managing the sale that would get the lowest numbers, but she thought she and Abby would still be fine.

Abby had brought two folding camp chairs. Olivia joined her at the head of the line while they waited for the numbers to be given out. Her friend was sporting a brand new tiny tattoo of a rose on the inside of her wrist. Olivia complimented her on it.

"So what is the scoop on this cop that's watching Molly and Sheyna?" Abby asked with a slight smirk. "Is he a hottie?"

Olivia laughed, "Alright, yes, he is definitely a hottie! He's a freaking drop dead delicious hottie!" She blushed, "He's also one of the sweetest, smartest, most wonderful men I've ever met."

"Oh my, girl, you've really got it bad, don't you?" Abby laughed. "So when am I meeting dream guy? Do you have to stop at his place to pick up Molly and Sheyna on the way home?"

"No, he's watching them at my house, well actually he's taking them to the park later. Right now, they're probably still eating breakfast in my kitchen."

"Wow! So he spent the night, and you were holding out on me?" Abby pretended outrage. "I want all the dirt!"

Olivia laughed, "No he came over at four-thirty AM to watch them so I could meet you. He didn't spend the night." She looked up to see the guy in charge of the sale coming out of the house.

Abby and Olivia picked up their chairs and walked up to the sale manager to collect their numbers. They received low numbers, so they would be in the very first group allowed in the house. They shared a look of triumph.

Olivia followed Abby to her van, and they put the chairs back inside, then climbed into the van to wait for the sale to actually open. There were a lot of people in the line for numbers now, and Olivia and Abby occupied themselves by people watching.

"There's Darlene . . . somebody, that woman who always grabs every single quilt and fancy pillow sham she can get to, and I am so happy to be going in ahead of her for a change." Olivia said. "I really need to get some nice quilts and I have a feeling this house will have them."

"You know it will!" Abby exclaimed. "Don't you remember hearing Melinda Pendergraft talking about the gorgeous antique quilts her grandma had in her cedar chests? This was her grandma's house." Abby looked like the cat that swallowed the canary.

"Oh my lucky stars!" Olivia beamed. "I have absolutely got to find those quilts before anyone else."

"We'll get them Liv. I'm looking for the cedar chests myself," Abby grinned broadly. "We'll go in separate directions and whoever finds the stuff, marks all of it sold, and moves on to whatever else she's looking for, then we'll work out the payment arrangements later. We've got this, girlfriend!" They high-fived.

The manager and his assistants opened the door at seven sharp and Olivia and Abby filed in behind four other people with fourteen more people following behind them in the first group.

Abby went left and Olivia headed right, each grabbing a few things they wanted that were on their way as they searched for the quilts in the cedar chests. Olivia grabbed a beautiful antique tall wooden butter churn and a simply stunning Dazey glass butter churn which was high on her list and hung on for dear life as she struggled through the house, bashing herself in the shins with the large wooden churn. She was afraid to take the time to ask a sale assistant to mark them for her.

Just as Olivia thought she was going to drop everything, she heard Abby give a shout of triumph. She breathed a sigh of relief and stopped to reposition the wooden churn, which was causing her to lose her grip on the other items she was carrying.

Once she'd gotten all her finds back under control, she headed to where she'd heard Abby's voice and found her with a sales assistant happily marking all the quilts, quilted pillow shams, antique crocheted bedspreads and two stunning cedar chests sold with their names.

Olivia got the assistant to mark the items she was carrying as well, and gratefully put them down with the quilts. As soon as they were sure all was well there, they each went back to their own agendas, agreeing to meet outside when they were done.

Olivia found a few smaller items from her clients' lists and a stunning antique Omega sterling silver man's watch that actually worked, that she could picture on Josh's strong wrist. She thought it would be a nice 'thank you for watching the animals' gift, so she added it to her purchases.

She bumped into Abby on her way to pay for her finds, so they went together to pay and helped each other carry everything to their respective vehicles, except for the cedar chests which were being delivered. Abby had found a beautiful oriental rug that she was pretty sure one of her clients would love, but she was so thrilled with the cedar chests that she couldn't stop running her hands over them.

They gave each other a hug and parted ways at Abby's van. Abby made Olivia promise to introduce her to Josh as soon as she felt comfortable doing so.

It was only eleven AM when Olivia pulled into her driveway. Josh's car was nowhere in sight and the front door was wide open. Olivia stayed in her car, making sure the door was locked and dialed Josh's number on her cell.

He was just about to leave the park with Molly and Sheyna when he answered.

"Stay in the car with the engine running and pull back into the street. I'll be right there," he ordered tersely. *"I'm calling it in, so you just watch to make sure no one is coming near you, then take your keys and get in my car with the girls and lock the doors when I get there."*

Olivia obeyed quickly, backing the car up and staying alert until she saw Josh's car pull behind her. As soon as he got out she turned her car off and rushed back to his car to stay with Molly and Sheyna while he walked toward her house with his gun drawn.

Before he got to the front door, they could hear sirens, so he waited until his backup arrived then they quickly went in and checked the house. The intruder had ransacked the house, spilling things out of all the drawers and cabinets, but luckily hadn't really destroyed anything. Obviously they'd been looking for something specific.

Once the detectives Josh had called were finished checking for fingerprints and such, Josh asked Olivia to see if she could tell if there was anything missing. Most of her jewelry was gone from her jewelry box on her dresser, and there were a few antique silver thimbles missing from her collection, but everything else seemed to be accounted for.

Olivia seemed to be feeling pretty freaked out by the break-in, and Josh wanted her to bring the animals and come to Headquarters with him so he could try to get protection for her again. She was so shaken up that she quickly agreed. Josh helped her put the house back in order and clean up the fingerprint dust. It was two hours later that they finally left for headquarters to file the official police report.

He escorted them into his office and made some coffee with extra sugar to try to help Olivia relax. Even when she'd been personally attacked, she hadn't seemed this upset. Josh was really concerned.

"I'll be okay Josh," she said quietly. "I just feel really violated, seeing all my things thrown around and walked on like that. My home is supposed to be safe."

Josh took her in his arms and just held her for a minute. She felt so small and fragile. He hated to see her looking so beaten down. She was such a strong woman.

He led her to a chair, "Sit down and relax for a few minutes, I'll be back as soon as I can." He looked back to see her with tears in her eyes, as he walked out the door.

He knew he would have an uphill battle getting the Captain to agree to spend any more of their meager budget on protection when nothing had happened the last time they'd had a guard at night, but he had to try. He steeled his resolve and knocked on his boss' door.

The aggravated look on Josh's face as he left his Captain's office eloquently told the story of his failure to secure police protection. He stopped to curb his temper before he went back to his office so he wouldn't display his frustration in front of Olivia by behaving like a surly idiot.

Okay, plan A was gone; did plan B have to entail sitting in his car in front of her house all night or could he come up with a better solution, he pondered? He knew the rules, but at this point he was more worried about her than about his job. He couldn't invite her to stay at his apartment, because pets weren't allowed, and it was a small apartment, too cozy for comfort with a woman he was this interested in. He wondered if she would consider letting him sleep on her couch. He didn't want to look like he was trying to take advantage of a scary situation. *Well, she won't let you for sure if you don't ask,* he told himself, opening the door.

"The Captain said the budget is too tight for us to have someone stay with you. I had a feeling that was what he would say, but I don't think you should stay there alone."

"It's okay," she sighed. "I wasn't sure how I felt about having a stranger stay in my house anyway. Molly is a very good watch dog and will bark if anyone comes near the house."

"I don't want you to think I am hitting on you or saying you aren't able to take care of yourself, because that's not the case," he said, watching his wording carefully, "But I would feel much, much better if you would let me sleep on your couch tonight just to make sure no one tries to get in. It would be safer for all three of you. This guy's aggression is escalating and I don't want to see any of you get hurt."

Olivia looked pensively at Josh for a moment. "Thank you," she said simply. "I would be grateful for your protection. Molly would never willingly let someone break in, but if he was armed, she wouldn't stand a chance. I know you would be able to defend yourself, and us."

Josh breathed a sigh of relief. "I was afraid you were going to say no, and I would end up spending the night sitting in front of your house in my car," he grinned.

"Well, we can't have that," Olivia smiled back, regaining some of her strength. "When will you be coming over, now or later on?"

"I can't come until my shift is over at 5:00," he said.

"I'll grab a few things from home and be there by 5:30 if that's alright.

"That's perfect," she said. "I will stop on the way home and pick up some food for supper. If you're protecting me, the least I can do is feed you well."

"Oh man! I'm getting the best part of this deal," he laughed. "I haven't had a meal as good as those breakfasts you cooked in ages. I never seem to feel like cooking for just me."

"Do you like eggplant parmigiana?" she asked. "I'm thinking of a slightly different version that I make, maybe with some homemade rosemary garlic bread and Caesar salad?"

"I'm wishing my shift was over already," he laughed. "I'll bring the wine," he said, forgetting for a moment that this wasn't just a dinner date with a woman who was gorgeous and fun to be with. He found himself wishing it was exactly that. Well, he'd take what he could get. She needed protection, and he would get to spend time with her, while making sure she was safe.

CHAPTER SEVEN

Despite how horrible she'd been feeling over having her privacy violated and her house trashed, and despite her misgivings about getting too close to Josh, Olivia was actually feeling cheerful and excited about the pending evening. She phoned her friend Julie, whose daughter Sandra had a summer job stocking shelves at the little grocery market near her house that she'd kept into the early autumn on a part time basis, and asked if she would see if her daughter could possibly come out and watch the animals for a few minutes while she shopped. Julie called back and said it was arranged.

Olivia shopped quickly, grabbing the nicest eggplants she could find, some fresh romaine lettuce for the salad, and all the other ingredients which she didn't already have at home. She gave Sandra a nice tip and a hug, then rushed home to make sure everything was back to its normally neat and clean state—well, clean anyway—neat was sometimes a stretch.

After a frenzied bout of house cleaning, Olivia prepped the dinner then she ran to the Suburban and dragged all her new purchases into the house and put them in the storage room to deal with later, and headed upstairs to see what she was going to wear.

Okay Liv, she told herself, *you know how your*

clothes look on you already, so you really don't need to try on every single thing in your closet and then make a mess, which you'll have to straighten before you can shower. Molly woofed her agreement.

Olivia was as excited as a school girl getting ready for her first date. She hadn't let herself get close to anyone since Danny. She'd dated a little, but nothing even remotely serious, usually not even a second date. She knew Josh would be different; if she let him in, she could fall for him way too easily. It scared her silly, and she had a feeling that it might already be too late for caution.

After her shower, Olivia dressed in a cute light brown sleeveless dress with golden orange accents. She decided on low heeled strappy brown sandals, as she really didn't want to suffer through leg cramps from high heels while she was cooking. Stomping and limping around the kitchen trying to relieve crampy calves would definitely not be sexy. Her fingernails and toenails were done in a French manicure style, and she applied only a tiny bit of eyeliner and clear lip gloss.

"There!" she exclaimed. "Did I get it right?" she asked Sheyna and Molly. "You guys like him as much as I do, admit it." She picked up Sheyna and hugged her. Molly head butted her free hand for pats, which she lovingly provided.

"Okay girls, he'll be here soon. Let's get this show on the road." She quickly straightened her room and headed downstairs.

Olivia finished getting the dinner ready for baking, then she fed Molly and Sheyna.

Molly heard or sensed Josh's arrival first and ran to

the front door wagging her tail. Sheyna followed a little more sedately, with Olivia actually waiting until he knocked.

She opened the door to find Josh holding a bunch of yellow roses and a bottle of wine. He held them out to her a little awkwardly, as if he were unsure of her reaction. Olivia smiled warmly and took the proffered gifts.

"Hi Josh, thank you so much for the flowers; they are lovely. The wine looks very welcome right now too. Please come in."

"Good evening Olivia, you look beautiful," Josh followed her into the house with Molly and Sheyna trailing behind him. "Something smells beautiful too," he grinned. "I hadn't even realized I was hungry until I smelled those aromas."

Olivia led him into the kitchen and pulled out a chair for him to sit, then put the roses into a vase with water. "We're eating in the kitchen if you don't mind," she smiled. "The dining room is full of stuff I'm cleaning and sorting for sale right now, so it's a bit of a mess, as you may remember from seeing it earlier today."

"I love your kitchen!" Josh exclaimed laughing, "Cozy atmosphere and the best food in New Hampshire. You don't need to worry about impressing me with your fancy dining room; I'm already very impressed with you, and not just with your cooking."

The look he gave her sent delicious goose bumps running up and down her skin.

"I'm pretty impressed with you too Detective," Olivia said, a bit flirtatiously, her breath catching in her throat, as he gazed at her with warm green eyes.

Sheyna broke the spell by jumping into Josh's lap and head butting his chin with a loud purr.

Josh laughed, "You sure know how to change the mood, don't you Sheyna?" He rubbed her head and reached down to pat Molly so she wouldn't feel slighted.

Olivia took a calming breath and turned back to the oven to check on the eggplant dish—just a couple more minutes. The bread was done and sitting in the still warm oven. Olivia poured the dressing over the salad and tossed it all together, putting some in two bowls and placing them on the table.

She quickly served the rest of the food and sat down across from Josh, who lowered Sheyna to the floor.

Josh spread a little of the garlic butter over a piece of bread and bit into it. He groaned in appreciation of the flavor. "My taste buds are in heaven," he said, as he followed the bread with a bite of eggplant. "You may be a great antique finder, but I think you're an even better chef."

Olivia grinned, "Thank you Josh," she said. "I love to cook almost as much as I love antiques, but it's not something I'd want to do for a living."

They engaged in friendly banter with flirtatious overtones while they ate, never once mentioning crime. The delicious food and the wine made them both more mellow and relaxed.

After dinner, Josh helped Olivia clear the table and they gave the scraps to Molly and Sheyna, then washed and dried the dishes together. Every time their hands touched as they handed a dish to each other, a tingle of electricity passed between them.

As soon as they finished, they carried their wine into the living room, and Olivia lit a small fire in the fireplace, just for the romantic atmosphere, as it wasn't a chilly night. Josh sat on the sofa and Molly and Sheyna hopped up beside him. He patted them both while Olivia got the fire going and put the screen in front to keep sparks from flying out. There were plenty of sparks flying between her and Josh already.

Olivia put on some soft music and Josh lifted Sheyna into his lap to make room for Olivia to sit beside him. They sat close to each other watching the small flames in the fireplace in silence for a while, then Josh shifted slightly to put his arm around Olivia and Sheyna jumped up onto the back of the sofa with a disgusted look. They both laughed and Olivia snuggled in closer as Josh's arm tightened around her shoulders.

Despite the huge attraction she was feeling and the hot electricity flowing between them, Olivia felt safe and comfortable with Josh holding her. For the moment, there was nothing scary or uncertain in her world. They sat, letting the music wash over them, enjoying their closeness and the dancing lights from the fire.

After some time had passed, Olivia got up and brought the bottle of wine in from the kitchen to refill their glasses.

"I feel comfortable with you Josh," she said quietly. "I can't even tell you how unusual that is for me."

Josh took her hand in his and they slowly intertwined their fingers.

"I've been thinking the same thing myself," he said. "Since Susan died, I haven't met a woman I could talk with, or just sit quietly with like this, without it becoming awkward and uncomfortable or something else altogether." He grinned, "Passion is one thing; communication is another. I have a strong feeling we could have both and I'm greedy enough to want it all."

He took her other hand and they twined their fingers together, as he leaned in to touch his lips to hers. Though sparks flew between them, the kiss was surprisingly sweet and hopeful as well.

They cuddled together on the sofa, with Molly and Sheyna, content just to hold each other and share a little about their pasts and their hopes and dreams for the future. Josh also finally managed to get Olivia to agree that he would come and stay in her guestroom until the danger was over.

Olivia and Josh were both startled when the antique grandfather clock started chiming at midnight. Reluctantly, they got up and put the wine glasses in the sink. Olivia showed Josh to the downstairs guestroom, and gave him towels and a washcloth so he could shower in the morning.

Josh left the door to his room open, so Molly and Sheyna could come and go as they pleased, and so he would be able to hear if anything was going on in the rest of the house. He unpacked his pajamas from the little overnight bag he'd brought and got ready for bed. Sheyna came and leaped up onto his pillow beside his head and began to purr as soon as he lay down.

Olivia locked up the house, turned off all the lights and headed upstairs to her bedroom with Molly trailing behind her. Once she'd changed into her nightgown she opened her door so the animals could go in and out. She lay down and Molly snuggled against her back. This was one night she was pretty sure her dreams would be good. She smiled as she drifted off to sleep.

~~~

Olivia awoke to the smell of fresh coffee brewing

and smiled as the memories of the previous evening came flooding back. She didn't think she'd ever felt such a wonderful emotional connection with a man, not even with Danny, not to mention the chemistry that was so obviously there. She stretched and got up, excited to see what the day would bring.

Once she'd showered and dressed, she went downstairs to find Josh reading the paper while Molly and Sheyna ate their food. An empty cup was sitting on the table waiting for her and Josh quickly got up, poured her coffee and gave her a kiss that she felt all the way down to her toes.

"Good morning Livvie," he said, his breath warm against her hair as he hugged her. "How did you sleep?"

She hugged him back. "Like a baby," she laughed, "all safe and sound. How about you? Did you get enough sleep?"

He gave her a sexy grin, "I slept plenty, but no baby ever had the kind of dreams I had last night."

Olivia blushed and laughed, "Okay, perhaps baby wasn't the right word. It sounds like we shared our dreams as well as the house last night."

Josh laughed, hugging her again, then letting go and stepping back slightly. "I am going to behave myself, if it kills me," he said. "We should take things slow and work on keeping you safe for now, because since you are still on the suspect list, I have to be careful not to be seen as impartial or improper. Even this, is completely against regulations and I am going to try very hard not to let anyone in the department find out I'm staying here." He gave her a light playful kiss, "After all of my protective services last night, do I get a free breakfast?"

Olivia smiled, "You bet you do!" She said, grabbing

a skillet and opening the fridge. "How do scrambled eggs with cheddar, scallions and soysage sound?"

"Wonderful!" Josh exclaimed, taking the skillet out of her hand and putting it on the stove so she could carry the food stuff. He got her coffee from the table and put it near her on the counter so she could drink it while she cooked.

"So," Josh said as he sat down, "I've decided to take you into my confidence on the case." He smiled, "I'm quite sure you are innocent of any wrong doing, and I like the way your brain works, so I think together we have a better chance of figuring this out quickly."

Olivia beamed at him happily. "Thank you for taking me seriously Josh," she said. "I would love to be a part of figuring out what's going on, since I seem to be involuntarily involved anyway."

Josh frowned slightly, "I don't want you to become involved in the dangerous parts of it. Leave the going out and physically investigating to me and the department." He watched her closely, "You and I can brainstorm everything and investigate on paper and verbally. Do we have a deal?"

Olivia knitted her brows, "Just because I am a woman, doesn't mean I can't investigate physically. I may not be as strong as a man, but I am very capable of thinking."

Josh smiled at her, "Yes you are! I don't think you are one bit less capable than anyone who hasn't been trained in police work, and self defense, but that's the point. My people and I have been trained and are better at protecting ourselves against criminals. It's the training, not the gender."

"Okay, I'll buy that," Olivia smiled, holding up her hands in surrender. "After all, I did very much welcome your protection last night. You're right that I wouldn't really know how to stop someone with a weapon, so I will take the deal." She gave him a coy look, "Maybe I will have to start taking a martial arts class."

Josh laughed, "That is a great idea, but for now, we'll play it my way, okay?"

"Yes, I'll play by your rules on this as long as you really will share your information with me," Olivia smiled as she stirred the egg mixture in the pan.

"I promise." he grinned. "Right now, we're still leaning toward Henry Larsson, since he was the first guy you picked out of the pictures, when you tried to identify the guy who'd attacked you, but so far, we have no physical evidence at all," Josh looked frustrated.

Olivia served the food onto their plates and sat down across from Josh. "Did you ever look into the robbery victims?" she asked.

"Yes, the captain himself looked into them, but he didn't find anything suspicious about any of them; they all collected insurance money on the missing stuff, but everything seemed straightforward," he said. "I also talked to one of the cops who worked on the case when Jamison's partner Larsson was convicted and he thinks it's likely that he is the one who killed Jamison." Josh sighed, stabbing a bite of soysage, "He said Larsson's got a temper on him, and he wouldn't be surprised if he'd done it. He doesn't have a clue where he is now unfortunately."

"Hmmm, if he killed Jamison, and left no evidence," Olivia frowned in thought, "why is he after me? I mean, I don't have anything he wants. Jamison is the one who cheated him, and he's the one who would have had the spoils from the robberies. I didn't even see him in the shop, so it doesn't make sense."

"That's another big question, isn't it?" Josh said. "He must think you saw or heard something that could incriminate him, or maybe that Jamison gave you something or sold you something that was very valuable to keep him from finding it."

"But that would mean that he hadn't seen or heard me come in, and didn't know I was there until later," Olivia mused. "Could he have been hiding outside somewhere when I walked out the door to my car the first time, but why would he, if he'd already killed Jamison, wouldn't he run away, not hang out, risking being seen?" Olivia's brain was racing, "Was he hoping for the chance to search the shop some more, but Sheyna and I thwarted his plans by going back inside and finding the body?"

They found themselves bouncing ideas off each other as naturally as though they'd been working cases together for a long time.

Once they'd finished eating, Josh reluctantly said he'd better get to Headquarters, since it was almost seven AM already.

Olivia refused to let him help wash up, so he quickly packed his overnight kit and rejoined her in the kitchen. Molly and Sheyna, followed as Olivia walked him to the door. He took her hands in his and they stood just looking at each other for a moment, then he bent and kissed her. Passion flared between them and they stepped back singed. Josh smiled mischievously, winked and turned toward his car.

Olivia laughed, then waved and went back inside as

he drove away. Molly whined to be let out and Olivia found herself grinning like an idiot as she walked to the back door. She hadn't dreamed that she could feel like this again after Danny, but here she was falling like a ton of bricks, and loving every minute of it.

CHAPTER EIGHT

Josh arrived at Headquarters a good five minutes before his Captain came in, so he immediately stopped worrying about being a half an hour late and busied himself with finishing some of the paperwork he'd postponed yesterday evening.

He soon finished with his neglected papers and started going through the Jamison file again. There had to be something they were missing.

He took out the picture of Larsson that the former Parole Officer had emailed him. It was from about two years ago, and was the most recent one they had access to. Josh thought again about putting out an APB on the guy, but decided it was just too risky, as it could too easily backfire and make him flee the area and go underground. Then they'd probably never get anything on him for the murder or for the break-ins and attempted kidnapping of Olivia either.

He studied the picture. Prison hadn't been too hard on Larsson from the looks of him. He was a fairly thin, though very muscular, athletically built middle aged man with pale blonde hair and Scandinavian features. In the picture he looked healthy, meticulously groomed and well dressed, unlike the vast majority of the parolees Josh had dealt with. He may or may not have gotten any or all of his payout for the Olander robbery, but he'd obviously either had some financial help from somewhere or a hidden cache of money from the robberies that the cops had never found. He knew they'd searched diligently, since there was so much money involved, but they'd never found anything but the swords. Larsson's bank accounts had held less than two-thousand dollars.

Josh read further through the information he had on Larsson. He'd be forty-nine years old now; he'd been married once about twenty years ago, but they'd divorced after only a year, so it was highly unlikely the ex-wife had anything to do with this or his earlier criminal activity, but he would try to locate her anyway to make sure.

Josh's phone buzzed on his desk. "Abrams," he answered. "Okay, give me fifteen minutes and in the meantime don't let anyone in." He hung up the phone with a bang.

"O'Brian," he stepped outside his office into the main squad room and called to the detective, "I need you and Hendricks over at the antique shop yesterday! Someone broke in and tossed the place pretty bad."

"Was it the killer?" O'Brian asked.

"How would I know, O'Brian?" Josh asked, throwing his hands up in exasperation. "A neighbor called it in and Fallon just got there a couple minutes ago. He said it looks like someone was looking for something specific and went through the shop pretty thoroughly." Josh turned to pick up his keys. "I'm headed over there now too, but I need you and Hendricks to dust for prints and work with Fallon and McNabb to canvass the neighborhood."

"You got it, Lieu," O'Brian grabbed his keys and a bag of potato chips from his desk and walked toward Hendricks' desk.

Josh drove out of the parking lot and called Olivia on his cell phone to let her know that he might be late getting to her house depending on how things went at the antique shop. He hung up a few minutes later feeling more cheerful just from hearing her voice.

Unfortunately, the cheerful feeling was short lived. O'Brian arrived with Hendricks shortly after Josh and proceeded to dust for fingerprints and search the inside and outside completely. Aside from a lot of mess created by the intruder and the fingerprint powder, they didn't find anything to help with the investigation. Once they'd finished at the shop and with canvassing the neighborhood, Josh dismissed Fallon and McNabb. Hendricks and O'Brian headed back to Headquarters shortly thereafter, grumbling about it having been a waste of time, and Josh was left on his own in the now dusty mess.

He methodically went through the shop again, taking a few pictures of areas that had been especially trashed, to compare with the pictures in the file from the day of the murder. Maybe he and Olivia could look through them all tonight after dinner. A fresh pair of eyes would be welcome, especially eyes that were so observant.

Olivia noticed things really well he thought; she probably would have made a wonderful detective. He wasn't about to encourage her too much in that direction though, as she still didn't have any self defense training and was already in way too much danger without even trying to solve any crimes.

He had to admire her courage. Most people would have been throwing a fit if the police denied them protection after being targeted so many times, but she had been calmly accepting until he offered to stay with her. He had a feeling she might have accepted more because of Molly and Sheyna than her own safety.

Josh was walking slowly across a small rectangular oriental rug in the room Jamison had used as a bedroom, when he felt a slight unevenness under his left foot. He knelt and tried to lift the long edge of the rug but quickly discovered that he would first need to move the heavy antique chest of drawers from which only about a foot of the outside edge of the rug was protruding. He put the camera on the bed and carefully scooted the chest off the rug, half lifting it as to not damage the fragile looking wooden casters. Before he tried to lift the rug again, he got the camera and took a picture of it with the chest off, then he lifted the outside edge of the rug to find a recessed hinge. He jerked the rug out of the way, exposing a trapdoor with all the hardware recessed to keep it from being easily detected. He examined the hinge he'd stepped on and realized that one of the screws must have loosened over time, causing it to stick up just enough for him to have felt it under the rug, when he was walking slowly.

Not knowing what or who may be below, he thought it was best to follow procedure and wait for backup before attempting to open the trapdoor. Josh used his cell phone to call headquarters and ask them to send O'Brian and Hendricks back. He had thought about going out to the car and radioing them, but decided he'd better stay by the trapdoor in case someone happened to be under it. He definitely didn't want to give anyone a chance to come out and hide, or get away out the front door while his back was turned.

While he was waiting on his backup to arrive, Josh drew his gun and stood quietly against the wall, facing between the open bedroom door and the closed trapdoor. He doubted there was anyone below but he didn't fancy being caught unaware by a killer either.

It was only a few minutes before he heard O'Brian yell his name from the front of the shop.

"I'm in the bedroom," he called. "Bring the big flashlight and come on back here."

Bob O'Brian came in quickly, carrying a huge flashlight, followed by Earl Hendricks. O'Brian looked a bit sheepish when he saw the trapdoor.

"We never thought to move that big old chest and take up the rug," he said. "I guess we figured anything that he might have hidden would be in the other rooms somewhere. We did search in here Lieu," he said hurriedly, trying to cover his tracks, "just not under the rugs."

"No sweat, O'Brian," Josh shook his head. "I didn't think of it either until I felt it. We all should have known better, but at least it's found now, so let's get it open and see what we have."

The trapdoor opened smoothly and soundlessly, as O'Brian lifted the latch and pulled. Josh shone the big light down into the darkness below. There appeared to be a partial basement below, with no windows or other exits that they could see from up top.

After shining the light into all four corners, O'Brian held the big light while Josh and Hendricks descended the stairs with their guns in one hand and flashlights in the other. Josh was turned slightly to the right and Hendricks to the left as they went down.

"Whoa!" Hendricks breathed, as they reached the bottom and he saw several cases of gold coins spread out on a table. "I think we hit pay dirt!"

Josh reached a gloved hand out to lift one of the cases. "Well, I think we might finally have our proof that Jamison was involved in the Olander robbery, which means most likely the others as well. He must have been waiting for the statute of limitations to run out before selling them. Hmmm," he murmured, "he only had about three months left to wait."

Josh and Hendricks continued searching the half-basement area, finding a couple of other items that looked like things that were on the lists of stolen goods from the robberies in Boston. Just as they were about to wrap it up, Josh found a metal box behind a loose board in the bottom of the stairs.

He pried it open and let out a whoop. "I think the insurance companies are going to be fighting over which robberies this came from for a long time." He laughed, looking at the stacks of hundred dollar bills inside.

He and Hendricks both were taking pictures, and O'Brian had joined them to start dusting the whole lower level for fingerprints. Josh finally left his subordinates to finish with the dusting and went upstairs to radio his captain of the first good break they'd had in the case.

Once he'd finished with that, he quickly called Olivia to let her know that he might be an hour or so late getting to her house, so she wouldn't worry or have dinner waiting for him too early.

Josh and the other troopers carried all their

discoveries out to Josh's car and loaded it up. He would have to catalogue everything as soon as he got back, and write up his report on the finds. It was a huge haul monetarily, but actually a fairly small amount of items, so it shouldn't take more than two or three hours, he hoped.

He drove off toward Headquarters, leaving his men to lock up the shop and replace the crime scene tape. He quickly got to work on writing everything up once he reached his office.

Looking through his case files on the old robberies, he was able to match the Salvadore Dali painting and the lesser known Van Gogh landscape to the Porter robbery which was the next to the last one.

No one had ever been convicted for that one or the other seven robberies they'd suspected Larsson and Jamison to have committed. Well, at least they now had proof that the dead man had been involved. Better late than never.

Josh studied the list of stolen coins from the Olander job against the cases of coins they'd found under his shop. The first case he went through was a bust. None of the coins matched the list, neither did the coins in two other cases, but five of the cases held coins from Olanders' list. Over half of the missing coins were there. His insurance company would be happy at least, even though there were still sixteen million dollars worth of items unaccounted for. They'd paid out four million for the coins, over two million dollars worth of which they could now recoup, well they could once the police were done with them.

Josh ran a hand tiredly through his wavy dark hair and sat back in his chair. *Besides finding proof that*

Jamison had been in on two of the robberies, and recovering a tiny portion of the loot, what else had they gotten that would help them solve the case? Well, he thought, *it was better than nothing.*

He took his report to the Captain, snagged his files on the case and headed to Olivia's house, only a half hour late.

~~~

After Josh left her house that morning, Olivia called her friend Pam McAllister who ran a visitation program for the elderly in the local retirement home. It had been a while since she had taken Molly to visit the residents and she wanted to make sure today would be a good day and also to ask if Sheyna would be allowed to visit too. Molly was a registered therapy dog, but Sheyna didn't have any therapy training that Olivia knew about, but then, aggressive cats were less likely to injure someone severely than dogs and Sheyna was a super sweet cat.

Pam was thrilled to have Molly come and Sheyna too, as long as she was sweet and was up to date on her shots. Olivia changed into nice but comfortable pale green jeans and a beige short sleeved blouse and got Molly and Sheyna into their harnesses. She took their leads, some treats and a collapsible water bowl and loaded the animals into the crates in the SUV.

Olivia admired the view as she drove down the street. The trees were beautiful right now on this autumn day, all bright green, gold and orange with a hint of vivid red starting on some of the leaves. It would be sweater weather in the daytime soon, already the nights were getting chilly.

She wanted to take Molly hiking in the mountains again soon, before it got cold. Maybe she could tie

Sheyna's small carrier onto her backpack somehow so she could safely go too, although, as quickly as Sheyna was picking up the leash walking, she might be able to just take her on lead. She could always carry her when the trail got too steep and rocky. Molly was so agile, she seldom had to help her up even the worst parts, only when it was so steep that she almost needed a boost herself.

She spotted a great parking place near the front and backed in so the animals could safely get in and out on the sidewalk. Both Molly and Sheyna wanted a walk before going in. Olivia was really proud of how well Sheyna was doing on lead now, getting better every day. Molly was a great teacher.

Pam was waiting for her in the lobby and the friends hugged each other.

"Oh my, look how beautiful she is!" Pam stroked Sheyna's silky fur, then bent to kiss Molly's head. "You're gorgeous too Miss Molly; don't think I'm ignoring you for your new sister."

Pam straightened and smiled at Olivia, "So, what's new in your life besides this lovely little creature?" She pushed her sandy blonde curls back from her eyes and gave Sheyna another pat.

"There is way too much to tell you right now, so we will have to get together for lunch or dinner and catch up soon," Olivia laughed, shaking her head. "It's been too long since we talked, and life has been pretty wild lately."

"You got it. Just let me know when."

"I'll give you a call in a week or so and we'll set it up," Olivia smiled. "So how many people do we get to visit with today?"

"I have five that would love to see Molly and probably Sheyna too, and there is one lady who had to leave her cat behind when she moved in, and she cries over her still, so we can see how she reacts to Sheyna."

"Oh, how sad!" Olivia cried. "I hope playing with Sheyna will make her feel better, not worse, but I guess there's no way of knowing until we try."

"It kills me that they can't bring their animals with them when they move in," Pam looked sad and angry. "Poor people, it's hard enough on them having to leave their homes, without losing their pets, who are like their children, and who frequently treat them a whole lot better than their human kids."

"That really is sad," Olivia's eyes filled with tears, imagining how devastated she would be if she were in that situation. "I'm not sure I could bear it. What happened to the lady's cat?"

"One of her kids found her a loving home, thank goodness, but I am sure some of these people's pets weren't so lucky."

"Hmm, I wonder if there is something we could do to help future residents and their pets?" Olivia thought hard. "Do you think we could find animal lovers who would be willing to not only adopt their pets, but actually bring them for visits once in a while? Would the facility allow it, if they weren't certified therapy animals? If not, maybe the residents could visit their pets in their new homes if the new owners were willing and we had volunteers to take them there."

"Wow, you are on a roll today!" Pam was amazed at the flow of good ideas coming from her friend. "I've been wishing I could do something to help them for a long time, but couldn't think of anything that would work. The facility wouldn't allow the pets to come if they weren't certified, because of insurance and liability, but yes! If we had volunteers to drive them and help, then they could visit their pets, at least the people who are physically able to travel." Pam hugged Olivia in excitement. "I am so glad you came today! This could actually work!"

"Oh, I hope so; it would be wonderful for them not to have to completely give up their pets, for them and for the pets too. You can put me on the volunteer driver list; and maybe as a tentative on the potential foster/adopter list too, if you get a dog or cat who would fit into our family." Olivia was as happy and excited as Pam, ready to commit to almost anything to see this idea work.

Pam led Olivia down the hall to the first resident on her list and left her, Molly and Sheyna for a while to visit. All five of the dog lover residents that they visited loved Sheyna too, so it was a sweet and fun time. Finally Pam took them to visit Mrs. Barnes, the lady who'd been crying over leaving her cat.

As soon as she saw Sheyna, her sweet wrinkled face lit up. Olivia gently laid Sheyna on the bed and Mrs. Barnes petted her, and cuddled her, forgetting and calling her Mona once in a while. It turned out, her cat Mona, had been a calico also, though short haired. Sheyna looked enough like her to bring back all the good memories, and to comfort her, even though she knew it wasn't really Mona. She cried, but there were a substantial amount of happy tears mingled in with the tears of grief she usually cried.

Olivia felt tired and content when she hugged Pam goodbye, promising to get together with her soon. It had been a wonderful, emotional day, and they were all a bit wrung out, but in a good way.

She stopped at the grocery store on the way home to pick up a few things for dinner and next couple of days. Her friend's daughter Sandra was there and cheerfully came out and petted Molly and Sheyna while she shopped, making sure no one came near them. Olivia wished she didn't have to be so paranoid, but she couldn't take any chances where her animals were concerned.

It was almost time to start cooking dinner when she got home. After she put the groceries away, she took a quick shower, changed and started on dinner preparations. She was tired, so it was going to be quick and easy food tonight. She tore up lettuce, cut a bell pepper, and a tomato to put in a salad, then made a delicious roasted tomato and red bell pepper soup. For the main course, she'd make something she'd stumbled upon while trying to use up leftovers. It was a quick dish to make, so she was going to wait until Josh arrived to prepare it.

She set the table and decided to add a candle to the center, and put on some soft music, not that she and Josh seemed to need any help getting romantic with each other, but it did make for a nicer atmosphere in the kitchen.

Molly let out a joyful bark and raced to the front door, just as Olivia heard the knock. She followed Molly to open the door. Sheyna stayed to keep watch over the sour cream container.

Josh kissed Olivia and handed her a chocolate torte from the bakery in town.

"Sweets for the sweet," he smiled. "Oh Molly, no,

you can't have chocolate. I brought you and Sheyna something much better." He handed Olivia some handmade dog and cat treats from one of the local pet stores.

"Oh Josh, you don't need to buy us things. You're doing so much for us already."

"Are you kidding? I'm getting to stay in a nice house, eat fantastic food, with great company and adorable animals for no rent!" Josh threw Molly's tennis ball for her to chase, and picked up Sheyna. "Can't tell me I'm not getting the best end of this deal."

Olivia smiled and gave him a peck on the check. "You're our hero, and we're enjoying your company too. Are you hungry? Everything is almost ready."

"Something smells good," Josh sniffed the air. "Is that bell peppers?"

"Yes, it is a pepper and tomato soup. I'll start the main course now." She smiled, "Go wash up, it'll be ready in ten minutes."

Olivia quickly threw together the veggies and fake meat for the main course and mixed it up in the pan with a little butter.

By the time Josh came back to the kitchen, the aroma was heavenly and Olivia was placing the covered pan onto a trivet on the table.

She served the food onto their plates and offered to pour him a glass of wine. He gratefully accepted, pulling her chair out for her, before seating himself. Wow, Olivia thought, "and he's a total gentleman."

They talked about their day. Olivia was excited over Josh's discoveries at the antique shop and eager to look at the pictures he'd brought, once dinner was over. She told him about her visit to the rest home with the animals, and about the ideas she'd had for helping new residents and their pets.

When she'd cleared their plates, she served each of them a slice of the chocolate torte Josh had brought, with a steaming cup of espresso. The torte was incredibly good, so rich and delectable. If she hadn't already been in a wonderful mood, the chocolate alone would have done it.

Josh jumped up to clear the dessert plates and started washing the dishes before Olivia could get up. She grabbed the dish towel, and swatted him with it playfully before starting to dry the dishes.

"So, I am hoping you will see something in these pictures of the antique shop that I might have missed," Josh handed her a rinsed plate. "I wish I could take you with me to the shop tomorrow to see if you can remember anything more from being there, but I don't think the Captain would allow it."

Olivia dried the plate thoughtfully, "Josh, I want to go and talk to the neighbors to see if anyone knows more than they told you. Sometimes people will tell someone like me something they wouldn't tell the police."

"I suppose that is safe enough, but only as long as I am following you," he splashed water in emphasis. "I'll park where they can't see me, but where I can see enough to make sure you're okay. It's too dangerous otherwise." Josh handed her another plate, but held onto it as she reached for it, until she met his worried eyes. "I don't want you to be in danger. The neighbors are probably perfectly innocent, but we don't know that for sure. One of them could have been in cahoots with Jamison or could even be the killer for all we know."

Olivia smiled, taking the plate gently from his soapy hand. "I'll be happy to have you following me Josh. I don't crave danger, especially for Molly and Sheyna, who haven't done anything to put themselves in harm's way. At least I have a choice in where I go and what I do. I will feel better knowing you are there."

When they'd finished with the kitchen clean up, Josh brought the crime scene pictures from his bag in the guestroom and laid them on the table. They sat and Olivia picked up the first group of pictures, which had been taken the day of the murder. She went through them slowly, taking time to absorb the contents, trying to let them take her back to that day.

She laid them down and picked up the pictures from today. Wow, everything was all over the place. It looked like a tornado had gone through. Nothing actually seemed to be broken, just shoved or thrown around out of place. She started comparing the old pictures to the new ones to see if she could find anything missing in the newer ones.

She took a second look at one of the pictures of Jamison's bedroom from the murder day, then quickly took today's picture of the same area and studied them excitedly.

"Josh, I think I've found something, or maybe lost it is more accurate. Look here at the dresser in the old picture, and then again in the new picture."

Josh quickly took the two pictures and scoured them with his green eyes. "You're good Olivia!" he exclaimed in excitement. "I looked at these all afternoon and didn't see that the mirror had been changed in the new picture. Wow!" he looked at her in awe. "You really would be great as a detective."

"But what good does it do to know that someone changed the mirror? He probably took it, and whatever secrets it held with him, so we'll never know what it was," Olivia sounded frustrated. "Jamison could have been using it to hide coins, drugs, jewelry or anything small. What a great hiding place, right in plain sight."

"Tomorrow, we'll go let you talk to the neighbors, then when you leave, I'll stop at the shop to check out that dresser again on the way back to see if there is anything left to find there."

"That's a great idea! It is possible that something could have fallen out when he changed the mirrors over. It may be unlikely, but it's possible." Olivia smiled, "I know when I am in a hurry or worried about something, I tend to drop things and get clumsier than usual, so maybe he's like that too. It would have to be a little nerve wracking to be breaking into a murder scene to try to remove incriminating evidence or something valuable that you'd missed, knowing that the police were likely to be watching the place."

They studied the pictures for a bit longer but didn't find any other discrepancies, and Josh finally packed them back into his bag to return to Headquarters tomorrow.

Olivia made them some hot tea and they went to sit in the living room on the sofa. Molly was already curled up on one end of the couch sleeping when they sat down, and Sheyna jumped on Olivia's lap and rubbed against her chest. Olivia scratched between her ears until she was purring like a motorboat. Josh laughed and put his arm around Olivia, drawing her close.

"So, tell me more about Olivia. Why are you single?" he stroked her arm with his long fingers. "If I am being too nosy, just tell me to shut up."

Olivia sighed, "No, you're not being nosy, it's a natural question for you to ask." She looked down at Sheyna. "I was engaged to a great guy named Danny. We had been dating for over a year, and were supposed to get married on April eleventh. On April ninth—he vanished."

"You mean he ran off or something happened to him?"

"I honestly don't know. I guess he must have gotten cold feet and couldn't bring himself to tell me, so he just left." Olivia looked distressed. "All of his things were gone from his apartment, and no one knew anything about where or even when he had gone. I went and talked to the police, but they said he was an adult, and maybe he'd just wanted to end it with no complications, so they couldn't do anything."

"I'm so sorry Livvie," Josh hugged her tightly. "Sometimes we cops can be pretty insensitive. I can't imagine someone not wanting to be married to you."

"I know they couldn't do anything. It just all felt so . . . wrong, and I wasn't ever able to find out what happened to him. She sighed again. "If he just got scared and ran off, I can live with that, but what if something bad happened? It's the not knowing that's hard."

"I understand that well, from dealing with the families of victims," Josh said quietly. "When we've gotten this case solved and things are calmer, I can try to help you find out what happened to Danny if you want me to."

"Oh Josh, you are the most amazing man," she buried her face in his shoulder, holding him tightly. Sheyna protested the shift in position and jumped to the other end of the couch by Molly, curling up between her legs in a little ball.

"I have finally gotten over Danny, though it took a long time. I just hate not knowing if he is okay, or if he's been a prisoner, or lying dead somewhere for all this time and no one even knows."

"He's probably fine, and was just a scared idiot back then, but I will help you find him once this case is over." Josh looked a little happier when Olivia said she was over Danny.

She sat up, looked at Josh and caressed the firm edge of his jaw, running her fingers down to the sexy little dimple in his chin. She leaned up and kissed it, smiling at his surprise.

Josh sat up and captured her lips with his own in a slowly deepening kiss. Olivia clung to him as the heat flared between them. Her foot slid out from under her on the slippery wood floor, knocking her hard into Josh. They fell back onto the sofa together, bumping Molly and Sheyna, who loudly expressed their displeasure at being awakened by clumsy, amorous humans, invading their sleeping space.

Olivia and Josh laughed at themselves, lying in a mad embrace, tangled with each other and half squishing Molly and Sheyna.

"You can't say it isn't interesting, living with animals," Olivia laughed, finally extricating herself from the sofa.

Sheyna flicked her tail in annoyance and strode off toward the kitchen, obviously expecting treats after such rude treatment. Molly stood, turned her back to them and shook, as if to rid herself of the influence of the humans' silliness, and joined Sheyna in the kitchen. Olivia and

Josh started laughing all over again.

Once they'd gotten their merriment under control, they went to give the girls some conciliatory treats.

"I think it's getting to be pumpkin time for me," Olivia yawned with her hand in front of her mouth. "It's been a long day, but a super good one."

"Yes it has. I have to be at Headquarters by seven tomorrow, because I have some people coming in early that I have to see, so I may not have time for breakfast," Josh looked disappointed.

"You're taking care of us, and keeping us safe, so you will not go to work hungry," Olivia laughed. "Set your alarm for a few minutes earlier and breakfast will be waiting."

Josh put his arms around her and kissed her goodnight, carefully making it a sweet kiss, but not overly passionate. They held each other for a couple minutes, then Josh headed into the guestroom. Molly followed him and jumped onto the bed.

Sheyna went upstairs with Olivia and curled up on the pillow. It was funny how the animals seemed to be taking turns sleeping with each of them so no one would feel hurt or left out. Olivia brushed her teeth, and got ready for bed, giggling to herself over their passionate klutzfest. Sheyna smacked her with her tail when she lay down, letting her know she was still annoyed and wanted Olivia to make up for landing on her earlier. Olivia patted her, stroking her fur until Sheyna was finally purring happily, and they both drifted off to sleep.

CHAPTER NINE

Olivia awoke at five AM from a wonderfully sensual dream in which Josh played a starring role. She didn't want the dream to end, but the reality of him being there in her house was sweet enough to get her out of her warm cozy bed.

After a quick shower, and such, she dressed and went down to the kitchen to start breakfast, stopping by the front door to collect the newspaper from the porch. She'd decided on waffles, so she made the batter, started the coffee brewing and sat down to read the paper and drink orange juice while waiting for Josh to appear. She could hear the shower in the guest bathroom, so she knew he was up. Sheyna batted at the newspaper with a paw.

"Good Morning Sunshine!" Josh kissed her, as he and a sleepy looking Molly joined them in the kitchen. She leaned into him for a moment, inhaling the spicy scent of his aftershave, then poured them each a cup of coffee.

"How did you sleep?" Olivia poured batter into the waffle iron and threw some soysage links into a pan with butter. "I hope Molly didn't keep you awake."

"Not at all, she slept like a log all night, and so did I."

Olivia quickly fed Molly and Sheyna, washed her

hands again and checked the first waffle. It was golden brown, so she plucked it from the iron with tongs and put it on Josh's plate, and held the pan close, handing him the tongs so he could select his soysage links.

He spread a little butter on his waffle and poured a healthy amount of syrup over it.

"I love Vermont maple syrup," he grinned, wiping his mouth on a napkin. "This is delicious. Thanks for getting up early to do this for me. I want to cook something special for you sometime soon. I just have to figure out the best way to make it vegetarian."

"You don't have to do that," Olivia took a second soysage link. "However, I will be more than happy to taste anything you cook, when you're in the mood to do it," her eyes twinkled.

Josh left soon after breakfast, promising to call as soon as he was able to meet her to go to talk to the neighbors.

Olivia brushed and trimmed Molly then gave her a bath in the bathtub. She let her out in the back yard for a few minutes to shake off the excess water, then towel dried her before finishing with the big dog blow dryer. Sheyna had wisely made herself scarce during the whole grooming session.

Olivia mopped up the bathroom, cleaned the tub, then took a quick shower and changed into a casual green and white dress with low heeled shoes to look presentable for her neighborly visits.

She decided to have some bagels ready to toast and top with cream cheese for herself and Josh, as she figured he might be hungry by the time they met. Having someone besides herself and Molly to cook for was so much fun, not that toasting bagels was cooking, but still... well, now she had Sheyna too, and she had Josh at least temporarily. She was afraid to think about that too much yet.

At eleven thirty her cell phone rang and Josh's name showed in the caller ID, bringing a little smile to her lips as she answered. He asked if she could meet him by the antique shop in a half hour. She agreed, letting him know that she was bringing a light lunch, so he didn't need to stop somewhere.

Olivia toasted the bagels, smeared them generously with cream cheese, put them, a couple sodas and two apples into a cute little wood vintage picnic basket with a red and white checkered lid, and loaded Sheyna and Molly into their crates in the Suburban. Five minutes later they were on Route 302 headed to the antique shop. When she arrived, there was a strange car in the parking lot, and she almost kept going, but just in time, realized Josh was in the driver's seat, so she braked hard and cut the wheel sharply to pull in near him.

"Yikes!" she scolded laughing, as she got out of her car. "You scared me. I thought maybe you were the killer, back to do some more searching and I was afraid to stop."

Josh chuckled sheepishly, "Sorry about the car. At the last minute, I decided if I was following you, it would be less noticeable if I was in my own car instead of a police car. I should have let you know."

He gave her a light kiss and said hello to Molly and Sheyna.

"I brought toasted bagels with cream cheese, if you'd like to eat first," Olivia gestured toward the little picnic basket on the passenger seat.

"I'm so sorry Liv, I would love to have lunch with you, but as it is, the Captain's in a bear of a mood today and I'm feeling lucky to be here at all. I told him I was going out for lunch, and he said I'd better not be late getting back. Not sure what's eating him, but I can't push it today."

"Don't apologize! Bosses are bosses and sometimes they're a pain, but it's not your fault." She smiled and handed him the picnic basket, "You are not going back to work hungry, and if you eat your lunch while I'm talking to people, you won't even have lied to your boss."

He gratefully accepted the basket.

"Okay, so I'll hang back out of sight, but please promise me to be careful. Keep your cell phone in your hand ready to call me, and program my number into your one touch dialing, so all you have to do is push one number and I'll come running." He spoke seriously, "If it gets late, or something happens and I need to go, I will call you. If you are in any kind of trouble and you can't speak freely, ask me how I liked the bananas, so I know."

Olivia programmed the number into slot one. "I will, and I'll be okay Josh, don't worry."

Olivia drove west down the street to the first house on the same side of the road and pulled into the driveway. It was a cute little green saltbox style house with an older blue Toyota Corolla in the front and a kid's bicycle lying across the dirt walkway. She walked past a pretty little herb garden with Russian Sage still blooming and climbed the steps onto the porch. She knocked on the door, and while she waited she admired the lovely rust colored mums in a white hanging basket with three beaded wires securing it to a large nail in the overhead wooden beam. Fall was definitely coming, when the mums were on display.

After a few seconds, Olivia heard footsteps inside the house and a thin, birdlike sixtyish woman with short curly grey hair and a flour covered apron opened the door, looking at Olivia with a curious smile.

"Hi there, can I help you?" the woman asked.

"Hi, my name is Olivia McKenna. I'm the person who found Mr. Ketterer in the antique shop after he was killed. I just wondered if there was anything at all from that day that you've remembered or anything that you know or had heard, that might have some relevance to his death." Olivia and the woman shook hands, while Olivia made her little rehearsed speech.

"Oh my! You're the one who found him?" she looked distressed. "That must have been terribly frightening for you. Please come in dear. I was just baking a pie for my grandson Jimmy, who I take care of now that his mama's gone. I'm Mrs. Tanner, Sally Tanner. It's nice to meet you," the woman said, not giving Olivia time to get a word in. "Let me just turn off the stove and we can sit and chat in the living room. Would you like some cookies and tea, or a bottle of pop?"

"Tea would be lovely," Olivia said quickly into the sudden silence. "Thank you for your thoughtfulness."

She followed Mrs. Tanner into the living room, to see a little boy of perhaps five years of age, working intently at building a castle from vintage Lincoln Logs, like the ones her mom used to play with when she was little. He had a beautiful pencil drawing of a castle with a moat laid out on the floor in front of him and was using it like a blueprint. Wow, the kid would make a great architect when he grew up, judging from both the drawing and the way that castle was progressing.

Mrs. Tanner told Olivia to make herself comfortable and disappeared, presumably to the kitchen for tea and cookies. Olivia sat in a padded wooden rocker, with bright hand quilted cushions and watched as the little boy added a new level to his castle.

"You're a good builder," Olivia said. "Have you built many castles before?"

The boy continued working on his castle, without answering her, and Olivia gave up trying to engage him, choosing to look around the room at the furnishings instead. It was as cute and comfortable inside as it was outside. Mrs. Tanner certainly wasn't wealthy, as everything looked to be older, and well used, but also loved and well cared for, and many of the decorations and accessories looked to have been lovingly handmade. She seemed like a woman who was good at making the very best of what life threw at her. Olivia had liked her immediately.

Mrs. Tanner was carrying a large metal tray, when she returned to the living room. Olivia hurried to help her set it on the coffee table. There were three small empty plates, a huge platter filled with delicious looking homemade chocolate chip cookies, two empty tea cups, a small steaming teapot, some napkins and a glass of iced lemonade.

"Wow! Mrs. Tanner, you didn't need to go to so much trouble," Olivia felt guilty causing her extra work, when she was sure she already had plenty raising her grandson.

Mrs. Tanner waved away her comment, "It's no

trouble at all. I've just taken the pie out to cool. I love having company, though it doesn't happen as often as it used to, now that Joanie died. That's Jimmy's mama, my daughter. She was such a pretty, fun loving girl; the house used to be full of her friends and happy noises, and once she was married, and had Jimmy, there was a different kind of happiness." She was silent for a moment, pouring tea and piling cookies on the three plates. "Once James Hill (that's Jimmy's daddy) took off and Joanie died, it wasn't so happy anymore."

Mrs. Tanner took one of the small plates full of cookies and the lemonade over and sat them on the floor beside Jimmy. He looked up, smiled and hugged her, then took a cookie and kept on building.

"I'm so sorry about your daughter," Olivia said, her eyes getting moist. "It must be really hard for you to have lost her, and now to be raising her child alone."

"We do alright," Mrs. Tanner smiled, as she sat down across from Olivia. "He's deaf, you know. That's why his daddy left. I would never tell Jimmy that was the reason, but James was a weak man, and as soon as they found out little Jimmy had gone deaf after he got sick when he was a year old, he told Joanie he wanted a divorce. He signed the papers giving sole custody of Jimmy to her and just took off," she took a bite of cookie and shook her head. I had to get him to sign those papers again after Joanie died six months later, giving me custody, but he has never come to visit or even asked about his son since he left." Her lip quivered, "even if he wasn't capable of raising him, he should have called once in a while. It's like he just washed his hands of him because he had a handicap. Jimmy is a wonderful, smart boy he should have been proud of."

Mrs. Tanner took a breath and a sip of tea. "I'm sorry dear, I so seldom have anyone to talk to that can hear me, I tend to run on when I do. You wanted to know about Mr. Ketterer and the day of the murder, right?"

"Yes ma'am, I am trying to help the police figure out who killed him and why, because the murderer seems to think I know something about him or that I have something he wants. He tried to pull me from my car, so I really want to get to the bottom of it."

"Oh my! I am so glad he didn't hurt you. I was at home the day of the murder, but I didn't see anything unusual that I can remember."

"The police tried to talk with you that day, but no one answered the door," Olivia said. "Were you afraid to talk to them?"

"Goodness, no child, I've never been afraid of the police in my life," she laughed. "I must have been out in the back shed where I keep my gardening tools. I remember being scared to death when I heard about the murder the next day. You see, I'd left Jimmy inside playing by himself and had gone out to the shed to try to fix my lawn mower. The murderer could have come into the house and hurt Jimmy and I wouldn't have been there to protect him."

"I'm glad he didn't Mrs. Tanner," Olivia smiled. "So you didn't see or hear anything at all that day that was different from any other day?"

"Not that I can think of sweetie, I'm sorry."

"It's okay, it was just wishful thinking on my part," Olivia smiled and stood to take her leave. "It was such a pleasure meeting you, and if you don't mind, I'd like to keep in touch with you."

"I'd love that!" Mrs. Tanner said warmly. "I had such a good time talking with you."

Olivia pulled a business card from her purse and gave it to Mrs. Tanner, hugging her goodbye and thanking her for the tea and cookies. She waved to Jimmy, who stopped work long enough to smile and wave back. She'd made a sweet new friend, but didn't seem to have learned anything helpful about the murder.

As she got into the car, she thought about the talented little deaf boy and wondered why he hadn't had a cochlear implant to help him hear. She quickly realized that Mrs. Tanner probably couldn't afford the kind of insurance for him that would cover such an expensive procedure. She'd have to talk to a friend of hers to see if there was anything that could be done to help them.

As Olivia pulled out of the driveway, her cell phone rang.

"Hi Liv, are you okay?" Josh was pulling into the road a little way behind her. "You were in there for quite a while, but my file shows an older woman and a kid living there, so I wasn't too worried."

"I'm fine Josh, she was a sweetheart. I'm sorry to have stayed so long, but I really liked her and I think we're going to be friends."

"It's okay Liv, I'm glad you made a friend. Unfortunately, I can't go to the next one with you today since it is almost time for me to be back if I don't want the boss pitching a fit. Meet me at the antique shop to say goodbye properly?" he asked teasingly.

"In half a minute," Olivia laughed, hanging up the phone and pulling into the parking lot of the deserted shop.

"You know," she said when he arrived, "Mrs. Tanner

sounded like she'd never talked to you guys at all since the murder. She was in the back shed when your people were there that day and she didn't hear you. Didn't anyone go back and try to interview her another day?"

"The local PD was supposed to keep trying to reach the ones that weren't available that day and report to Sergeant O'Brian, but we haven't stayed on them as much as we should have obviously." Josh looked annoyed with himself. "I'll send O'Brian personally to check on the others."

He pulled her close and kissed her. "I have to get back now. I really wish I could stay and finish this, but we'll just have to continue tomorrow, and hope the Captain is in a better mood."

Olivia kissed him back, "Hmmm, I wish you could stay too, but I'm not sure it's for the same reason." She nuzzled his neck playfully.

"Hey, no fair!" he laughed backing up. "I can't go back to work if I need a cold shower."

She laughed and squeezed his hands. "See you tonight Josh, and thanks."

Olivia watched Josh back out and drive off. She backed out too, "Hey girls," she said. "What do you think about going to the next house without Josh? Will he be too upset?" she bit her lip, contemplating the risks. Molly's eyes seem to reproach her from the rear view mirror. "No, it's not worth risking your lives or Josh's trust," she decided after a few moments' thought. "Home it is; you're a grownup now Livvie, no games."

CHAPTER TEN

The next day, Josh and Olivia met at the antique shop again for a quick lunch in his car, then he followed her discretely to the next house on the list, which was just up the street about a half mile to the west of Mrs. Tanner, on the same side.

In contrast to Mrs. Tanner's neat and cozy little home, this one, though about the same style and size, looked run down and slovenly from the weed infested driveway as she pulled in. Olivia exited the car with trepidation, watching carefully where she put her feet as she walked through the stickers and knee high weeds to the porch steps.

The steps creaked as she climbed them, bringing starkly to mind many horror flicks she'd seen over the years that contained creaking steps and weed filled lawns. She gave herself a silent scolding. You are not twelve and this is not a haunted house. Josh is a one touch phone call away, literally, so get a grip Liv. Still her hands were trembling slightly as she knocked on the door.

After a minute or two a face appeared at the window of the door, and it opened to reveal a young man with stringy, dirty brown hair, bad teeth and a bad complexion. He looked suspiciously at Olivia, then glanced to see that she was alone and his expression became more of a leer.

"Yeah babe, what can I do you for?" he slurred, looking her up and down.

The smell of strangely harsh smoke drifted from the open door and wafted off the man's clothes as well. His breath was rank and smelled of alcohol under the smoke.

Olivia backed up and turned to walk back to her car, but he grabbed her arm, twirling her toward him. Olivia pushed the 1 button on her phone and held it down calling Josh. He roared up in his car almost before she'd released the button. Brakes squealed and he jumped out running. The young man stumbled and let go of Olivia, trying to get back inside and shut the door before Josh grabbed him, but his reflexes were obviously too impaired by whatever he'd been smoking and drinking.

"Don't hurt him Josh!" Olivia cried, afraid he might think it had been worse than it had. "He only grabbed my arm."

Josh grabbed the guy's shirt and dragged him over to the filthy, ripped overstuffed chair that was near the front door and tossed him none too gently into it.

"I won't hurt him Liv, don't worry." Josh said quietly to her, "Please just stay here while I talk to this idiot."

The guy started to get up and Josh pushed him back into the chair again.

"What are you smoking buddy?" he asked in a companionable voice. "You got any more? Will you give me some or sell me a little?" he made his voice sound whiny.

"No man, I don't know you, and I don't got nothin'." The guy was definitely either drunk or otherwise impaired. "Just leave me alone man."

"Aw, don't be like that friend," Josh said in the whiny voice. "I just need a little bit so I'll feel good."

"Aw man, I don't got enough to be givin' it out to everybody," he sat up unsteadily, "okay, come on, you can have just a little bit if you go away and stop buggin' me." He led Josh into the house and handed him a pipe. Josh sniffed the pipe, looked at the little off white rock sitting next to it and snapped the handcuffs on the man, leading him outside and reseating him in the dirty chair while the guy complained bitterly about being tricked and how mean cops were. Josh shook his head and called headquarters asking for someone to come, search the house, then take the prisoner in.

Josh knew it would take a while for the other cops to get there, so he uncuffed one of the guy's hands, and recuffed it through the metal column of the porch next to the chair so he couldn't get up and leave or bother Olivia.

Josh grinned at Olivia. "Wait here, out of his reach. I need to make a phone call privately. Are you okay?"

She grinned back, "I'm fine. He was drunk and acting like a grabby jerk, that's all."

He squeezed her hand and strode down the steps to his car.

Olivia looked at the drunk guy who was sprawled in the chair. "Hey, did you know Mr. Ketterer at the antique shop?" she asked. "Do you know what happened to him?"

He focused bleary eyes on her face, "Who, the old fart with the cat?" his speech was getting a little less slurred.

"Yes, what happened to him?"

"Some dude bumped him off, babe. He was always messing around in people's business and prowling in their yards."

"Do you know who killed him? Did you see anyone over there that day?" Olivia asked quickly.

"Not that day, it was this morning," He sniffled. "Three blondies, looked like two brothers and their hot li'l sister sneaking in the door lookin' over their shoulders like they was up to somthin' bad." He giggled, "I went over and peeked in the windows to see what they were doin' and one of the dudes was knockin' on the walls like some crazy fool."

Josh walked onto the porch just as the state trooper car pulled into the driveway. The guy, who Josh called Fergusson, saw the car and Josh and stopped giggling and started yelling about being tricked again.

Troopers Michael Fallon and Joe McNabb walked to the porch to collect the prisoner and McNabb escorted him to the back seat of the car, then joined his partner and Josh to search the house.

"Wow," Josh chuckled to Olivia once everyone else had gone. "We seem to only be able to get to one house per day. It's a good thing there aren't that many out here."

She laughed, "Who knew it could be so exciting out here in the country."

He followed her in his car back to the antique shop parking lot so she could take the girls out for a walk away from weeds and stickers. She opened the back hatch of the Suburban and let Molly out, snapped a lead to her harness, and put Sheyna on lead for a walk. Josh took Sheyna's lead so Olivia could let Molly go faster without getting her arms pulled in opposite directions.

She filled Josh in on her conversation with the drunk

guy while they walked.

"So, Jamison was prowling around the neighborhood. Looks like he was missing his cat burglar days," Josh knitted his brow in thought. "That just opened a whole new can of suspicious looking worms."

"Right!" Olivia sighed loudly. "It could have been one of the neighbors, if he was robbing them, or if they were up to something and he saw it while he was prowling. We have way too many suspects now."

"I am going to have to get my guys to go back and canvass every single house in the area." Josh was both frustrated and hopeful. New suspects added to the pool might actually give them a much needed break in the case. "Unfortunately, that means I can't let you question them anymore right now, because my captain would have my head." He looked at her worriedly.

"I understand Josh." Olivia smiled at him. "It's police business and I am not supposed to be doing this at all officially. I would never want to get you in trouble. It's been a fun experience for me though, helping you on the case."

He picked up Sheyna and put her in the little crate, then as Molly jumped into hers, he closed both crates. He pulled Olivia into his arms and kissed her. When the thunder rumbled, they both thought it was their own reactions from the kiss for a minute until the huge cold raindrops started falling on their heads. They each ran laughing to their own car and talked to one another on their cell phones while the sky opened up above them.

After agreeing that they'd see each other at Olivia's when Josh was off work, they hung up and drove in opposite directions. Josh went to back headquarters, and Olivia drove to her friend Nora's house to pick her brain about little Jimmy Hill and possible ways he could get help with his deafness. Nora's little dogs were friends with Molly and should adjust to Sheyna easily, since Nora used to have a cat, so they all ran inside out of the rain, Olivia carrying Sheyna until the front door was securely closed.

Nora worked as a nurse in the otolaryngology department of the local hospital, so Olivia knew she would be a good person to talk to about Jimmy.

Sheyna hissed at the little dogs when they started sniffing her too eagerly, and they backed off immediately with their little tails between their legs, prompting laughter from Nora and Olivia. Even Molly seemed amused. Sheyna, just gave everyone a disdainful look and licked the back of her paw flicking her tail in warning whenever the stranger dogs came too close to her.

"It's been way too long since we've seen each other," Nora popped open a canned soda and handed it to Olivia. "When did you get the kitty?"

Olivia sat on a loveseat and took a long sip of the cold beverage, "You're right, it's been ages. I got Sheyna almost three weeks ago. Her previous owner was murdered and I happened to be the one to find him."

"Murdered! In our little town? Oh, you must be talking about Mr. Ketterer out in Eastman's Grant."

"Yes, there wasn't any family to take her, so she came home with me, and Molly and I adore her."

"She is beautiful." Nora smiled, dangling the end of a ball of yarn from her knitting bag that lay next to her on the couch. Sheyna batted at it, then went into stalk mode for a moment and pounced on it, grabbing it so hard that the whole ball fell out of the bag on top of her, causing her to shriek and run under the loveseat Olivia was sitting on.

"Well, she sure has good reflexes!" Nora laughed retrieving the yarn ball and burying it in the bag again out of sight.

Olivia looked puzzled for a moment, then chuckled and knelt down to pull Sheyna from under her feet. "Silly kitty," she laughed, rubbing Sheyna's head. "I thought I remembered something about the day of the murder for a second, but it was gone before I could catch it."

"Have they found out who killed him yet?" Nora lifted one of her dogs to her lap so he'd stop pawing at her jeans. "I haven't seen anything in the paper lately about it." She grinned at Olivia, "I certainly don't have to ask why you were at an antique shop."

Olivia wasn't at liberty to say too much, since she'd gotten her information mostly from Josh, "No, I don't think they have. The paper will probably run a big piece on it when they do." She shifted in her seat, putting Sheyna back on the floor to terrorize the little dogs again.

"I have a favor to ask you Nora. I met a woman who is raising her little deaf grandson. I have a feeling she either doesn't have health insurance coverage for him at all, or what she has is pretty lousy. I was wondering, do you know of any way he could get a cochlear implant if his insurance doesn't cover it?" She didn't mention names because she felt it wasn't her place to do that, and she really didn't even know the circumstances yet, it was just guesswork on her part so far.

"There is an organization called the Hearing For All Foundation that is really good at helping people get their insurance companies to cover cochlear implants, and I believe they can even help people who don't have insurance at all. I'll give you their information so you can contact them." Nora's dogs followed her as she went to find what Olivia needed.

Molly leapt to her feet barking loudly and rushed toward the window near the front door, startling Olivia into yelping involuntarily and Sheyna into fleeing under the loveseat again.

Olivia jumped up and ran to look out the window in time to see her Suburban backing quickly out of the driveway. She could barely see the driver, but it looked like a blonde man. Nora rushed to Olivia's side, the small dogs barking along with Molly.

"No!" Olivia ran out of the house, slamming the door behind her so the animals couldn't run out. "Don't take my car!" she sprinted hard down the street for almost a block, too far back to have a chance at catching it as it sped away, and she finally bent over, hands on her knees, winded.

~~~

Josh received Olivia's call while he was in the process of sending O'Brian to re-canvass the neighborhood around the antique shop.

He hung up his cell phone and turned back to O'Brian, "Put that on hold and follow me to 89 West End Road. Olivia McKenna's Suburban was just stolen from her friend's driveway. I'll need you to canvass that neighborhood right now instead, the other will have to wait. I'm having Hendricks put out an APB on her car. Let's go."

Josh gave Hendricks the information to issue the APB, and hurried out the door with O'Brian on his heels.

Ten minutes later, Josh was trying to calm an irate

Olivia, while O'Brian was going around to ask the neighbors if they'd seen anything.

"He took my car! It wasn't enough that he trashed my house?" Olivia was fuming. "The girl's crates and traveling toys are in there." She burst into tears, "Molly and Sheyna could have been in there! I've left them in the locked car for a few minutes before, as long as it's cool enough. These things don't happen here!"

Josh put his arms around her and she cried into his shoulder for a couple minutes, then pulled herself together with a little shake, dried her eyes on her sleeve and straightened up, stepping away from Josh slightly, in embarrassment.

"I just can't understand why these things keep happening. What on earth do they want from me?" Josh handed her a tissue from his pocket and she blew her nose. "I told you on the phone that it was a man with short blonde hair driving, but really, I was too far away to be sure, I suppose it could have been a blonde woman with short hair. I couldn't see the face at all." she sighed in frustration.

She led him into the house and introduced him to Nora.

"Pleased to meet you Nora, though I'm sorry the circumstances are so bad. I hate to be abrupt, but I need you to tell me what you saw and heard right away while your memory is fresh."

"There isn't much to tell. I was in my bedroom looking for something, when Molly started barking like crazy, Olivia screeched and I ran into the living room to see her looking out the window at her car being driven away. Then before I could say anything, Liv took off out the door chasing her car and yelling." She looked at

Olivia, "You scare me sometimes. They could have turned around and run you over or shot you or something."

"Could you see the driver at all?" Josh asked quickly before Olivia could respond to Nora's comment. "Was there anyone in the passenger seat?"

Nora shook her head, "It was too far away for me to see anyone inside the car; there seemed to be one person vaguely visible through the window, but that was all I could tell."

Josh sighed, "Thanks Nora, I figured you probably hadn't seen much, since you got to the window after Olivia, but I had to ask." He turned to Olivia, "Would you be okay driving my car until we find yours? I can drive the state car, so it would be easier that way than you having to rent one."

"If you're sure it would be okay and not inconvenience you, that would be wonderful."

"It won't be a problem at all. I'll take you to my place to pick it up, and follow you home to make sure you get there safely."

Nora raised an eyebrow and looked questioningly at Olivia in surprise. Olivia grinned and mouthed the word 'later' at her silently.

As Olivia and Josh were getting the animals into his car, Nora came out and handed Olivia a piece of paper.

"Here is the information on the Hearing For All Foundation. Let me know how it works out."

Olivia gave her a hug, "Thanks Nora. It was so good seeing you, and let's get together for dinner to catch up soon."

"Yes, we really need to do that," Nora laughed

pointedly, waving goodbye at Josh. "You've been holding out on me."

"See you soon Nora," Olivia laughed, as Josh put the car in reverse and backed down the driveway.

He stopped two houses down, where O'Brian's car was parked and went to let him know they were leaving. O'Brian said he hadn't gotten any information from the neighbors so far, but would keep at it until he'd talked to everyone in the area who was home.

They pulled up beside Josh's blue Chevy Traverse at his apartment building. Josh helped Olivia get Molly and Sheyna out and on leashes, then handed her the keys to his little SUV. He opened the back and checked to make sure his toolbox was there and closed the hatch.

"When I get off work, I'll remove the back seats so you can put the crates in once we find them, or I guess new ones if we don't. Your insurance should cover everything, right?"

"Yes, thank goodness, I have full coverage." Olivia sighed. "I'd be a lot more freaked out if I was underinsured."

Josh opened the back door and gestured to Molly, who hopped in happily, then he placed Sheyna in the seat beside her. Sheyna looked around for a minute and lay down contentedly. Josh walked to the front and opened the door for Olivia, but before she got in, he put his arms around her and held her for a few moments.

"It's been a pretty rough month for you, hasn't it? September is gone and we still haven't gotten this creep." Josh brushed her hair back from her face and caressed her cheek tenderly.

Olivia wrapped her arms around Josh's waist, holding him tight and looked into his eyes. "It hasn't all been bad. As a matter of fact, some of it has been pretty great."

He leaned down and kissed her slowly and deeply. "It's been a great month for me," he said when they came up for air. "Actually, this was the best month in a very long time."

Olivia smiled and stood on her tiptoes to kiss him again. "It has for me too, believe it or not," she stepped back. "What time will you be off work? I thought I'd barbeque some veggies on the grill, and we could have them with pasta and a vegetarian spaghetti sauce."

"You're making me hungry," he laughed. "I should be there around five-thirty, if all goes well. I just need to check in with O'Brian again and with Hendricks, who issued the APB on your car and write up my report at headquarters. Well, maybe five-forty-five is more like it." He kissed her again and closed the door for her once she was inside. "Drive safely and call me if you have any problems."

Olivia held her hand out of the window, palm down and Josh reached to take her hand, and she dropped an extra house key into his palm. "See you later," she smiled.

Olivia found she enjoyed driving Josh's small SUV. It was much easier to turn and park than the Suburban, though it didn't have as much room. Maybe getting a smaller vehicle wasn't a bad idea, if she didn't get her car back. She parked in front of her house and put Molly and Sheyna on lead to go into the house.

It was chilly inside and Olivia decided to light a fire. Once the house was warming up a bit, she checked her mail, and her email, then decided to call the client,

Andrew, who'd wanted the Dazey butter churn to report her success. He was a friend as well as a client and the same one she'd found the cute little iron bank for. He was thrilled, and so was Olivia's bank account. That should cover her mortgage for next month. She felt bad that she'd waited so long to give him the news. It was to be a present for his wife, and Andrew was more excited than Olivia'd been when she found it.

Abby called while Olivia was chopping the zucchini and yellow squash for the grill. Olivia filled her in briefly on the latest bad news, and they made a lunch date for the following Monday. It was nice talking to Abby, she was such a spitfire that she could always cheer you up. Once the veggies and the spaghetti sauce were ready for cooking, Olivia sat and watched TV, then took a shower and dressed for dinner.

She's been terrified to think about it too much, in case she jinxed it, but she realized now how much she loved having Josh staying with her. They hadn't done more than kiss, but the togetherness, the communion they experienced was incredible. Even with Danny, she hadn't had such closeness. She'd always scoffed at the term 'soul mates', but that's exactly how it felt with Josh, like they were two pieces of a whole. Oh, the fire was there too, no doubt about that, but there was so much more. At this point she could only cross her fingers and hope like mad he felt the same way she did. It was too late to wish for anything else.

Olivia was putting the pasta into the big pot and had the grill lit when Molly barked happily and Josh walked into the kitchen with Sheyna trailing behind him.

"I kinda like having my own key," he put his arms around Olivia from behind, kissing her neck. "You are so beautiful." His breath was warm on her neck as he trailed kisses down her back as far as her shirt allowed.

"Hmm, I think I should have given you a key a long time ago," her knees turned to rubber. She swiveled to face him, still in his arms and their lips met. Oh yeah, the fire was definitely there. She knew she could lose herself in him but just maybe she'd find herself too.

The hissing sound of the spaghetti pot starting to boil over, jerked them both back to reality. Josh grabbed the pot and lifted it while Olivia turned the heat down and wiped up the spilled water.

"We're a bit of a menace together in the kitchen sometimes, aren't we?" Josh laughed, setting the huge pot back on the stove eye. "We seem to always be getting everything all wet."

Olivia burst into laughter, "I'm not touching that one!"

Josh roared with laughter, "I don't blame you, I wouldn't either if I hadn't said it."

Molly nudged Olivia, then Josh, wanting to get in on the fun.

"Sorry Molly, that was just a silly people funny, we'll play with you and Sheyna after dinner." She kissed the top of her head and patted her silky ears. "Let me get your food ready now, so you won't feel left out." Olivia mixed the food for the animals and put it in their spots for them, then washed her hands and stirred the pasta.

"Josh, would you mind watching the sauce while I put the veggies on the grill? We don't want any more boil-overs," she grinned.

"Not unless it's for something really worthwhile," he teased with a grin, raising his eyebrows in a suggestive leer. They both started laughing again and Olivia went to put the sliced vegetables on the grill, still chuckling.

"Is there any news on my car or whoever stole it?" she asked walking back into the kitchen from the deck. "I somehow didn't get a chance to ask when you first came in." she teased back.

Josh sighed, "Unfortunately, you and Nora appear to be the only ones who really saw anything more than your Suburban going down the street. One neighbor heard squealing tires, but that was it. Hopefully someone will spot it soon and we'll get them."

"Maybe, if it was a woman driving, it was the one that drunk guy, Fergusson said he saw with the two blonde men. Maybe they're all in it together." Olivia said. "Then again, maybe it was random and totally unrelated to everything else." She shook her head, "This is unreal. I just can't figure out what they want. Why take my car if they're after me because they think I know something?"

"It really is weird," Josh agreed. "It is also worrying me that they haven't stopped stalking you. They seem to change their plan of attack every time, but they don't stop attacking." He scratched his head, "I'm going to speak to the captain again on Monday about day time security for you, but I have a feeling the answer will be no."

"Josh, thanks so much for all you're doing for me." Olivia hugged him and took the spoon from his hand to stir the sauce. "I'm not sure I could have managed so many things happening without you being here."

"It has been my pleasure, and I think you know that." Josh turned her to face him and took her hands, setting the spoon down. "I'm not going to say 'it's all part of the job'," he smiled. "This is not part of the job description. This is me wanting you to be safe. It's me falling in love with you."

Olivia caught her breath, "I'm falling in love with you too Josh. No, I'm not falling; I'm pretty sure I'm already there." He kissed her and they held each other tightly. "I'd like to keep taking it slowly Josh, because it's too important not to," Olivia whispered against his neck. "It's only been a few weeks since we met and I don't want either of us to get hurt."

Josh nodded, "As soon as it's safe to leave Molly and Sheyna at home alone, I want to take you on a real date, out somewhere." He smiled, "dinner and dancing, the movie theater for a chick flick or whatever you'd like best."

Olivia pulled him close and whispered in his ear. Josh roared with laughter for the second time that night.

CHAPTER ELEVEN

Josh helped Olivia adjust the harness of her parachute and pulled it tight.

"Are you sure you really want to do this?" he yelled over the drone of the plane's engine. "I don't want you to do it just for me. It's too big a thing for that."

"I'm sure Josh," Olivia laughed, grinning broadly. "Ever since you mentioned that you used to teach skydiving, I've wanted to do this with you. It's something I've always wanted to do, and with you I'll be safe; it's perfect! The girls will be safe in the airport office with the guys watching them until we are down, what's not to love?" She kissed him happily.

Josh was grinning in delight as he secured her harness to his, positioning her with her back to his chest, below him so she would be able to see everything unobstructed.

Olivia took a deep breath, trying not to panic, and held Josh's hand tightly as they walked over to the door of the plane. Josh opened the door, bracing them both from falling out.

The pilot gave Josh a thumbs up and Josh stepped backward out the door onto the ledge of the plane with Olivia in front of him. Olivia felt a rush of cold air and their legs lifted into the air behind them, with only Josh's

ANTIQUES & AVARICE

strong hands holding the doorway on each side to keep
them from flying free. She gasped in fright, panicking.
She screamed trying to grab onto the doorway and Josh.

He pushed them in and out of the plane twice,
pushing out harder on the third time and letting go, so
they were flying face down and Josh tapped Olivia on the
shoulder, which was his prearranged signal for her to
spread her arms wide, and they were flying like a giant
tandem bird, free falling with the wind rushing through
their hair like being caught in a dry hurricane, surrounded
by endless blue sky and fluffy white clouds. Olivia was
still screaming as she somehow forced herself to spread
her arms. Josh's strong hands covered the backs of her
hands comfortingly and it suddenly seemed they were
one being riding the wind from the top of the world.
Instantly, Olivia's fear evaporated and she opened herself
to the crazy wonderful feeling of flying. Her heart was
racing from fear, adrenaline and sheer ecstasy. Olivia
wished that moment never had to end.

All too soon, Josh had to open the chute, slowing
their descent with a sudden jerk. Olivia discovered that
she loved slowly drifting down too, but not as much as
the free falling; she'd never, ever forget that incredible
feeling.

Once they were low enough to see clearly where they
were going to land, about thirty feet from the ground,
Josh flared the chute, slowing them down for a soft easy
landing which they managed nicely thanks to Josh's
experience and Olivia's trust and agility, though she did
scream again, as they touched ground, whether it was
from fear or excitement, she wasn't telling.

As soon as they were free from the harnesses, Olivia

131

was jumping up and down, grinning like a little girl with her first puppy. "That was the most exciting thing in the whole world! No wonder you love it so much!" her eyes sparkled. "I wish we could free fall like that forever."

He grinned boyishly at her enthusiasm, "It's a high like no other. You handled it like a pro Liv!" He hugged her as they walked toward the plane. "I always love skydiving, yet I think that might have been my favorite jump yet, because I got to see it all through your eyes and live your excitement. What a rush!"

Olivia was still floating on a cloud of adrenaline and happiness as they collected Molly and Sheyna and headed out to the lake for a picnic lunch. It was a beautiful sunny day, cool enough for a long sleeve shirt, but not cold. The air so high up when they'd jumped had felt cold but the exhilaration from jumping kept it from being bothersome. Now, lakeside, it was pleasant in the sun.

Josh spread a blanket on the grass and pulled out the picnic basket while Olivia got Molly and Sheyna out and made sure Molly was going to be okay off lead. She put Sheyna on a long lead and looped the handle around her foot.

Olivia unwrapped the breadless sandwiches she'd made from tomato slices with steamed asparagus, mozzarella and basil layered upon each other and drizzled with a homemade anchovy-less Caesar dressing. She passed Josh a double paper plate and plastic knife and fork and took a set for herself.

"This looks delicious!" Josh helped himself to one of the sandwiches and slid one onto Olivia's plate too. Sheyna and Molly gave Josh a pathetic look, since they knew Olivia wouldn't fall for it. He laughed, "Oh no, you don't! I'm not about to get myself in trouble with your mom. You'll just have to wait until we're done. I know the rules as well as you do by now."

Olivia chuckled, "They're obviously hoping you'll forget. They're hopeless beggars, both of them, but at least they're polite about it."

Josh petted both Molly and Sheyna and told them to wait, and they'd get treats later. Molly gave up and ran to the lake and jumped in splashing around, blowing bubbles and playing while she swam. Sheyna looked at Molly like she was crazy and carefully stayed clear of the splashes.

Once they'd finished their lunch, Josh gave Molly and Sheyna some cheese they'd saved for them and some of their own treats as well. Olivia looped Sheyna's leash through the handle of the cooler so she couldn't take off if she became startled by anything. Then Josh lay back on the blanket, pulling Olivia down to lie beside him. She put her head on his shoulder and her right arm across his broad chest. He kissed the top of her head.

"What do you want out of life Liv?" he asked after a few moments. "Kids? Marriage? Illicit affairs?" he grinned.

She swatted him playfully on the chest, "you wish," she laughed. "I think I'd like to be married. I'm really not sure about kids. I know all women are supposed to want them, and I'm not saying I don't, just that I'm not sure. Having Molly and Sheyna is so much like having kids anyway. What about you?"

He thought for a second, "I feel pretty much the same. I wouldn't mind having kids, but it's not super important to me. In fact I'm not sure I wouldn't rather adopt a kid who needs a home rather than bringing another child into the world just to satisfy the 'mini me' mentality, because I don't really buy into it myself." He looked at her to see her reaction. She was smiling.

"I don't either, and yeah, I think adopting might be a great plan if we decide we want kids." She realized her slip and blushed furiously. "I mean if I do someday."

Josh laughed, "I hope you meant what you said the first time. I know it's too soon, and you said you wanted to take things slowly, but however slowly we may go, I'm already completely sure that I want to marry you Olivia McKenna. That's not going to change." He pulled her closer.

Olivia drew a shuddering breath, "So ask me already Detective Abrams."

He got up and pulled her to her feet, then knelt in front of her holding one of her hands in both of his. "Olivia McKenna, you are the moon, the sun and all the stars in my sky. I'd hike every trail in these mountains barefooted in winter to be with you, and with Molly and Sheyna too," he winked, glancing at them, before turning back to Olivia. "I love you with all my heart, mind and soul. Will you make me happy beyond all my dreams by marrying me?"

She didn't hesitate for a moment, "Yes! I will marry you Joshua Abrams. I'm too happy and excited to think of all the beautiful words I should say like you did, but I love you with all my heart, mind and soul too." She lifted him to his feet and threw herself into his arms. He kissed her and spun her around and around until they fell onto the blanket dizzy and laughing. Molly barked excitedly at them and Sheyna flicked her tail in annoyance and stayed out of the way of the crazy humans.

Josh sat up and rummaged through the picnic basket,

coming up with a twist tie, which he quickly formed into a ring and placed it on Olivia's left ring finger. He kissed her again and they lay back holding each other and kissing until it started getting too intense for a public lakefront, then Josh ended the kiss, caressing her face and lightly kissing her eyelids.

"You are so beautiful. I could look at you all day and never get enough."

"You're not too hard on the eyes either Josh," Olivia laughed, running her hand over his muscular abs through his shirt. "All my friends will be jealous."

"Mine will be jealous of you too," he laughed. "They'd better keep their distance too." He sobered for a moment, "We need to wait on announcing our engagement until this case is solved though, as I could lose my job, and it would be a lot harder to solve it without having access to everything like I have now."

"That makes sense Josh, and waiting a while is not a bad thing," Olivia smiled.

He got up, helping her to her feet. "We'd better get going, the sky is getting a little cloudier than I like, unless we want to get soaked."

They quickly packed up all the trash and their stuff, got the animals into the car and drove onto the road. Josh was right, the first raindrops started pelting the windshield just as they reached Olivia's house. They grabbed everything they could carry, including Sheyna, let Molly jump out with them and they all ran to the door, getting under the porch overhang just in time.

Molly was still damp from her swim, so Olivia dried her with a towel before she could jump on the couch, while Josh lit the fireplace. The autumn chill in the air quickly evaporated with the cheerful flames licking the wood logs, and once Molly was dry and cozy, Olivia went to the kitchen to get a pan of buttered popcorn they could pop over the fire.

"Josh, what is the department focusing on now, the neighbors at the antique shop, Nora's neighbors or what? I know my car is not nearly as important as the murder, but we know it has to be tied in together somehow."

"Yes, it does. No way can that be a coincidence," he rattled the popcorn pan. "I'm going to have O'Brian and Hendricks go back to talk to all the neighbors at the antique shop on Monday. "Right now, we only have Larsson as a real suspect, but I suppose we can still count all the victims of the robberies too, even though the captain didn't find anything suspicious there."

He sat the popcorn pan aside for a moment and went into the guestroom. A few seconds later he emerged carrying a file and a portable folding whiteboard with two different color markers.

"Would you like to write up the suspect list formally, and then we can see what else we have that we can put up here to study?" he grinned. "I'll bet you and I can crack this thing together, before my guys have gotten anywhere with it."

"So, we have Larsson, as suspect number one, right?" Olivia wrote Suspects on the left top of the board, then wrote Larsson just underneath. "Was the last homeowner to be robbed Olander?"

"Yes, then Porter, Martin, Weinstein, Morrow and Humphries. These are the robberies that we are pretty sure were carried out by Jamison and Larsson. There were a couple others before that but we weren't as sure of those, so I think we should concentrate on these for now."

Olivia wrote Olander, then each of the names he recited on the board in order under suspects. "Did all of them collect insurance for all the losses?"

"Actually, no not all. Morrow had just recently purchased some expensive jewelry for his wife and had failed to obtain insurance on it before the theft occurred. He collected for the other items taken, but was out about a hundred and twenty grand for the jewelry. He was not a happy man."

Olivia wrote Underinsured by Morrow's name. "Did anyone else seem especially angry or upset? I mean, I'm sure no one was happy, but did anyone strike the officers who investigated as being more 'over the top angry'?"

Josh looked through his case notes, "Martin seemed pretty upset, but more sad than angry, as the jewelry and paintings that were stolen from him were family heirlooms, and Lattimer, the cop I talked to in Boston, thought the sentimental value was worth more to him than the insurance money." He set the file down and opened the popcorn, which smelled wonderful and poured it into a bowl. He salted it a little then held the bowl out to Olivia and they both took a handful of the buttery goodness.

"Hmm," Olivia wrote 'sad' by Martin's name. "Unless he fooled Lattimer, or was so depressed that he turned homicidal, he sounds much less likely than Morrow to have killed Jamison." She frowned in puzzlement, "How would the victims have known about Jamison, if he was never charged or even arrested for the crimes? It would make more sense for one of them to have killed Larsson rather than Jamison, wouldn't it?"

"See! That's why I think you and I will crack this

thing," Josh laughed. "You have a detective's instinct and plenty of brains to back it up." He hugged her, "plus you're not a bit lazy, unlike a particular higher ranking cop I won't name."

Olivia smiled, squeezing his arm, "What about Porter, Weinstein and Humphries? Did Lattimer mention anything standing out about them?"

"Porter is the one whose paintings were recovered from Jamison's basement, at least two of them were," he amended. "Lattimer didn't mention anything specific about him or Humphries; he said he didn't think they would have bothered since they seemed fairly calm about it and were fully reimbursed by their insurance companies. Weinstein was eighty years old at the time he was robbed, and in a wheelchair, so unless it was a relative, or he hired someone, it is pretty unlikely that he's guilty, if he's even still alive. I'll look into it first thing on Monday," he grinned, seeing her open her mouth to protest because he hadn't checked on him yet. "We've been slowly checking up on everyone. He just seemed so unlikely. Out of all of them, he was kinda last on my list."

Olivia wrote 'wheelchair, 80 yrs old, relative? Hired Killer?' by Weinstein's name. "How about Olander? Did Lattimer say if he seemed overly upset?"

"No, he said he took the whole thing pretty well, and had also been fully reimbursed by insurance like most of the others. Lattimer really thinks Larsson is the killer, and it certainly makes the most sense from what we know." Josh stretched his back and took a handful of popcorn. "Olander is still living in Boston, married to the same woman, kids in private prep schools, all the same as before, so we haven't found any red flags with him.

Porter is also still living pretty much the same life as before, had another child since then, but that's all we found."

Olivia dutifully wrote 'new baby' by Porter's name.

"Morrow, is our best suspect after Larsson because he lost a good chunk of money, not that he really felt a pinch from it, but he apparently isn't a man who likes to lose anything," Josh glanced at his watch and muttered an oath. "I can't believe how late it is. I'd hoped we could talk about our wedding and have a romantic evening, and it's after midnight and we're still talking shop," he laughed, shoving the file out of the way and pulling Olivia close.

"Maybe we could start a detective agency some day," Olivia grinned running her fingers though his wavy hair. "With your beauty and my brains, we'll make a fortune at it."

Josh laughed and tickled her, "Oh yeah? Who's got the brains, huh, who?"

She was laughing and trying unsuccessfully to evade his tickling fingers. "I do!" she giggled and squirmed. "I do! Okay, okay! You do!" she collapsed in helpless laughter as he stopped tickling.

He kissed her, "No Livvie, you do. You have the beauty *and* the brains and I am the luckiest man alive."

CHAPTER TWELVE

Sunday morning was cold and grey, showing the first signs of a rapidly approaching winter. Olivia walked out onto the porch to retrieve the Boston Globe from the steps and the air was raw, the frigid little breeze scraping her skin like sandpaper, quickly sending her shivering back indoors.

"Ooh Molly, I'm going to start letting you fetch the paper again from now on unless it's actually touching the door. It's chilly out there!" Olivia dropped the paper on the kitchen table and rubbed her hands together to warm them before starting the coffee brewing. Her cell phone rang as she put down food for Molly and Sheyna.

It was Abby, making sure they were still on for lunch the following day. After agreeing to meet at a Thai restaurant in town at noon, Olivia hung up and started preparing breakfast. She poured herself a cup of coffee and took a sip after she'd mixed the blintz batter and put it in the fridge to rest. She could hear Josh moving around in the guestroom, so she quickly mixed the filling, made the blueberry compote to top the blintzes, then she sat to read the paper until he came out.

She scanned the headlines while sipping her coffee, then turned the page. A few seconds later Olivia leaped up so quickly that she scared Sheyna into a panicked flight to the next room.

"Josh!" she yelled. "You have to see this!"

Josh rushed into the kitchen shirtless, wearing only jeans, his hair still damp from the shower.

"What happened? Is everyone okay?" He was as panicked as Sheyna.

Olivia held the paper out to him, turned to the second page. "Larsson is dead. He committed suicide by jumping from his apartment window last night."

"What?" Josh was astounded. "Where was this?" He stopped talking to read the article, taking Olivia's vacated chair. "Apparently he was still living in Boston. Seems this made the news because the robberies he was accused of were well publicized, and because when he jumped, he landed on a passing car, scaring the life out of the people inside, but lucky for them, hitting the hood instead of the roof." He shook his head in amazement.

"Why would he kill himself?" Olivia leaned over his shoulder to read along with him. "He must have gotten something from Jamison when he killed him, or afterward when he went back to search. Was he so broke that he was desperate, and when he couldn't get the loot after committing murder, he freaked out and gave up?"

Josh sighed. "It just gets more convoluted all the time. We still don't know why he was after you." He ran his fingers through his damp hair in frustration. "I guess I know where I'll be going tomorrow."

"Oh, yes, I guess you would have to go there, and I suppose I will be safe now too, since he is dead. What a horrible thought, but it's true. I am relieved at not having to be afraid all the time anymore."

"It's not horrible, it's perfectly natural." Josh reached

and pulled her into his lap, snuggling her close. "Anyone who's been stalked or victimized in some way would feel relief to have it end, even if it ended badly for the aggressor. It shows what a kind person you are, that you feel bad for being relieved."

Olivia hugged him and sighed. "Okay, let's get some hot coffee into you and I'll get back to fixing breakfast; at least we have today together." Leaning against Josh's bare muscled chest was more than she could handle first thing in the morning. She reached for her cooled coffee and popped it into the microwave to warm up for a few seconds, while pouring Josh a fresh hot cup from the pot.

"There were a few interesting yard sales for today listed in Friday's Sun that I'd thought of checking out if we can handle the cold." Olivia smiled with a half fake shiver. "Until I stepped outside this morning, it had seemed like a fun idea. Now I almost think staying in by the fireplace sounds more appealing."

Josh laughed, "How about if we take the girls and go for a short brisk hike, then hit the yard sales? We can make some hot cocoa and take it in a big thermos so we'll stay warm. I promise I won't let you be cold," he said with an enticing smile.

"I'm sure you won't," Olivia grinned delightedly. "It sounds like it's going to be a fun day." She pulled the blintzes off the pan and spooned the filling onto them one by one, then rolled them and put them back into the pan with a little more butter. The delicious smell of blueberries filled the kitchen as she used the spatula to transfer the golden brown blintzes to their plates.

Josh made a quick trip to the guestroom to grab a shirt and was buttoning it by the time Olivia put the blintzes and blueberry compote on the table in front of him.

"I hope you like blintzes," Olivia said. "I forgot to ask. I think they are my favorite breakfast food because they remind me of childhood so much."

"I love them!" Josh took two of them and liberally spooned the compote over them. "Childhood memories can be sweet," he bit into a blintz, "sometimes even as sweet as this." He moaned in pleasure at the delectable taste. "Even better than my mom used to make, and believe me, that's saying something."

"I'm so glad you like them," Olivia smiled. She spooned compote over a blintz and took a bite. "So, do you really enjoy going to garage sales and things like that, or are you just humoring me?"

"No, I enjoy them too. Both of my parents loved antique things. My mom liked glassware and china. She had a Wedgwood collection that was incredible; she had something in every color of Jasperware they ever made. My dad collects old books. He's a sucker for old first editions, especially old children's books."

Olivia looked at Josh in fascination. "I've never heard you talk about your family before. Does your dad live in this area? I'm so sorry about your mom. When did she pass?"

"How did you know my mom was dead and my dad was still living?"

"You said everything about your mom in the past tense, but used the present tense for your dad."

"You really are observant. I didn't even realize I did that. I think you may just be onto something with that detective agency stuff," He grinned. "My dad lives in Boston and is still an avid book collector. He's gonna love your business, and he'll drive you crazy looking for books for him too. He's a good guy; you'll like each other for sure."

"I can't wait to meet him; he sounds terrific. What happened to your mom, if you are okay with talking about her?"

"She got breast cancer and by the time it was diagnosed, it was too late for them to save her. She died ten years ago."

"I'm so sorry Josh. She must have been a wonderful mom, to have raised you to be the kind of man you are."

"Thank you. She really was. She was just an amazing person. She had a real sense of right and wrong, you know? I don't mean that she saw things in black and white either. Just that she hated injustice and worked her whole life to help people. She was a doctor and quite an activist for social justice."

"I would have loved to have met her," Olivia said quietly.

"She would have adored you," Josh smiled at her tenderly, "just like I do. I know my dad will too."

Olivia smiled and started clearing their empty plates. Josh took them and put them in the dishwasher as she rinsed them.

"We can run it tonight after dinner," Olivia said. "Let's go get ready for the cold, cold hike," she laughed.

They were both dressed in light layers they could easily shed once the physical exertion from hiking warmed them up. Olivia wore a day pack with a three liter water bladder inside, a small first aid kit, a compass, knife, matches, an ultra-light waterproof tarp, and a few snacks, with plenty of room left over for whatever clothes they wanted to take off during the hike. They both wore spring gloves, which were warm enough for the weather without being as hot as winter gloves would have been. Josh didn't have a pack or even his favorite hiking boots with him, but luckily he had an old pair of boots he carried in the car that would suffice for a short hike.

"I really have to remember to put my emergency pack in my police car, I should never be without it. I took it out the other day to change some things and still haven't gotten it back in there."

"I'm taking plenty of cash for the yard sales afterward," Olivia laughed. "I hope we find some cool stuff."

"I'm hoping for some nice old snowshoes or wooden skis, but I'm not holding my breath," Josh laughed. "Good ones are hard to come by in garage sales nowadays."

Olivia put Molly's little backpack on her back and cinched it securely. It had her collapsible water bowl, a little dog kibble and cat kibble in case of emergency and a few treats for her and Sheyna.

Olivia's pack wasn't heavy until the water bladder was filled, but water is amazingly heavy. Josh offered to strap her backpack on himself, but had to agree that it wouldn't begin to fit his much larger, muscular frame.

"It's okay Josh, I am used to carrying a lot more than this, so don't worry," Olivia smiled at his consternation. "I am a seasoned backpacker. This weighs about a quarter of what my pack weighs when I am backpacking for a week."

"Yes, I am sure it does, I just feel bad that you're carrying everything."

"Oh, I'm not carrying everything; Sheyna's chest-pack carrier is very adjustable and will actually fit you, so you get to carry her when she gets tired of hiking on lead," Olivia laughed.

"She is so light, I won't even notice," Josh picked up Sheyna's carrier, adjusted it to fit and strapped it to his chest for a second to make sure.

Once they had everything and everybody loaded in the car, Josh got behind the wheel.

"How about doing Mt. Crawford, instead of the trail by Moore Reservoir since most of the yard sales we want to hit are in North Conway? That will put us closer and should give us enough time to get to them before all the good stuff is gone since we are leaving relatively early."

"It's a more strenuous hike and maybe a little longer, but much closer, so yeah, that makes more sense," Olivia agreed. "There won't be much of a view today, but it is a fun hike, even in fog or rain; at least it's only overcast, not socked in today."

The drive was pleasant with not too much tourist traffic so early in the day and they were at the trailhead by nine-thirty. There were a couple other cars in the lot where they parked, so it seemed they weren't the first on the trail.

Josh clipped Sheyna's lead to her harness and set her on the ground. Olivia tucked Molly's lead into her backpack, since she was fine off leash most of the time. Only near busy roads, did Olivia really worry about her, even though she was well trained not to go near the road.

Josh strapped Sheyna's empty carrier to his chest and helped Olivia adjust her pack and they were off up the trail. The air was brisk and they were glad for their gloves. The path was smooth at the bottom compared to most of the rough rocky trails in the White Mountains and they went along easily, admiring the peaceful beauty of the dark red, burnt orange, gold and brown leaves strewn across the forest floor. The path was so covered with leaves, it was like a multi-colored carpet.

It soon became steeper and a little tougher going. Josh picked Sheyna up and put her in her carrier, as the path became the typical New Hampshire bolderfall type trail, with rocks way bigger than Sheyna could climb. There were a couple of spots where Olivia had to boost Molly, as the next step up the rocks was over her head. Josh gave Olivia a hand up one super steep section, as it was slippery and her heavy backpack was making it harder for her to not fall over backward on the steepest spots.

After a while, they came to a fork in the trail and headed toward Mt. Crawford's summit instead of the side trail. Though there were a few steeper spots, the trail was easier now, and they soon reached the lower ledges where the views on a sunny day were awesome. Even on a grey day like today, they had great, though overcast views. In less than an hour, they reached the summit and Josh took Sheyna out of her carrier and put her back on lead so she could prowl around with them and eat and drink easily.

Olivia took off her pack and handed Josh some trail mix. They sat for a few minutes enjoying the splendid views. Sometimes the views were even nicer when it was grey, Olivia thought. It made everything look so moody and powerful.

"Here, stand right here next to this little section of rock and hang onto Sheyna so I can get a picture of you guys. Molly stay!" Olivia positioned everyone to her liking and snapped a couple pictures with her phone.

Josh pulled her close to him and reached a long arm out to take a selfie of all of them. Then he kissed Olivia and they stood arm in arm looking out over the massive ravines, valleys and surrounding mountains until the chill wind persuaded them to get packed up to go. The hike down was easier than the hike up and went much faster, except for a couple of the steepest sections.

It was one PM when they reached the first yard sale in North Conway. They didn't have anything that was on Olivia's list, and no snowshoes or skis for Josh, but Olivia found a beautiful vintage Tiffany style table lamp with beige and green stained glass that would look wonderful in her green toned guestroom and could replace the contemporary white lamp which she'd never really liked.

The next sale was almost a complete bust. Aside from finding a cute little ceramic food dish with the initial 'S' on it for Sheyna, there was nothing that was interesting to either of them. At the third stop, Josh found a pair of old snowshoes. They weren't antique, but they were vintage and they were unusual, so he bought them, looking very pleased with his find.

The last two yard sales were quickly gone through, with Olivia finding a nice old Amish quilt in good shape, though a tiny bit pricier than she'd have liked, and an antique coffee pot she was pretty sure one of her clients would like.

"Why don't we stop and pick up some take-out from the restaurant on the way home?" Josh asked. "It's been too long a day for cooking at the end."

Olivia agreed, "They have a really good cheesy spinach dip with bread that we could share to go with our main course if you like it."

They called ahead and ordered their food so it would be ready when they got there and Josh ran inside to pick it up. The aromas tantalized their senses for the rest of the drive to Olivia's house.

CHAPTER THIRTEEN

Josh left early the next morning for Boston, having called his captain to clear it with him. He had a green light as long as he didn't overstep his jurisdiction and tick off the Boston PD. He hoped to be back the following day, figuring he'd be stuck there at least one night checking up on everything. Olivia kissed him goodbye and sent him off with extra coffee and a couple of homemade breakfast sandwiches to help him stay awake on the three hour drive.

She thought about the situation while she fed Molly and Sheyna and fixed her own breakfast. Now that Larsson was dead, there was no legitimate reason for Josh to stay on at her house. She loved having him there, and was very much looking forward to being married to him but on the other hand, it wasn't always that easy to maintain their distance, thus keeping their relationship a bit simpler for a while, as they'd agreed to do for Josh's job's sake, because she was still technically a suspect in Jamison's murder until it was solved, as she had no alibi. He couldn't afford to be seen as 'sleeping with the enemy' so they weren't going to cross that line yet.

They were planning to wait to announce their engagement until after the murder was solved too. All the more reason to solve it already, Olivia thought impatiently. It had been long enough since the murder. With Larsson dead, it was definitely not going to be easier to solve the crime, but it should she supposed, be a lot safer.

Now that she wasn't wearing a figurative target on her back, Olivia decided she would go back out to visit the rest of Jamison's neighbors, after her lunch date with Abby, to see if anyone had any information that might help. Before she went however, she sent an email to the Hearing For All Foundation about Jimmy Hill, not naming names, to see if they would be able to do anything for him. Maybe next time she went out by the antique shop, she could stop in and talk to Mrs. Tanner and she might have some real help to offer, if she was interested.

Olivia found she still felt uncomfortable leaving Molly and Sheyna alone at home, so she called Abby and asked if they could stay with her mom for the day. That way, when she and Abby had finished lunch, she could continue to Eastman's Grant to investigate without worrying about them.

Abby said she was sure her mom would be thrilled, so once Olivia had finished cleaning the house and doing a little work for her antique business, she packed some toys and treats for the girls and loaded them into Josh's SUV.

The day was cool, but not windy or damp, so she was comfortable in a long sleeved zip necked shirt and jeans. She wore a new pair of trail runner shoes she was trying to break in gradually since she shouldn't be doing too much walking today. At the last minute she decided to take a jacket and gloves along in case it got colder unexpectedly.

Annie was happy to see Sheyna and Molly and quickly pulled out some special treats she had for them.

"I'm so glad you brought them by Liv," Annie said laughing. "I was bored to tears with the cooler weather, not wanting to go out as much until my body adjusts. Now I can have company and enjoy myself, and still be warm."

"Thanks for watching them Annie, I'm going out to talk to some of the neighbors of the antique shop where I found Sheyna, after Abby and I have lunch and I'll be back to pick them up after that, maybe around four o'clock. Is that okay?"

"Stay out as long as you like, just be careful out there by yourself." Annie said as Olivia walked to the door. "And call me if you're going to be late, so I won't worry; you're like my second daughter you know."

Olivia gave Annie a hug, said goodbye to Molly and Sheyna and closed the door. She called Abby to let her know she was on the way, and tell her to go ahead and grab a table if she got there first. Her stomach grumbled. It hasn't been that long since breakfast, she told herself. She really should order take-out Thai food for dinner once in a while. It was so good, the thought of it always made her hungry. She wondered if Josh liked it. Hmmm, maybe she should look for some recipes and learn to cook it herself.

Abby was early so she was already seated at a table by the window when Olivia arrived. Olivia took the chair across from her and plopped down with an exaggerated sigh.

"I'm starving! Well, okay, just craving that delicious Tofu Miracle they have on the menu," Olivia laughed. "I know, I know I really need to eat out more often."

Abby was her usual cheerful self and the lunch was fun. Olivia enjoyed her food immensely and even thought about getting a batch to take home for dinner since Josh wouldn't be there, but decided against it, promising herself that she would bring him there soon instead.

Olivia gave Abby several pairs of beautiful vintage rhinestone earrings she'd found that she knew were on one of Abby's clients' lists and Abby insisted on picking up the tab.

"So how are things going with dream guy?" she asked impishly. "Has he spent the night for real yet?"

Olivia laughed, "He's stayed in my guestroom for the past two weeks. We've been getting to know each other really well though," her expression sobered. "If I tell you something, you have to promise you won't tell anyone else."

Abby's eyes grew wide, "What happened? Don't tell me you think he's the murderer?"

"Oh no, of course not!" Olivia burst out laughing.

Abby threw her hands up laughing, "Well, what then? You looked so serious all of a sudden, I figured it had to be something scary."

"He asked me to marry him and I said yes."

"Oh my! Really? Yay!" Abby jumped up and hugged her best friend. "Congratulations Liv! I am so happy for you!" She looked at her, "Why can't I tell anyone?"

"Because technically I'm still a suspect in the murder and Josh could get in trouble or even get fired if it got out that he's involved with me." Olivia said in a soft voice.

"Oh, yeah, I guess that makes sense. Well, I won't say anything until you tell me I can."

"Thanks Abs, I just had to share the news with someone and I know I can trust you."

Abby hugged her again. "This is the Best. News. Ever!"

"Will you be my Maid of Honor?"

"As long as you don't make the dresses Blaze Orange. You know how lousy I look in Blaze Orange." Abby grinned. "Livvie, I am so excited!"

Olivia grinned back, "You aren't the only one. I love him so much!" She drank the last sip of her tea.

The waiter came and brought the check which Abby promptly grabbed before Olivia could blink.

"I was already going to pay the bill, but now... No, sheesh woman, hands off that wallet!" she laughed, waving away Olivia's money. "It is definitely my treat after that announcement."

"By the way," Abby said as they got up to leave, "have you decided when the wedding will be yet?"

"No, not yet. We are still hoping to solve the case first so there won't be any controversy about Josh and I being together."

"I hope you can get it solved soon then Liv; it's a shame to have to wait for that."

Olivia hugged her as they reached their cars, "Hopefully we'll find out all the answers soon. I'm going to question the neighbors now to see if I can get anything."

"Be careful. Are you going alone? Does Josh know you're going?"

Olivia made a wry face, "No, I didn't get a chance to tell him, but the murderer killed himself you know, so it shouldn't be dangerous just to try to wrap up the details."

"Okay, I guess you know what you're doing. Call me

when you get back though, okay?" Abby got in and shut her car door.

"I will," Olivia promised, getting into Josh's SUV and starting the engine. It was almost one PM, so depending on how long each interview took, how many of the neighbors were actually home, and how many refused to talk to her, she might be able to fit them all in and be able to get back to Annie's house by four, but it wouldn't be easy. It was about forty-five minutes to Eastman's Grant, so she went as fast as the speed limit allowed. She definitely didn't want to get stopped for speeding by one of Josh's subordinates.

The first house she came to on her list was a cute little beige cape style house with burgundy shutters and trim. It looked neat and well kept on the outside, and had an adorable little flower garden in the front with stained glass butterflies on copper posts placed strategically throughout.

Olivia knocked on the door expecting a sweet grandmotherly type woman to answer. She was gobsmacked by the sight of the huge leather clad, tattooed biker gang member looking guy who opened the door. She stood frozen for a few seconds before her mouth would open.

"Hi," she squeaked, "My name is Olivia McKenna, and I was wondering if you saw anything the day of the murder over at the antique dealer's place?" Her voice was pretty well back to normal by the time she finished the sentence.

"Hi Ma'am, I'm Tiny Dawson, pleased to meet you," he said holding out a massive hand.

Olivia gamely shook his hand which totally engulfed

her own. "I'm please to meet you too Tiny, please call me Olivia."

"Oh, please come in," he stepped back and motioned her inside.

Taking a deep breath to steady her nerves, Olivia decided he really didn't feel like a threat to her and stepped inside.

He led her to a cheerful kitchen with white walls and yellow cabinets and pulled out a bright yellow vinyl chair with chrome legs for her to sit at the gorgeous 1950's Formica and chrome table. Her heart almost stopped from the sheer beauty of the dining set and she immediately lost the last smidgeon of her fear.

"This set is gorgeous!" she cried. "Where did you find it?" she touched the flawless Formica tabletop reverently.

"It belonged to my ma," he said, opening the adorable yellow 1949 Hotpoint fridge. "Can I get you some pop or iced tea?"

"I'd love some iced tea, if it's not too much trouble," Olivia smiled. "So do you live here alone? Everything is so well kept, I kind of expected a woman was taking care of it."

Tiny grinned ruefully and blushed, "Well, yeah, I guess I'm not the type of guy you'd expect to be living here, but when Ma got sick, I came and stayed with her until the end, and then when she died, it didn't feel right not to keep it up the way she would have, you know?" He poured tea from a full pitcher into a tall glass with ice and set it on the table in front of Olivia, then poured a second one for himself and sat across from her. "She was a great mother. She helped me build a big tree-house way in the woods back behind the house when I was a kid. Climbed up there every day working with me until it was done. It's still standing strong today. I wanted to make sure her home was always standing strong and beautiful like she was."

"I can understand that. It's a beautiful, cozy feeling home."

"Thanks," he said. "So you asked me about the day of the murder over there," he gestured with his head toward the antique shop. "I was out most of the day, but I was here when they say the murder happened. I told the cops that the only thing I saw was some guy on a bicycle riding by."

"Can you remember anything about him?"

"He had on a black helmet. I think he was wearing those tight shorts, black also, and a white shirt. It was too quick and I wasn't really looking at him. I just happened to see him when I glanced up."

"What made you glance up?"

"Huh? What do you mean?"

"Did you hear something, or what? What were you doing when you saw him?"

Tiny thought for a few moments, rubbing his forehead with his big meaty hand. "I was in the front yard, weeding the flower bed. I'm not sure what made me look up." He paused, "I think I might have heard something, but danged if I can remember what it was right now."

Olivia sighed, "Tiny, if you remember anything else at all, please call me. It's really important to me to solve this murder."

"Why are you involved in it, are you with the police? I never even thought to ask why," he chuckled. "You know, that guy that was murdered was up to something over there."

"What do you mean?"

"He was always sneaking around on other people's property. I saw him out digging around on Mrs. Tanner's property near the woods, back behind her old shed, in the dead of night. I mean, somebody's doing things like that, they're definitely up to no good."

"Do you know if he was sneaking onto the other properties around here too?" Olivia asked.

"I've seen him walking down the road at night looking around like he didn't want anyone to see him, but I never saw him actually on anybody else's land, no." Tiny offered her more tea.

"Thanks Tiny, but I'd probably better get going," Olivia thought for a second. "Well, actually, maybe I'll take a little bit more. What can you tell me about the neighbors around here? Is there anyone I need to be careful with? I already met Mr. Fergusson, up the street, and I think I'd rather be warned ahead of time if there are any more like him," Olivia said with a wry expression.

"Oh, you met him, did you?" Tiny rolled his eyes, "Yeah, he's a piece of work. Even when he's not loaded to the gills, he's not all there, he's a creepy kinda weird." He thought for a moment, "Sanders, down the road a ways, is a cantankerous pain in the neck, but he isn't dangerous, just a mouthy jerk. Oh, and old Wendy Rankin, she's a nasty bit. Not dangerous either, but she's got something bad to say about everything and everybody. I'm not sure why she's like that, but her place is worse than a pigsty, yet she complains if anybody has a dog or a cat, not to mention farm animals . . . and kids, she hates them!"

"So there isn't really anyone I have to watch out for, as far as being dangerous?" Olivia smiled. "Mrs. Rankin doesn't sound like a lot of fun, but she won't shoot me if I knock on her door or anything, right?"

"No, if you can stand the smell of the place, you're safe enough. I wouldn't touch anything though, that place is just plain nasty." He grimaced in distaste. "You'd be more likely to get cooties than to be shot," he laughed.

"Yuck!" Olivia laughed, "Okay, I am forewarned. Thanks so much for your hospitality Tiny. I probably don't have time to go to the other places today, but it'll help me for next time," she said glancing at her watch.

"The other neighbors around here are all pretty nice. Mrs. Tanner with her grandson over there, he gestured with his head, and young Edwina Parson down at the end are both sweethearts," Tiny stood to walk her to the door. "It was real nice meeting you Miss Olivia. Good luck figuring it all out and be careful."

"Thanks Tiny, it was great meeting you too and thanks so much for the tea and all the information," Olivia shook his hand and headed back to the car. "Oh, here is my card, if you happen to remember what made you look up that day, or if you remember anything else for that matter, please call me," she turned back and handed him the card, then continued to Josh's SUV and waved as she drove out.

It was already three-fifteen, so she headed back toward Annie's house to pick up Molly and Sheyna. She hadn't really learned much about the day of the murder, though if there was something that Tiny remembered later, it might be helpful, but she did at least learn a little about the neighbors and would feel safer interviewing them alone when she went back.

A grey van passed her suddenly just before a curve, flying by from the other direction, so close to her that she almost drove into the ditch to avoid being hit. She stopped the car, shaken and looked in the rearview mirror, but the van was already too far away for her to see anything more about it.

Crazy kids trying to see how fast they can get away with driving on the back roads, she thought. She pulled back into the road and drove to Annie's house without further incident, arriving just before four PM.

Annie opened the door with a smile, "I'm glad to see you back safely. They were angels!"

Molly and Sheyna were happy to see Olivia, but it was obvious they'd had a great time and probably had loads of treats too. Olivia hugged Annie and thanked her for watching them.

"I want you and Abby to come over for dinner sometime soon," she said. "It's been too long since we had a 'family night'."

"I'd love that Livvie, just let me know when," Annie walked Olivia to the car and put Sheyna into her crate in the back. Molly jumped in and lay down in her own crate. Olivia waved and pulled into the road, picking up her cell phone to call Abby before she forgot and made her worry. Josh called as soon as she'd hung up from reporting her well being to Abby.

Things were going well in Boston, and he should be back the next afternoon. The cops investigating the suicide, were satisfied that there had been no foul play, but Josh wanted to talk to people who lived in the building and the ones adjacent to it himself, to make sure all the 'T's were crossed and 'I's dotted. Olivia decided to save the story of her afternoon for when Josh returned, so she could tell him in person. Some things were best not said over the phone.

When she got home, she fed Molly and Sheyna, then made some comforting Risotto for herself, along with a salad and sat down to try and sort out everything they knew about the case. There was still something in the back of her memory from the day of the murder that she couldn't reach, and she had a feeling it was important. She decided to make a list.

1.   The murderer killed Jamison while I was in the shop.

2.   He used a weapon he found in the shop rather than bringing one with him or he brought one and changed his mind about using it.

3.   Two blonde men and a blonde woman broke into the shop after the murder. Well, that's if Fergusson wasn't too loaded to know what he saw.

4.   Some of the robbery loot was found in the shop basement.

5.   Jamison was seen prowling in neighbors' yards and digging in Mrs. Tanner's woods.

6.   Larsson is dead, apparently a suicide.

7.   The next best suspect is Morrow who lost money due to being underinsured.

8.   Some of Olander's and Porter's stolen stuff had been recovered by Josh and his guys.

9.   The insurances companies were out tons of money from the robberies and could have had a motive for wanting Jamison dead, but probably only if they could recover the loot.

10.   Jimmy Hill was alone in the house during the murder and possibly saw something out the window?

Olivia stopped writing, as she couldn't think of anything else pertinent that they were sure of. She would have to make time to check on Jimmy Hill and see if by any chance, he'd seen something, and she thought, I should check and see if that organization wrote back about him.

Sure enough, there was an email from the Hearing For All Foundation, saying that depending on the circumstances, they thought they might very well be able to help him. Olivia was thrilled. She'd really liked Mrs. Tanner and Jimmy was such a talented little guy, she'd been hoping pretty hard that something would work out to help him hear. Now she definitely needed to get by to talk to Mrs. Tanner soon.

Well, aside from teasing in the back of her mind, she wasn't much further along in the investigation than before, except that at least her thoughts were written out succinctly. Maybe Josh would have something more when he got back from Boston. Olivia decided to call it a night, and after letting Molly out for a while, then bringing her back in and locking up, she went to bed and fell asleep almost immediately.

CHAPTER FOURTEEN

Josh's trip to Boston had felt like an exercise in futility. From the time he'd arrived, he'd been relegated to the back seat figuratively, and frequently quite literally. At the moment, his six foot frame was jammed into the back seat of the lead detective's tiny personal sports car, while the two detectives occupied the small front seats.

They'd agreed to allow him to sit in on their interviews with the neighbors in the apartment building, but firmly suggested that he ride with them, leaving his New Hampshire State Police car at the station. He'd had little choice in the matter, and so it was that he could now testify as to exactly how a sardine would feel jammed into a little tin can. He was pretty sure they'd made him ride like this just to dissuade him from coming.

The detective in charge of the case was obviously not pleased to have a New Hampshire State Trooper horning in on his investigation, and was upfront about it. He also informed Josh that he was not welcome to go off on his own questioning possible witnesses. He was being allowed to sit in on their interviews, but was to keep his mouth shut and listen only.

Despite having made it to the rank of Lieutenant, or maybe because of it, Josh hated the petty politics and uncooperative attitudes of some police departments, and many individual cops. How were they supposed to solve cases if they refused to help each other? To him, it was the results that were important, not who got them.

Nothing of consequence had been divulged during the interviews, as it seemed most of the people in the building had been inside their apartments, or out for the evening and no one reported having seen or heard anything. Josh itched to be able to ask questions of his own and to go looking for additional witnesses, but without departmental cooperation, his hands were tied.

He was contemplating going ahead and doing his own investigating anyway and risking the wrath of the Boston PD, as well as his own captain who'd probably not only fire him but have his head mounted on a pike in the parking lot of Headquarters to serve as a warning to any other lowly cretin who might have the audacity to consider flouting his instructions. Finally, he decided to play it by the book for now, as he really didn't want to lose his job.

It wasn't that he really needed the job. He actually could afford to quit if he chose to; he had enough money, but he loved his job for the most part. It was a way for him to give to the community without anyone having to know that he was wealthy. He quietly donated his entire salary and more to various charities, and easily lived off a small portion of the interest from the money left to him by his mother and grandparents.

He hadn't told Olivia about the money yet, and had been trying to figure out the best way to do so. He'd learned long ago not to tell women he was interested in dating that he came from wealth, as it either made them want him for his money or made them think he was a spoiled trust fund baby type. He knew Olivia wouldn't be like that, but still, it had never been an easy subject for him to broach.

He decided he would figure out a way to tell her as soon as he got back from Boston, waiting wouldn't solve that problem. For now, unfortunately he was planning to stick to his job, which meant leaving Boston with nothing to show for the trip except a lot of frustration and a sore neck from being crammed into a car designed for small children. If nothing else, he would stop on the way out and buy a bunch of Cannolis to take back tomorrow, so it wouldn't be a totally wasted trip, and he just might try to stop by the Cambridge Antique Market and see what he could find for Olivia. Right now, he was going to Regina's to find a large puttnesca pizza with extra Pecorino Romano and a big salad for dinner.

~~~

Olivia woke early the next morning, fed Molly and Sheyna and went for a run before breakfast. She'd been lax about her exercising lately and she could feel it in her legs after the first mile. The second and third miles were actually a little easier, but the fourth was no fun at all and the fifth was pure torture. *See why it's bad to slack off Liv?* She scolded herself. She reached her house and squatted on the porch gasping.

When she caught her breath, she picked up the morning paper and went inside to make herself some eggs and toast. Molly wanted to play, so Olivia threw a plush toy for her while she cooked, and Sheyna watched until she finally ran and grabbed the toy and darted under the couch with it. Molly stood barking at her until Olivia had to go and fish her out, and give Molly the toy while skillfully substituting an almost identical one to give back to Sheyna. She barely managed to grab her eggs off the stove before they burned.

"Well girls," she said cheerfully, "Josh is coming back from Boston today. He said he'll have to go to Headquarters for a while, but he should be home early." Molly watched her with her head tilted. "What should we do to welcome him back?" she paused, then laughed, "No, not that you naughty girl."

"Oh, I know! I never gave him the watch I found for him at that estate sale." She patted Molly's head, "That will be perfect." She ran upstairs and got the watch, then back downstairs to her storage room for a nice box and some wrapping paper. Once she had it wrapped in pretty brown and gold paper, which was the most masculine wrapping paper she had, she took it and laid it on his pillow in the guestroom.

"I think I'll go and deliver the rest of the stuff I have for my clients today, you wanna come with me?" she asked Molly. Sheyna was still being a little sulky over the toy from the morning. Olivia laughed at her, when she flicked her tail. "You know I love you Sheyna girl," she crooned, rubbing between her ears. Sheyna gave in and rubbed up against her face.

Olivia packed up all the antiques and vintage items she had to deliver and got the girls into the car. Just as they pulled out, her cell phone rang. She spoke to Josh while she drove, then hung up looking perplexed.

She drove to State Police Headquarters and parked in the lot to wait for Josh to come out.

~~~

Five minutes after he saw Olivia pull into the parking lot, Josh made an unobtrusive exit from the building and climbed into the passenger seat beside her.

He took her hand and held it, running his fingers teasingly over her palm.

"I wish I could kiss you right now," he said in his sexy voice. "This is killing me." He laughed and squeezed her hand. He took a deep breath.

"Your poor Suburban is toast, both literally and figuratively. I'm sorry sweetie," his tone sobered as he delivered the news. "It looks like they went through it thoroughly, looking for something, and maybe tried to burn it so we wouldn't find fingerprints. There was nothing left of the girls' crates or toys except for a charred mess. It was totally trashed and burned."

"Wow, I was kind of expecting it to be trashed, but hearing it still feels bad," Olivia sighed. "Do I need to do anything, or sign anything? I know I will need some kind of report from you for the insurance."

"You can come in and get it now and I will need you to sign some things too, or I can bring everything to your house tonight after work. Whichever works best," Josh felt a little awkward, wondering if the guys had noticed him getting into the car and were now watching through the windows. He decided it just didn't matter that much.

Olivia rubbed his hand, "If it isn't a pain for you to bring it, I think that would be better for me, so I don't have to bring the girls inside."

"It's not a pain at all," Josh smiled. "Nothing about you has ever been a pain," he rubbed his fingers over her palm seductively.

"Okay, now this is killing me!" Olivia laughed. "I want to kiss you and hold you without worrying about whether people are watching or not. I'm going to go do my errands and I'll see you at home later. What time will you be there; do you know?"

"I should be there around five. I'm getting off early, but I need to make a couple stops."

"Alrighty then, I'm off!" she squeezed his hand laughing. "See you later big boy."

Josh climbed out and shut the door, waving as she drove off. He wasn't sure, but he thought he could see the blinds moving in the windows of the HQ. Nosy bunch, they were. He chuckled as he went back inside to see everyone pretending to be so busy they didn't notice his entry, even the receptionist, who kept giving him sidelong glances.

He immersed himself in his work, trying to forget the argument he'd had with the captain that morning. He'd complained to his boss about the way he was basically shut out of the case in Boston, and seeing his boss' apathy, told him in frustration that he'd almost decided to go ahead and conduct his own investigation. Captain Corwin went ballistic, yelling that he'd had his orders, and he'd be out on his bum looking for work immediately if he ever did anything to get him on the wrong side of any other police department. Josh took the tirade calmly, inwardly rolling his eyes and thinking of a few choice words he wished he could say.

This certainly wasn't the first time they'd clashed over politics, nor would it be the last, he was sure. Captain Frank Corwin was definitely a politician, first and foremost. Being a cop took second chair to his need to be promoted as high as he could get and make as much money as possible. Josh had major issues with his boss' attitude, as it all too frequently made doing his own job difficult to impossible. Sometimes he wondered if what he was doing was worth the frustration. He was able to help people he couldn't have helped if he wasn't a cop, but there were times he could have done as much or more as a civilian.

Maybe Olivia's idea, though said jokingly, of them starting their own detective agency someday wasn't a bad idea at all. He had plenty of experience, she had plenty of intuition, and they were both intelligent, hard working people with a flair for figuring things out. Hmm. He'd love to be able to tell the Captain that he quit, and to let him know exactly what he thought of his brown-nosing, greed and laziness. Well, now wasn't the time. He didn't want to leave the department until the Jamison case was wrapped up, as that would forever leave Olivia under a slight shadow of suspicion. He needed to get it solved already while he was still in a place where he could easily do things civilians had a hard time doing.

O'Brian entered his office with a light knock on the door. "Lieu, we found a good latent partial fingerprint on the underside of the door handle on the back passenger side and another partial of the same print on the inside of the door frame on the other back door," he looked properly elated to present his boss with this good news. "Baker's running it through AFIS now."

"You mean it wasn't Larsson's or Ms. McKenna's?"

"No, and it wasn't yours either boss. I checked that myself," he added hastily, seeing Josh's expression darken and his eyebrows rise. "Sorry boss, but I've seen how you two are when you're together. Don't worry," he said with an irrepressible grin, "I haven't said anything to anybody. I like having you as my boss."

Josh shook his head and had to chuckle, "Okay O'Brian, it was good thinking, just see that you keep your mouth shut about that particular piece of information. When will she have the results for us?"

"Baker said she should have something back in a couple hours if it goes well, but the system was acting up, so it could be tomorrow if it doesn't come back up."

"Big surprise there. We really need to get someone in here to figure out why it keeps going down."

"I hear you Lieu. Seems like there's always something not working around here," O'Brian muttered, glancing toward the Captain's office to make sure his door was still closed. "I know the budget is tight, but come on . . .."

"Yeah, I guess it depends on your priorities," Josh agreed shaking his head. "Alright, thanks for the information O'Brian. Keep me updated."

Josh sat in thought for a couple of minutes, reaching into his desk drawer to take out a little velvet ring box. Olivia had saved the twist tie he'd given her as an impromptu engagement ring, but it was high time she had the real thing. He'd give it to her tonight. This had been his mom's ring, and her mom's before that. He couldn't wait to see it on Olivia's slender finger. Speaking of fingers, Josh turned back to his case files with a renewed sense of purpose and a glimmer of hope that with the discovery of a fingerprint they might get it wrapped up soon after all.

CHAPTER FIFTEEN

Olivia happily pocketed a generous check for the Dazey butter churn, stopped by the bank to deposit it along with the money she'd gotten from the other two clients she'd delivered items to that morning, and finally stopped by a roadside stand that was selling pumpkins, fancy decorative squashes and dried corn stalks for decoration. She chose one large pumpkin, and a few smaller ones of various sizes, along with several types of squash, she could place strategically around the house, then later cook. She passed on the corn stalks but couldn't resist an adorable wreath with a crow dressed as a scarecrow, and a gorgeous full sized handmade hearth broom, designed to look like a witch's broom. She also bought a couple large pots of mums for the porch, one brilliant purple and one bright orange. They were the nicest mums she's seen for sale all year.

She wanted to make the house look as festive as she felt, which despite the murder and it's scary aftermath, was pretty festive, thanks to a certain tall, dark and wickedly handsome cop, not to mention the lovely warm butterflies she had in her stomach most of the time when they were together.

She stopped at the park on the way home to throw a Frisbee for Molly for a while, walking Sheyna on her leash. The wind picked up after a bit, sending the leaves flying from the trees like autumn colored snow. Olivia zipped her fleece jacket up to her chin and pulled her gloves from her pocket. It was chilly in the wind, but too beautiful to run for the warmth of indoors just yet. With her hands securely in her warm fleecy gloves, Olivia threw the Frisbee, jumping up and down when Molly leaped and caught it in mid air. Sheyna rubbed against her legs asking to be picked up. Olivia bent and picked her up, cuddling her to warm her in case she was cold. As she straightened, she had a strange feeling creep up the back of her neck. She turned quickly to see if someone was nearby watching her, and thought for a second that she saw a figure duck behind the trees several yards away, but though she stood for a while watching closely, she didn't see anything.

No longer feeling comfortable in the park, Olivia called Molly, put her on leash and they headed back to Josh's car. She looked around, scanning the trees as she pulled away, but as far as she could see, there was nothing there. Molly hadn't barked, so that was a good sign, but then, she'd been taught not to bark at people and other animals in the park, so unless they were doing something that upset her, she wouldn't have been likely to bark. *Oh well,* Olivia sighed to herself, *it was probably just her overactive imagination at work.*

When she arrived home, she got the girls in the house, then unloaded her decorations from the car and spent the next half hour arranging them to her liking. There—the porch looked cozy, warm and very festive. It was already three o'clock by the time she'd finished, so she decided to get a jump on cooking dinner. She was planning to use one of the pumpkins she'd purchased to make a pumpkin risotto.

Olivia prepared the pumpkin and the other stuff for the risotto, then straightened the kitchen and went upstairs to take a shower and get ready for dinner. She dried her hair, taming its wild waves as best she could, then put on a little black dress that was very sexy in a subtle understated way with plain black heels and a tiny bit of mascara and lip gloss.

She added a gold bangle bracelet to her wrist and a thin gold chain with a tiny diamond around her neck. Spritzing a little perfume behind her ears and on her wrists, she was as ready as she was going to get, so she went down to feed the girls and light the fireplace.

Molly was happily tired from playing Frisbee, and both she and Sheyna were acting hungrier than usual from the cold weather, so Olivia put a little extra of the vegetable mixture into their bowls with their kibble.

Once Molly'd gone out to do her business and returned, Olivia started the fire in the fireplace and sat on the floor patting and brushing Molly and Sheyna until Josh arrived.

~~~

Josh walked into Olivia's living room to find a picture perfect scene. Olivia was sitting on the rug, with her back against the couch, reading a book in front of a dancing fire with Sheyna in her lap and Molly's head on her feet. His heart felt so full of love for them, he wanted to embrace the whole world.

"Hi sweetheart, you are so beautiful; you know that?" he came over and sat next to her, taking her into his arms and kissing her, as she half rose to greet him.

"Mmm, you're not looking half bad yourself stranger," she murmured when they came up for air.

Molly and Sheyna both crowded around vying for attention. Josh scratched their ears and tickled their bellies laughing at their jealousy.

"Okay, enough guys!" he laughed, getting up and helping Olivia to her feet. "Both our faces are thoroughly washed now; why don't you go groom yourselves for a while?"

Olivia laughed, "It's so much more fun to groom their people. I think our reactions are more amusing to them than they are to us."

They kissed again then Olivia led Josh to the kitchen and handed him a glass of wine. She had set the table with a candle in the center, which she lit now.

"Can I help you cook?" Josh asked. "That's a lot of stuff I see sitting out there," he said, eyeing all the chopped veggies and pumpkin.

"You can make a salad if you'd like, and boil the water for the pasta" Olivia smiled. "I've got the rest ready to cook."

When everything was done, she served the risotto in small bowls and the rest of the food onto their plates. Josh put the salad into little bowls also and sliced a couple pieces of bread.

"Now that's multitasking at its finest!" he said laughing. "Wow, I like to cook, but I would never have been able to make risotto while cooking anything else at all."

Olivia smiled happily, "Risotto is easier than it looks, really. As long as you add things slowly and stir consistently, it's a piece of cake."

The meal was delicious, warm and mildly spicy, perfect for a chilly fall evening. Josh told her all about his trip to Boston while they ate and complimented her on the new decorations outside. They decided to carve a jack o' lantern together and Josh promised to find a suitable large pumpkin the next day.

After they'd cleaned up the kitchen and put the dishes in the dishwasher, washing the larger pots and pans by hand, they retired to the living room. Josh sat on the couch and Sheyna jumped into his lap purring. He petted her and Molly jumped up beside them licking Josh's face enthusiastically. Olivia laughed and sat next to Molly, hugging her. Josh reached over Molly and hugged her and Molly both. Then he threw Molly's toy for her and let her fetch it to him for a while until she settled down on the rug by their feet.

"Oh, I'll be right back," Olivia jumped up and ran to the guestroom to get the gift she'd put on his pillow since he hadn't gone in there yet. Shyly, she held it out to him.

"Wow!" he said in surprise, "What's this for?" he took the little box with a happy smile. "It's not my birthday."

"It's actually something I meant to give you a long time ago, but got sidetracked by all the chaotic things that were going on back then and somehow never did. It's a thank you for all the wonderfully kind things you've done for me, especially the ones you did before we even really knew each other."

He smiled again, "You didn't need to get me anything. I wanted to do everything I did." He tore off the paper and opened the box. "Oh," he said in a stunned whisper, "Liv, that's beautiful!" he lifted it out of the box and held it up. "Thank you so much," he hugged her and held her to his chest tightly.

She hugged him back, then took the watch and fastened it on his wrist, after removing his old rather battered looking one.

He grinned, "That one can go for donation, if anyone is desperate enough to want it. I beat it up pretty badly when I wore it skydiving a few times. What a wonderful, sweet gift! Thank you!"

"You're very welcome Josh. It just seemed to have your name on it when I saw it."

"I am so glad it did!" he grinned, flashing his wrist around to show it off.

"Okay, it's your turn to wait for a minute," he went out to his state car and retrieved a strangely shaped package, gaily wrapped in green glittery paper with a big yellow bow. He held it out to her tentatively. "I hope you like it. It's a rather odd sort of gift."

Olivia took the package with a puzzled smile. "What on earth could that be?" she shook it lightly. "Is it some kind of banjo?"

Josh laughed, "Open the paper and see for yourself."

Olivia ripped the paper open to find a gorgeous seventeenth century brass and copper bed warmer that was in beautiful condition. She was so excited she almost dropped it.

"Josh, this had to have cost way too much money! It's simply stunning!" She set it down carefully and threw her arms around him. "You are the nicest man I've ever known. Thank you for being so wonderful."

"I'm glad you like it. I had a very hard time finding something that had your name on it, when there were so many things to choose from," he chuckled, "I stopped by the Cambridge Antique Market while I was in Boston to see if I could find you something special. This was it."

"It so is!" she cried. "It's absolutely gorgeous! I hope you didn't spend too much on it though, I would feel really bad if you overstretch your budget for me. I know cops don't make tons of money like they should," she kissed him, then picked up the bed warmer to look at it again, running her fingers reverently over the old metal.

"Liv, we need to talk," Josh said, sobering. "There is something I need to tell you."

Olivia gasped and turned pale, "You're breaking up with me."

"No! Oh, never Sweetheart!" Josh took her suddenly rigid body in his arms. "I love you and want to marry you more than anything in the world." He smoothed her hair back as the color returned to her face. "No, it's not something bad, in fact it's something I hope you'll be happy about, once you get used to the idea."

Olivia pulled away and sat down, holding Josh's hand and drawing him down with her. "So, okay, I'm calm now, go ahead," she smiled sheepishly. "My mind just went to one of the worst possible scenarios and jumped on it. Sorry."

Josh smiled, "I should have worded it differently, it did sound ominous." He took a deep breath, "Okay, so what if I were to tell you that I am from a wealthy family and I'm only working as a cop in order to be able to give something to my community, and because I absolutely love the work?" he held his breath waiting for her answer.

Olivia gave him a skeptical look, then pulled away angrily. "What kind of joke is that? First you scare me half to death, then give me a ridiculous story about being rich?" she looked hurt. "Why?"

"Ah Liv, I'm so sorry I messed it up," he ran his fingers through his hair. "I never meant to scare you sweetheart, and I really am rich. It's not a story or a joke. I'd wanted to tell you several times lately, but just hadn't found the right time, then when you said what you said about cops not making enough money, I knew I had to tell you right then," he looked miserable. "I'd never lie to you Olivia."

Olivia's breath caught in a swallowed sob, "I believe you now Josh. It just caught me so off guard coming right after thinking you were dumping me."

"I'm sorry love, sometimes my mouth starts working before my brain I think," he took her in his arms and hugged her tight. "So are you okay with that? You won't hate being wealthy?"

"Not unless I have to join some stuffy Ladies' Groups and dress like the Queen of England all the time or something," Olivia's sense of humor restored itself. "So do you have a big house somewhere or do you really just live in that little apartment? Do the other cops know?"

"No! There's no way I could work there if they did," he said. "They'd never accept me as one of them. That's why I live in the little apartment, not that I mind living there usually. I do miss being able to have pets, and a tiny bit more room wouldn't hurt," he grinned. "I don't have a big house somewhere, though my dad does. I do have a fairly large cabin on the lake."

"Really?" Olivia's face lit up. "I love being on the lake. I think I could get used to being rich fairly easily," she grinned. "Can we stay at your cabin sometimes, and take a rowboat out on the lake? It always looks so romantic in the movies."

Josh laughed, "You know we can. I can't wait to be married to you! We're gonna have so much fun together. We really need to get this case solved and over with."

"Yes we do. I want to go and talk to the rest of the people in Eastman's Grant, just in case somebody has some information they haven't shared with you guys," she lowered her head apprehensively. "I was out there yesterday and talked to Tiny Dawson. Do you know him?"

"What?" Josh held her back from him so he could see her face. "You went out there by yourself when I wasn't even in town? Olivia, what were you thinking?"

"I was thinking that the murderer is dead and that it wasn't so dangerous anymore!" she retorted with her eyes flashing at the reprimand. "Obviously I survived the experience."

"Yes, thankfully you did," he said calming his jolted nerves. "Listen Liv, I'm sorry I scolded you, but there is something I haven't gotten to tell you yet. They found a couple of fingerprints on your car, that didn't belong to you, me or Larsson. One was in a place that seems unlikely to have just been a passing stranger or a friend who rode with you, so it's a little suspicious. It may mean there was someone else involved. We don't know yet, I mean, they could conceivably have been from your mechanics. We'll soon know if the prints are in the database."

"Oh," Olivia said in a small voice, "does that mean someone may still be after me?"

Josh felt like a jerk for having to shatter the peace

she'd finally managed to regain after almost a month of being stalked, but he had no choice. It wasn't safe to keep her in the dark about things, even though he wasn't sure if the print meant anything. On the off chance it did, he had to play it safe.

"Yes, it could. We don't know for sure though. It may be something else and have nothing to do with the case. When did you have your car serviced or cleaned last?"

Olivia thought, "About a month ago I had it washed and cleaned inside and all. It's been a few months since servicing."

"Great," Josh said feelingly. "They were fairly fresh prints, so that's why we were worried. It could easily have been the people who washed your car then." He smiled in relief. "Please promise me not to take any chances until we know for sure though," he hugged her hard. "I don't want to lose you."

She hugged him back, massaging his back gently. "I don't want to be lost."

Speaking of how much I love you," he reached into his pocket, pulled out the ring box and removed the ring, dropping the box on the floor. Then he knelt on one knee, took her left hand in his and said, "I want to do it right this time. Olivia, I love you so very much. Will you still marry me?"

Olivia dropped to the floor with him, taking him into her arms. "Yes! I love you too and want to be with you forever."

He put the ring on her left ring finger. "This ring was my mom's and her mother's. I know they would want you to have it now."

It was a stunning ring, gold with a large center

diamond, surrounded by small sapphires. It fit perfectly. Olivia's face glowed. Josh had never felt happier in his life.

CHAPTER SIXTEEN

The remaining weeks before Halloween passed quickly. Josh and Olivia carved a wonderful Jack 'O Lantern and set it by the front door. They'd bought candy together and were all ready for Trick or Treaters to arrive when Josh realized that he shouldn't be seen staying at Olivia's unless he wanted to let the cat out of the bag and risk losing his job. He just couldn't afford to do that until the case was solved, and that meant either leaving until the kids had all come and gone or hiding each time someone knocked at the door. After all the preparations and excitement they'd shared getting ready for the night, Josh felt a letdown.

"It's not fair, sweetie," Olivia said sadly. "I want to be able to share this with you. It's our first holiday together. The heck with the job. Nobody really thinks I killed Jamison, do they?"

Josh swallowed his disappointment to respond, "I don't think so love, but you still shouldn't have this hanging over your head. And, even though the prints we found weren't in the AFIS Data Base, we aren't sure there wasn't someone else involved in it, though it seems unlikely. I can't lose my job yet. I won't leave the force without clearing your name and making sure you're safe."

"It's really too hard sometimes, living like this, with you staying here in the guestroom, but us not really being together, and having to hide our relationship." Olivia stopped and put her hand over her mouth as if to pull the words back in.

The elephant that had been hiding in the room for so long finally roared.

Josh had to admit it was tough on both of them, living together 'sort of'. He knew for sure it was tough on him, and he was pretty sure it wasn't much easier on Olivia, if any. Then there was the constant worry over someone saying something to his boss, who'd love to get rid of him in a way that would make Josh look bad; it really was all getting to be a bit too much. Now that it seemed the danger was over, as nothing more had occurred since Larsson died, it had been getting harder to justify Josh's continued presence in Olivia's guestroom. But he was going to miss the closeness that came from sharing a house, if not a bedroom. He sighed.

"So, maybe it's time for me to move back into my apartment until we get this case solved."

"Josh, no!" Olivia blinked back tears from her lovely hazel eyes. "I'm sorry I said it. I don't want you to leave." She ran to him and held him tightly.

He brushed her hair back from her face and kissed her tenderly. "I know, sweetie, but it's for the best. We'll get to be a normal dating couple now. We never really had that," he smiled. "It'll be fun."

"I've loved having you here. Yes, it's been hard sometimes, but mostly, it's been wonderful."

"It has for me too Liv. It will be nice to actually date you too though," he smiled. "We only ever really had one date, and that was skydiving. I think we're going to enjoy this."

"Well, maybe," Olivia tried to smile. "But Josh, how are we going to date if we can't be seen together too much?"

Josh knitted his brow, "I didn't say it would be easy. I am the cop in charge of the case and you're a witness, so we can be seen together legitimately to a certain extent. I suppose taking you to dinner might not seem inappropriate, as long as we act cool," he thought for a moment, then grinned mischievously. "I've hardly ever used my money to do anything extravagant, but why not once in a while?" he held his hand out to her gallantly. "My dear, I would be very pleased if you would join me for dinner on Friday evening."

Olivia raised her eyebrows, "And what pray tell, my good sir, are you up to now?"

Josh laughed, "You'll see on Friday. Now, I should go so you can finish getting ready for the scary kiddies." He went into the guestroom and quickly collected his things. When he re-entered the living room Olivia put her arms around him silently. He bent and kissed her, pulling her against his chest. "I love you sweetheart. It will all be okay, I promise. Have a fun night and we'll talk tomorrow."

~~~

Olivia felt sad to see Josh moving back to his apartment, but inside, she knew it made sense. She didn't have the slightest doubt of her love for him or her desire to marry him, but it had been a strange and sometimes awkward situation with him staying in her house before they even really knew each other. Now that they did, and were engaged, it was actually even harder in a way. But it

ANTIQUES & AVARICE

had been wonderful too. She now knew they would be able to live together and get along. It had been like a test run.

She smiled as she wondered again what he was planning for Friday night. She loved it when he was mysterious. Sheyna meowed as she and Molly followed Olivia up the stairs to her bedroom.

"Okay girls, it's time to get ready for Halloween!" Olivia reached into the closet and pulled out three hangers. They'd been hanging in order of size—smallest for Sheyna, middle-size for Molly, largest for Olivia—in the center of the closet.

Olivia coaxed Sheyna into her adorable Cowardly Lion costume, then got Molly into her Scarecrow outfit, quickly donning her own Dorothy get up. She felt a pang that Josh, the Tin Man was missing. She hoped he was wearing his costume and giving out candy at his place, and that he wasn't lonely. Shaking herself, she put on a smile and herded the girls downstairs just in time to answer the door to greet the first group of kids who knocked.

Molly and Sheyna, while not ecstatic over wearing costumes, were thrilled with all the kids coming to visit. They both adored people, especially children. The kids were equally happy to see the costumed animals and gave them lots of attention. *What a win-win situation,* Olivia thought happily.

She had another thought and decided to make a quick call to Pam to see if she could bring Molly and Sheyna by to give out some candy to the residents. Pam agreed excitedly, promising to have some sugar free candy available for the people who weren't allowed sugar in their diets. She quickly called Abby to see if she would give out the candy at her house since Abby never got any trick or treaters where she lived. Abby said she'd be right over.

Olivia got Molly and Sheyna loaded in the car, showed Abby where everything was as soon as she got there, then hurried to go to the grocery store and get more candy before going to the retirement home. She decided to grab some fruit as well, since it was better for the people's health; that way she'd feel less guilty about giving them so much candy.

Pam greeted her at the front door, helping her with her bags of goodies, as she led Molly and Sheyna on their leashes.

Olivia had been bringing Molly and Sheyna to visit regularly since her first visit, but this was her first time going in the evening. Pam had done a good job in making the place festive for the holiday, and Olivia complimented her on all the adorable little pumpkins and such that adorned the hallways and the lobby. The grand finale was the dining room, which sported a gorgeous sparkly garland made of black and orange pumpkins wound all around the room, draped from the ceiling in huge swags.

"Wow, Pam, you really went all out this year. I love this!"

"It was fun," Pam said smiling. "The residents like Halloween next best to Christmas I think, so I wanted to make it nice for them. So few of them get many visitors, you know, so I am thrilled that you brought the girls tonight. You're going to make Halloween special for these people."

"Oh, I hope so, Pam," Olivia said, looking around at

the tables with elderly people sitting, eating their deserts. She and Pam sat at one end of a semi empty table and waited until all the desert dishes had been cleared, then Pam stood up at the front of the room and announced that Olivia, Molly and Sheyna would be doing some reverse Trick or Treating, by visiting each resident's room to bring them Halloween treats and visit for a moment.

As the residents hurried to get back to their rooms, most of them excited over the impending visit, Pam took Olivia aside.

"I haven't been able to make much progress on setting up volunteers to foster or adopt new residents' pets, but I am still hoping we can make it work. I've just been too busy with work here to give it enough energy yet."

"I will start helping you to look into how to find volunteers and maybe we can get it going soon. In the meantime, let me know if you do have anyone new coming in that needs help placing their pets and I will try really hard to find someone agreeable to our plan."

"Thanks so much Olivia, it means the world to me and even more to them," she gestured to the residents who were still filing out the door.

As soon as the room was empty, Pam led Olivia and the animals down the deserted hallway to first room. They stayed with each person for about five minutes, doling out candy, fruit, and hugs and kisses from Molly and Sheyna where they were wanted. Everyone liked the costumes and the visit passed happily for everyone.

"Happy Halloween, Pam!" Olivia called as she drove away, waving at Pam who stood at the lobby door waving back. "See you in a few days."

Olivia sighed contentedly. It had been a really good night, and while she missed seeing all the adorable little kids in their cute and scary costumes, she'd enjoyed the happiness of the old people at seeing Sheyna and Molly in their costumes even more.

Abby was still handing out candy when they arrived home.

"I've had a blast." she said grinning. "That's the only thing I don't like about my house . . . no trick or treaters ever. It's just such a secluded, and very adult neighborhood. Any time you want me to come and help out on Halloween, just let me know."

"Abs, if I'd known you missed it so much, you'd have had a standing invitation forever. Well, you do now!"

"Aww, thanks Liv," Abby hugged her. "So where's Josh? I never got a chance to ask before you rushed out to the nursing home."

"Sorry, I had to get there quickly, because they go to bed pretty early," she smiled. "Josh moved back into his apartment because I'm not in danger anymore and it wasn't easy for either of us living like this."

"But you're still together, right? You're still getting married?"

"Yes, definitely. There isn't anything wrong, it was just getting too hard to live together without his boss finding out. As long as this case is unsolved, and I am a suspect, even an unlikely one, us being together could get him fired."

"Okay, I'm glad that's all it is. You had me worried for a minute." Abby smiled and went to answer the door for another group of kids. She handed out lots of candy.

"So, I am going home to watch old movies until I fall

asleep. You're on your own with the kiddos now," Abby got her jacket, grabbed a handful of Halloween candy and headed out the door scaring two children who were about to knock.

"Thanks again Abs!" Olivia waved, then greeted the kids with several pieces of candy. The children giggled as Molly and Sheyna joined Olivia on the porch. Sheyna rubbed against their ankles and Molly head butted their hands. The kids were delighted to pat them and had to be stopped from giving them half their candy.

"Candy isn't good for dogs and cats, especially chocolate," Olivia said smiling, "but they love getting pets way more than candy anyway." Okay, maybe that last part was a fib, but the first part was spot on. Chocolate could be deadly to animals and any candy was bad for their teeth.

The rest of the night passed too quickly, with the last of the trick or treaters leaving at around nine-thirty. Olivia waited until ten PM then turned off the outside lights, blew the candle out of the Jack O'Lantern, locked the door and put away all the candy. She missed Josh a lot. She'd really been looking forward to spending Halloween with him, and hadn't even thought about the appearances of it.

Once she was in bed and ready to sleep, she finally succumbed to the urge to call him. She shared her whole evening, as best she could through the phone, taking Molly and Sheyna to the retirement home, how much Abby had enjoyed being there and how much more wonderful it would have been if he'd been there too. He said he'd gone to a Halloween party one of his subordinates had invited him to, and it had been fun, but that he'd missed her a lot. It was a nice conversation, and Olivia felt better when they'd hung up. She drifted to sleep to dream of happy old people, carved pumpkins, adorable kids and Josh.

~~~

Olivia spent the next few days between looking for estate sales, yard sale and auctions that sounded good and restoring an old antique oak press back rocking chair that had gorgeous carved spindles beneath the arm rests. It had been painted a very unattractive green color, so she had to carefully strip the paint off without damaging the beautiful wood underneath. The work on the carved spindles was slow and painstaking. She was practically holding her breath, hoping there wasn't something wrong with the piece that she couldn't fix. Sometimes, antiques had been painted for a reason, like covering up a bad repair. So far, what she saw was perfect.

She found a couple giant yard sales that sounded promising, and called Abby to see what she thought of them. Abby agreed that they ought to be worth checking out, so Olivia's Sunday suddenly became busy. She also arranged for Abby's mom to keep Molly and Sheyna when they went to the sales and for Abby to babysit them on Friday evening, spending the night at Olivia's, just in case her date was a long one, which she hoped it would be.

She was wearing rubber gloves that were covered in a nasty combination of old green paint and paint stripper when the phone rang around four o'clock. By the time she got her gloves off and made it to the phone, it had stopped ringing. The number in her caller ID didn't look familiar, though it did look fairly local, so she decided to wait until she was done with the stripper to call back, as it was getting a little chilly outside and she wanted to finish before it got any later, thus colder, forcing her to quit for the day and come inside.

It was almost dark when she finally finished with the paint stripper and got the chair washed down with mineral spirits. She brought it inside and stuck it in her storage room to dry. Molly sniffed it and sneezed loudly, startling Sheyna, who was exploring the underside of the rocker, into yowling in alarm. Olivia laughed and shooed them both out of the storage room and shut the door, leaving the ceiling fan on to help disperse the smell of mineral spirits that still lingered on the chair.

Once Olivia had gotten herself cleaned up, she fed the animals then dialed the number of the earlier call on her cell phone. She let it ring for a long time, but no one answered, and it finally went to an answering machine. The male voice on the machine sounded vaguely familiar, but she couldn't place it, so she left a message stating that she was returning the call and hung up.

She warmed up some leftovers for herself, ate quickly, then cleaned up the kitchen and headed to her living room. Once she'd settled in her comfy padded antique Victorian chair at her roll top desk with a cup of Green Chai Tea and some paper and pens, she tried to focus on the case, as Josh and his guys hadn't been able to make any headway recently.

She reviewed the notes she'd made before, then added a column and wrote 'Fingerprints – Whose?' Under that she wrote, 'Why search my car?; Why did Larsson kill himself?; What did Tiny hear?; What was Jamison doing on Mrs. Tanner's property?; WHY was Larsson or whoever it was after me?'

Since the fingerprints hadn't been in AFIS, Josh and the other cops had no way of knowing who they belonged to unless they had a suspect to match them to, so . . . no answer to the first question yet.

The fact that they had searched her car so thoroughly, must mean that they thought she had something they wanted. Probably they thought Jamison had given her something, or that something she'd bought from him was more valuable than it was. Or maybe they thought she was in cahoots with him. *Yikes,* Olivia thought, *that's all I need, to have the bad guys thinking I'm one of them. Evidently the cops still aren't sure I'm not a murderer. No wonder Josh is worried about leaving the department before this is settled. I could never marry him if we don't solve it because he would always be under suspicion too then. They would always wonder if he'd been in on it with me, and maybe we'd killed Jamison together.*

To save her life, she couldn't figure out why a hard-boiled criminal like Larsson would throw himself out of his fourth story apartment window. The way she'd worded it in her mind, suddenly told her the most likely answer. He wouldn't have; someone else threw him out the window. He didn't fall or jump, he was thrown, which is probably why he'd landed on a car way out in the street, rather than the sidewalk or one of the parked cars next to it. She'd have to call Josh and tell him what she'd figured out once she was done studying all her questions.

Tiny had most likely heard something that day that caused him to look up in time to see the bicyclist go by. Also, she hadn't thought to ask where the bicycle was when he saw it. Was it past the shop already or going past it? Could it have come from the shop? Maybe she could run out to Tiny's house on Sunday or Monday to see if he'd remembered anything else. She could also check in at Mrs. Tanner's to find out if Jimmy has seen anything that day, and try to tactfully ask his grandmother why he didn't have a cochlear implant. Some people just weren't good candidates for it she knew, but if it was because of the money, she had some very good news for Mrs. Tanner.

She had no idea whatsoever of what Jamison had been doing on the Tanner property, with a shovel at night, aside from the obvious. But why he'd been digging was beyond her. Was he burying some of the loot from the robberies in case Larsson came looking for it? Why on her property and not his own? Wouldn't it have been safer for him to find a good spot on his own land where he wouldn't have to sneak around at night and risk the neighbors seeing him or even calling the police on him for trespassing? Olivia sighed.

Her last question was possibly the same as her second one. If Larsson or the person who left their prints in the car thought she had some of the robbery loot or something else from Jamison, it would make sense that they were after her, and that they searched her car. But she didn't have anything. Why would they think she did? She was just a random customer who happened to be in the store when Jamison was killed. She hadn't seen anything. Again, she felt the tickling at the back of her memory. There had been something unusual, but she still couldn't quite get it.

She sat up and massaged her lower back. She'd call Josh to see if he'd gotten anywhere and to make sure they were still on for the mystery date tomorrow evening. *I'd better ask him what to wear,* she thought. *Knowing him, and how well he already knows me, it could be anything from another skydiving trip to a fancy dinner out.* She smiled at the thought of him.

He answered on the first ring. After they'd shared their days with each other, Olivia told Josh what she thought about Larsson's supposed suicide. He agreed with her that it was very likely that Larsson had been murdered, even though the Boston PD had ruled it a suicide. Since he hadn't been allowed to investigate it, he obviously didn't know for sure one way or the other, but she was probably right about that. Whether Larsson's murder had anything to do with Jamison's murder or was due to some other aspect of his criminal life, they had no way of knowing yet.

Josh said yes, they were still on for their date tomorrow, and he suggested she wear that sexy black number he'd seen her wear before, with shoes that were good for dancing, and bring a change of clothes and shoes that were comfortable for walking. He wouldn't give her a clue where they were going aside from the clothes suggestions and though he couldn't see it through the phone, she stuck her tongue out at him.

CHAPTER SEVENTEEN

Olivia was excited from the time she woke up on Friday morning. As much as she had teased and tried to wrangle the details of their date out of Josh on the phone last night, she found the anticipation from not knowing was even better.

She gave Molly a bath in the shower then took her own shower before letting Molly out of the tub. She spent the next few minutes drying Molly, herself and then the bathroom. Luckily Sheyna didn't need a bath very often, as she was an impeccable self-groomer.

It was a nice day, chilly, but not really cold. Olivia went through her clothes, pulling out the dress and under garments she wanted to wear for the date, then finding a pair of beige wool slacks, an off-white sweater and a nice scarf. She'd wear her brown leather bomber jacket with it for whatever walking activity Josh had planned. Her brown leather mid calf boots with the lower heels would go perfectly too. She packed the change of clothes in a small overnight case so it would be ready.

Josh called at noon and asked if she could possibly be ready to leave by five instead of six. She called Abby, who said she could be there earlier, so Olivia agreed.

Even though Larsson was dead and there hadn't been any further incidents, Olivia still felt uncomfortable leaving Molly and Sheyna alone. She wasn't sure she could do that until the case was solved.

Abby got there at four-thirty and Olivia showed her where Molly's and Sheyna's dishes were, mixed their food so it was all ready to give them and added their vitamin supplements.

"Thanks so much for doing this, Abby. I didn't want to ask your mom, because it may be really late when I get back. You're spending the night in the guestroom, so hopefully I won't bother you coming in, but I would have had to awaken your mom if I'd left them with her."

"No problem Liv. Go and have a great time. I'm going to watch a couple of those movies you're got in your cabinet, then go to bed, so you won't bother me, no matter what time you stagger in," she grinned.

When she heard a car drive up, Olivia peeked out and saw Josh pull into the driveway. She picked up her overnight bag and her little clutch purse, hugged Molly, Sheyna and Abby, and walked out to meet Josh.

He was dressed in a dark suit with a white shirt, opened at the neck and no tie. Wow, did he ever dress up nice, Olivia thought, wanting to throw her arms around him, but acting casual in case anyone was watching.

"Hi Josh, you look awesome."

He helped her into his police car, took her overnight bag and put it in the back seat and closed the doors.

"You look pretty amazing yourself Liv," he got in and gave her a quick kiss, then started the car and backed into the road. He held her hand as he drove, heading toward the airfield where they had done the skydiving on their only other date.

ANTIQUES & AVARICE

"Josh, we're not going skydiving at night, are we? Oh, I guess we wouldn't be dressed like this for skydiving." Olivia laughed at herself.

"No love, we're definitely not going skydiving," Josh grinned, raising her hand to his lips and kissing her palm. "You're just going to have to wait and see. Patience is a virtue, remember what your mom taught you? I'm sure she said that, I think all moms said that back when we were kids."

Olivia chuckled, "Yes she did, and I hated it then too. Okay, I will be patient . . . for now."

Josh pulled into the parking lot of the little airfield where they'd skydived and opened Olivia's door for her, grabbing her overnight case and taking her arm to lead her into the building.

"Hi Mr. Abrams, ma'am, your ride is all ready for you," the man behind the counter greeted Josh and Olivia, gesturing out into the field.

"Thank you Sam," Josh slipped a bill into the man's hand and led Olivia out to the waiting Cessna. He helped her into one of the rear seats, then sat beside her in the other. The pilot taxied down the runway, talking on the radio.

Once they were airborne, Olivia looked out the window at the twinkling lights below and sighed happily, leaning against Josh and taking his hand.

"It's so beautiful up here at night. I've flown at night in commercial planes, but this is different. It's like we're all alone in the universe. Wow!"

Josh held her and they looked out the window in reverent silence. Olivia thought it was one of the most romantic places he could have possibly brought her. He

197

poured them some wine, and they sat back with Olivia in Josh's arms to enjoy the view.

Outside the window was mostly darkness, interspersed with tiny lights here and there, then more darkness. After an hour or so they had a lovely light show as they flew a little lower over Boston, then more darkness for a while. A couple hours later, the lights started becoming more frequent and suddenly, there were brilliant patches of light in all directions as they arrived over New York City. Olivia was awed at how much more beautiful it was from the small plane.

"So, are you going to tell me where we are yet?" Olivia smiled.

Josh laughed, "You can't tell?"

"Boston?"

"New York," Josh grinned. "We're going to have a wonderfully delicious dinner at Candle 79. For later there is a wonderful little piano bar called Brandy's I'd like to take you to, where the wait-staff sing for you, and they are pretty amazing. After all that, if we can still walk, we can take a stroll, that's why the extra clothes, just in case."

"Wow! Just like that, we're in New York?" Olivia laughed, "Yup, I think I could get used to having money. This is pretty awesome."

Once they'd landed and disembarked, there was a cab waiting for them and Josh seated Olivia and got in beside her. There was quite a bit of traffic getting out of the airport, but the cabby was a good driver and before long, they were on their way to the Upper East Side. The cab dropped them at the door of the posh little vegetarian restaurant, Candle 79.

The restaurant was not quite as romantic as Josh had

wanted, he explained to her, but just wait until she tasted the food. The waiter seated them at an upstairs table by the window. They were the only customers upstairs, though there were quite a lot of diners downstairs.

Olivia studied the menu, amazed at all the delectable sounding choices.

"I've never seen so many wonderful sounding dishes in a Vegan place before. This is so cool!"

"I was hoping you'd be surprised," Josh smiled. "I've eaten here before a few times, even though I'm not totally a vegetarian yet, because the food is so good."

"Yet? Are you planning to go vegetarian Josh?" Olivia was surprised. "I know I've been cooking all vegetarian for you, but I assumed you were eating meat elsewhere and would probably continue to after we were married."

Josh smiled, "No, I really am not that fond of meat, and have often thought of quitting it, so it seemed like a good time to take the plunge. It's been a couple weeks since I ate meat and if anything, I feel better, so that's a good sign," he grinned.

Olivia smiled happily at him, "As long as you're doing it for you and not me, I am thrilled with your choice."

"I am," he leaned over and squeezed her hands, then sat back to look at his menu. "So, what looks good to you? I think I may have the Portobello Steak, and if it sounds good to you, maybe we can share the Pomegranate BBQ Seitan Skewers for an appetizer."

"Oh yum! I haven't had BBQ Seitan in so long. It's one of my favorites ever." She said. "That sounds heavenly, and I think I will go for the Seitan Piccata for my main course. I used to adore Chicken Piccata when I still ate meat."

"Their Seitan is really good, and they do a decent job with most of the food here."

The waiter took their orders, filled their water glasses and glided away silently. There was soft music coming from hidden speakers, and despite how unromantic the restaurant had seemed when they walked in on the first floor, in the dimly lit upstairs, with a candle glowing on the table, away from everyone, looking out onto the people walking by in the street below, it was incredibly romantic.

The food, when it arrived was even better than Josh had made it sound. The appetizer was delicious, and the entrées even better. They sampled each other's food feeding each other choice little bites.

"Josh this food is so good; angels are dancing on my tongue!" Olivia sighed happily. "This has to be the best date anyone ever had! Have I told you lately how wonderful you are?"

Josh grinned, "You have, but you can tell me that anytime you want. You're some kind of wonderful yourself Miss McKenna."

When they exited the restaurant, Olivia noticed that there were people waiting outside to be seated, yet the whole upstairs had been empty except for them.

"Josh, how did we end up being the only people upstairs with all these people waiting? Did you pay them loads of money so we could be alone?" Olivia's eyes were huge.

"What's the use of being rich if you can't enjoy it once in a while?" he smiled. "I wanted tonight to be as special as I could possibly make it, and that meant making an unromantic restaurant into at least a semi romantic one."

Olivia kissed the dimple in his chin, "Being anywhere with you is romantic." They stopped and kissed on the sidewalk.

Josh hailed a cab and they were soon dropped off at Brandy's Piano Bar. They could hear lively singing as soon as they reached the door.

Olivia loved the atmosphere immediately. The waiters and waitresses, bartenders and half the guest were singing along to the piano player, and they all looked like they were having a great time. Once they were seated, she ordered a Bushmills Irish whiskey on the rocks and Josh ordered his Ardbeg Uigeadail Scotch neat. They traded sips, ordered another round, and after a while were happily singing along with everyone else.

It was getting late and it was a good thing neither of them was driving by the time they left the bar. Josh hailed a cab and they headed back to the airport, not drunk exactly, but not feeling any pain either. The pilot helped them onboard and made sure they had everything they needed before he taxied down the runway to await takeoff clearance.

The flight home was just as beautiful as the first flight and just as romantic. There was a lot of time spent kissing and simply holding each other while gazing at the lights below. It had been a magical night and Olivia knew she'd remember it for the rest of her life.

When they arrived back at the little airfield, Josh called a cab to come and get them, as he knew it was very unwise to drive after drinking. He'd have to deal with getting his car tomorrow.

"Josh, I can come and get you in the morning and we'll pick up your car." Olivia picked up on his thoughts. "I think I want to go and look for a new car tomorrow too if you would like to come with me."

"That's a great idea sweetie," Josh said as they got into the cab. "I think we'd better make it late morning though, as we may not be feeling quite up to par first thing."

Olivia grinned, "I think you might be right. I'll call you before I come, but probably around eleven." She leaned her head on his shoulder and he kissed her hair.

"Here we are folks, first stop, are you paying individually or at the end?" the cabby asked pulling into Olivia's driveway with a flourish.

"I'll pay at the end," Josh said. "I'll be right back."

He got out and held his hand to help Olivia out, then walked her to the door, handing her her overnight bag and waited until she had unlocked and opened her door. Molly came to greet them and Josh patted her for a moment, then kissed Olivia goodnight and went back to the cab before the driver got nervous.

Olivia closed the door and dropped her stuff on the bench in the foyer. She'd just had one of the most fabulous nights of her life. She was tired, tipsy and absolutely wound up. She couldn't stop smiling—how would she ever sleep?

~~~

Olivia awoke the next morning to Molly's tail thumping the bed and Abby's way too cheerful sounding voice saying good morning. Her head felt decidedly unhappy with her for last night's drinking escapade. She propped her eyes open to peer blearily at Abby.

"Good morning Sunshine!" Abby said grinning. "Did

we have a bit too much to drink last night? I could hear you singing after you went to bed, but I couldn't quite figure out which song it was."

"Oh Man!" Olivia groaned, sitting up and trying to clear her head. "I was singing in bed? I'll never live this down will I?"

"Not likely," Abby agreed impishly. "It's about time I had something juicy to hold over your head, after that thing with the mechanical bull."

"Hey Abs, thanks for watching the girls for me. I owe you big time!"

"That you do dearie!" Abby laughed. "I'm off to a yard sale or two. See you tomorrow for the sales."

"See you tomorrow and thanks again!" Olivia yelled after her friend who it seemed was galloping down the stairs like a herd of noisy elephants. Sheyna hopped onto the bed and flicked her tail in annoyance that Olivia was still in the bed instead of up and feeding her. Olivia rolled out of the bed and stumbled into the shower still half asleep. The hot water helped a lot, and after a couple aspirins and a cup of coffee, she was almost feeling back to her normal self.

She checked her email, poured herself a second cup of coffee, and fixed an egg on a bagel, then called Josh to see how he was feeling. He sounded like he was on the mend as well, so she arranged to pick him up in an hour.

She loaded Molly and Sheyna into the car and stopped at the park for a quick romp, then headed to Josh's apartment. He was just coming outside when she pulled up.

"Hi Handsome, how can you look so perfect after all that Scotch you drank last night?"

"The same way you managed to look stunningly delicious this morning after consuming so much Irish whiskey, they almost had to order more from down the street," Josh teased with a grin, kissing her, and getting swatted playfully on the head. "I did remember this morning why I so seldom drink. So, does it make sense to pick up my car and drop it back here first, in case you find the perfect car and want to actually drive it home?"

"Oh, that is a great idea! I've been thinking about the Ford Expedition EL, since it is really similar to the Suburban. For a while I thought maybe I'd rather get a smaller one, but I really need the extra cargo space for carrying my stuff from the sales and for delivering it too sometimes."

"You can always use my car to just tool around town in too, as I have the State car," Josh said. "It will be really easy once we're married and living together."

"I love the sound of that," Olivia smiled.

It didn't take long to reach the airstrip and for Josh to get his police car. Olivia followed him back to his apartment and waited while he parked and ran inside to get a jacket, as he'd forgotten to bring one and the day was on the chilly side. They were soon headed toward Concord, as there were a lot more dealerships there than in their smaller town or any others close by.

They stopped briefly in the Lakes region to walk along beside Lake Winnipesauke for a few minutes, and enjoy the view while letting Molly and Sheyna do their business and enjoy all the new smells to be found there. It was one-fifteen when they arrived at the first dealership. Olivia wanted to look at a couple other manufacturers before deciding, but was fairly sure she would be getting the Ford.

She took a tape measure and checked out all the SUVs she was interested in at each of the three dealerships, and the Ford was the best for her needs. They had one on the lot that had just been delivered the day before that had everything she wanted and more, and was in the color she wanted, blue, with brown leather seats. It cost a little more than her insurance would cover, but Josh persuaded her to buy it and insisted on paying for the difference.

"Yes, you could wait and order one and have it in six to eight weeks for less money, and smaller wheels, cheaper leather and all that. I know you don't need the DVD player in the back, but it will make the resale value higher, and maybe I'll ride in the back with Molly and Sheyna once in a while and we'll watch a movie while you drive," Josh laughed, pulling out his checkbook.

Olivia laughingly gave in and agreed to buy the gorgeous SUV. She loved it but she would have ordered the slightly less expensive one with a few less bells and whistles if Josh hadn't been so insistent on her having the nicest one and not having to wait. It was a stunning vehicle and it smelled so good inside. She loved that new car smell. Molly and Sheyna seemed to like the new car too and wanted to climb in, but Olivia wouldn't let them until she had new crates for them. She and Josh wanted to leave the old ones in his car, so it would be easy for them if they wanted to go somewhere in it, and buy new ones to leave in her new car. She would only have to remove them if she was going to a sale and wanted the space open.

Finally all the paperwork was done and she and Josh had both written checks, and she had the temporary title and tags.

"Let's run to the pet superstore and get the new crates so we can get you all set up to carry the girls in your new car."

"That sounds like a plan. Thanks so much Josh! I absolutely love it!" she hugged him tightly.

"You're welcome sweetie, I'm really glad you do."

Olivia drove in front and Josh followed with Molly and Sheyna in his car to make sure everything was okay with the car and no problems occurred. They found parking easily side by side. Josh took Molly, and Olivia took Sheyna on lead and they walked them carefully past a dog that was sitting in a nearby car sticking his head out the window to bark and growl loudly at them.

Molly started to bark back, but a soft command from Josh stopped her and she ignored the other dog. Sheyna ignored both dogs, her bristled tail held high in the air. The humans laughed.

It didn't take too long for Olivia to pick out the crates she wanted and to grab some dog and cat food bags as well.

Sheyna acted more like a dog than a cat frequently, Olivia thought. She had her definite cat moments, but she always loved to cuddle, she loved to chase toys, and actually bring them back for you to throw again, she loved meeting new people, she loved riding in the car, and aside from having her aloof moments and her occasional airs of superiority, she really did act like a cat shaped dog.

Once Olivia had paid for everything, Josh followed Olivia back to her place with the girls still in their old crates in his car and helped her carry the stuff in the house. She didn't plan to set them up in the SUV yet because she was going to yard sales tomorrow and might need the room available.

"If you'd like I can come in the morning and stay with Molly and Sheyna while you do the sales," Josh volunteered.

"Oh Josh, it's so sweet of you to ask, but I think it would be better to leave them with Abby's mom. She loves to see them and that leaves you free to do whatever you want for the day. I mean, if you really have a strong desire to spend tomorrow with them, that's one thing, but otherwise, enjoy your day and Annie will be thrilled to have them," Olivia smiled, hugging him.

"Okay," Josh agreed affably. "I'm fine with it either way, but I wanted to make sure you had everything set up so you were comfortable. I've noticed that you don't like to leave them alone anymore, and I can definitely understand it."

"Thanks Josh. I know it may not be completely rational, but I just don't feel safe having them be by themselves until this whole thing with the murder is over with."

"I know Babes, I don't want them alone either. It may be fine and nothing will happen, but why take a chance?"

"How about if you come to my apartment for dinner on Monday night, and I'll cook. You can bring Molly and Sheyna too, as long as we are careful not to let anyone see them," he grinned. "It's nice to live dangerously sometimes."

"Great! That will be fun Josh," Olivia hugged him.

Josh put his arms around Olivia and lifted her up to kiss her, then twirled her around and set her down. "I'm gonna run now, so I can look at some case notes I brought home from work. Have a fun day tomorrow and get lots of good stuff. I'll miss you."

"Thanks sweetheart; I'll miss you too. Don't work too hard tonight."

They kissed, and Josh gave Molly and Sheyna a kiss too then headed out to his car.

Olivia shut the door behind him after waving goodbye and went to feed the girls. The house phone rang as she set their bowls on the floor. She answered it, but there was no one there. That reminded her of the call on her cell the day before, and she decided to try calling the number again . . . still no answer except the machine. Again, the guy's voice sounded so familiar; she tried to remember where she'd heard it. Why didn't people say their names on those silly out-going messages? She hung up in frustration. Oh well, she consoled herself, it may just be a telemarketer or something, otherwise he would have called back after she left the message yesterday, right?

She made herself an enormous salad and sat down to watch TV while she ate. Molly bummed a few bites of lettuce, which she loved and Sheyna bummed one bite which she spat.

Just before she went to bed, Olivia prepared a light lunch for herself and Abby, got her clients' list together, and made sure she had enough cash as well as her credit cards and checkbook all ready to go, as it would be a fairly early morning. These sales were not starting as early as the estate sale she and Abby had last gone to, but even with yard sales, it was never good to get there late. She was thankful the weather was supposed to be warmer tonight.

As she lay down the phone rang again. Again, there was no one on the line. Olivia got up, and donning a headlamp she kept handy for power outages, she headed down to double check all the doors and windows. Everything was locked up tight. One call like that hadn't bothered her. It was the second one that set her nerves on edge. She went back to bed, with the girls locked in her room with her, and with the headlamp, her cell phone and a baseball bat all close beside her she finally fell asleep.

CHAPTER EIGHTEEN

Sunday was a very warm day for November, and Olivia happily put on a light beige and teal long sleeved blouse and pale blue jeans for the sales. After feeding Molly and Sheyna, making coffee and making a smoothie for the road, she loaded the girls into the back . . . crateless, hopped in her new car and drove super carefully to Annie's house to drop off the girls. Annie was delighted to keep them, and they were happy to see her too.

It was seven-thirty when she picked up Abby. One of the sales they were going to opened at eight and the other at nine. They were the first customers at the eight o'clock one and waited politely in their car until the homeowner in charge waved at them to come on over. It was a pretty big sale, with several people in the neighborhood pitching in to have it together. There was a lot of stuff. Olivia felt like she was at a flea market.

They had it set up all across the driveway and lawn in rows. She and Abby split up to better find things of interest quickly, so they could get to the next sale as soon as it opened. Olivia found several nice items for herself, among them a gorgeous little handmade basket, and an old cobalt blue bottle, and she also found a couple of things for her clients. She headed back to the driveway and saw a really old wooden toolbox full of rusty, but decent antique tools. One of her clients would be very happy. She paid for her finds and loaded them into her car, then headed back to see how Abby was doing.

As she walked through the grass swale toward the gate into the large driveway, she felt someone grab her purse from behind her, almost ripping it from her body. She screamed and hung onto it, and the large blonde man shoved her hard, ran down the street and jumped into the passenger side of a waiting grey van which immediately roared away.

Abby and the yard sale people came running to help her. Olivia had fallen when he pushed her, but she was standing up now, covered in grass stains and spitting mad. Abby saw her expression and headed her off before she could jump into her brand new car and chase after the guy.

"Whoa Rambo! Settle down, he may have a gun, besides, there are obviously two of them, since he wasn't driving. What happened? We heard you scream, saw someone run past, and a blonde guy jumping into a van, then heard the squeal of his tires peeling out. Did he attack you?"

"He tried to grab my purse, but it was strapped across my body, not just hanging on my shoulder, otherwise he'd have gotten it." Olivia was trying to calm down, since everyone was crowding around to find out what happened. She really just wanted to yell and throw things. She wanted to shove that guy down and hit him with her purse, preferably with something heavy in it.

"Let me call Josh and tell him what happened. Maybe he can put out an APB on the van, not that I got enough information on it," she said sadly. "It's okay everyone, just a purse snatcher, or actually a wannabe purse snatcher. My fiancé is a cop, so I'm calling him now."

The garage sale owners headed back to the sale and left her and Abby alone.

"Go ahead and look for stuff Abs, I'm fine now, I'm going to be here inside the gate with everyone else while I call him, so you don't have to worry," she smiled wryly. "Go!" she laughed, pushing her friend who looked reluctant to leave her alone. She dialed Josh on speed dial.

"Josh, someone just tried to steal my purse, and I don't think it was a random thing."

She held the phone away from her ear as Josh yelled *"What?"*

She explained what happened and told him what little she had seen of the man and the van, "It was an older model grey van, like a typical old Chevy or Ford or something like that. It was too far away for me to see the name on it. I think it had a Massachusetts license plate, but I am not sure and I couldn't see the numbers." She listened for a moment.

"I'm not sure if it was the same guy that tried to grab me last time. I don't think so. I think this guy was shorter and heavier. The other guy was leaner and more fit; this one had muscle, but was on the heavy side. They looked a lot alike though I think, both blond. Why does it always happen too fast for me to get a good look?"

She turned her back toward the people around her and listened, then said "I promise I will be careful and stay close to people. I love you too sweetheart. See you later." She hung up and looked around for Abby. She was still collecting things to purchase, so Olivia asked the people who'd been there if they'd seen the license number of the car or the model. Unfortunately no one had. By the time she'd finished talking to people, Abby was paying for the items she gotten, so they left when she was done.

"Are you sure you still want to go to the other sale?" Abby asked as Olivia started the engine. "You're sure you're not hurt, right?"

"No, I'm fine, a little bruise on my shoulder where he pushed me I think; mostly I'm just mad that it seems to be starting again. Yes, I'm ready for the other sale," she paused. "Wait, call your mom for me and ask her to be careful not to let anyone in. We're going to pick up the girls and your mom too and we're all going to the next sale. I'm not taking any chances." Olivia made a U-turn and headed back toward Annie's house.

Meanwhile Abby called her mom to let her know.

"This creep is not scaring me away from my business, but I'm not going to endanger your mom, Molly or Sheyna either." Olivia dialed Josh again and asked if he wanted to go with them just in case. He said he was happy to, as the whole situation was making him very nervous about her being out there without him.

Olivia picked up Annie, Molly and Sheyna and met Josh at her house. He'd decided it would be best if he followed in his personal car, so there was enough room for everyone and the car wouldn't draw attention like his police car would have. He wanted to meet at Olivia's just to make sure her house was okay. She went inside and checked and all was in order, so she locked up carefully and they left again.

Annie was happy to be going to the yard sale with them and insisted on walking Molly around the sale. Josh carried Sheyna in one arm and he and Olivia held hands. Olivia spotted a beautiful pair of antique snowshoes and hurried Josh over to them so he could snag them before someone else did. He was grinning from ear to ear carrying them. Sheyna liked them too, as they had cool leather dangly things she could play with.

"These are from around 1890 or so, definitely Native American or First Nation, possibly Cree. I can't believe I found these at a yard sale!"

Olivia beamed, "Stick with me kid and you'll go places."

Josh laughed, "I'd hug you for that, but my arms are too full. No, Sheyna, don't eat the leather. It's okay to play with it, but no chewing." He pulled the string out of her mouth, and let it dangle so she could smack it.

"Do you want me to carry her for a while?"

"Nah, we're good," he grinned watching Sheyna bat the strings with her paw. "I'm keeping my eye on her. She isn't going to hurt it unless she chews it, so as long as I watch, it's cool."

Annie and Abby were ahead of them and Abby was already laden with a nice old carved wooden chair and her mom was carrying a quilt in one hand and Molly's lead in the other. Olivia let go of Josh's hand and darted off to a nearby table to grab a box filled with antique chandelier crystals. Beside it was a gorgeous old dusty and rather spooky looking chandelier. Olivia picked it up with one hand, juggling the box of crystals onto her other arm and turned to find Josh frowning at her.

"Liv, did you forget that someone attacked you earlier today?" his tone was frustrated. "Why would you go running off like that and scare me half to death thinking someone was chasing you or something?"

Olivia was immediately contrite, "Josh, I'm so sorry! I didn't even think. I saw that chandelier and the box of crystals glittering and just had to grab it before someone else got there." She hugged him. "I didn't mean to scare you."

He bent and kissed her since he couldn't hug her with Sheyna and the snowshoes in his arms. "It's okay, I didn't mean to be a jerk about it, I just freaked out for a minute thinking something bad had happened to you."

She kissed him back. "I'll think before I run from now on," she grinned sheepishly. "Let's catch up with the McElhattans and see what other rare and wondrous things we can find to drag home."

"You stay with Abby and Annie and hold Sheyna for a minute and I'll go pay for all this stuff and put it in the car so we don't have to carry it around," Josh was making up for being upset with her. He disappeared quickly in the crowd.

"This is a huge sale," Abby said happily. "It's much better than the last one."

Olivia smiled, "Yeah, it's got a lot of good stuff. Oh my! Look at that gorgeous green and gold upholstered Victorian chair!" she knelt and looked it over thoroughly, sat in it, looked at the price tag and picked it up. "Sold!" she chortled happily. "Even the wooden wheels are in good condition."

Josh caught up with them and laughed at Olivia holding Sheyna in one hand and the fairly heavy chair in the other. He took the chair from her. "Should I go pay for this now or wait five minutes for you to find another heavy thing you'll have to carry?" he laughed.

She giggled, "It's just too hard to predict what's around the corner. Oops," she stooped to pick up a pretty little wooden bread box. "Like I said, it's hard to predict."

Josh grinned and took the bread box and went to pay for the two new items and put them in the car. The women and the animals kept looking around. Just as Josh came back to them, Abby found a very old typewriter that was in beautiful condition and was on one of her clients' lists. Right next to it was an old sewing machine that was on Olivia's list. Josh laughed and shaking his head, he took both items, Abby's chair and Annie's quilt and went to pay and stow them in the car.

They waited for him to come back and Olivia put her free arm around his waist, hugging him as they walked. Abby and Annie both thanked him and tried to pay him for their stuff but he wouldn't let them.

Finally they'd seen everything and bought quite a lot and were ready to leave. Both cars were a bit full between people, animals and antiques. Despite the trouble at the first sale, it had been a really fun day.

They drove first to Abby's house and dropped off her and all her finds. Josh helped carry the things inside. Then they stopped at Annie's house to let her off.

"Annie, thanks so much for watching the girls earlier. I want you and Abby to come for Thanksgiving dinner at my house. Josh, of course, you too." Olivia touched his cheek with her hand.

"I'd love that Livvie!" Annie said happily, giving her a hug. "You be careful now and you too Josh." She gave him a little hug too. "She's like my second daughter, so be good to her."

"I definitely will Annie," he promised, kissing her cheek. "Have a great night and I'll see you on Thanksgiving if not before."

They waited until Annie was inside with her lights on and waving to them, before Josh followed Olivia back to her house. They got the girls in the house, then unloaded all the antiques and carried them in.

Once everything was put away in the storage room to be dealt with later, Olivia made them some tea, Josh started the fire and they sat down on the sofa to relax and unwind for a few minutes. Olivia leaned back against Josh's shoulder and he put his arm around her. Molly and Sheyna joined them, taking up the other end of the couch.

They sat in companionable silence for a little while, then Josh sighed. "I guess I'd better get going. I have to be at work at seven."

"Are you too tired to drive? Do you want to stay in the guestroom?"

"No, it's not a problem to go home," he smiled. "Just wishing we could solve this crazy case. I'm tired of having you be afraid all the time."

"I'm not really afraid most of the time now. I think today may have just been a fluke after all."

"I hope so," Josh said. "I really don't want to think that it is happening again." He got up and lifted her to her feet and into his arms. She melted against him and they kissed. The electricity was fierce. They stepped back from each other breathlessly and Josh blew out a quick breath. "That burned all the way through." He grinned crookedly.

Olivia bit her lip, "Me too. Who knew cops were so hot? I thought that was supposed to be firemen."

Josh laughed, "Firemen are for putting out fire. You want hot, call a cop. They don't call us 'The Heat' for nothing."

Olivia howled with laughter, "Joshua Abrams, you are too much!"

"No Babes, I am just right," he joked, hugging her and laughing. "I wish I could stay for a while, but I have some files I absolutely have to go over tonight and I'll be a zombie at work tomorrow if I don't get any sleep." He took his car keys from his pocket.

"I'm going to go out and talk to Tiny Dawson and Mrs. Tanner tomorrow to see if they've remembered anything, and also to ask her about Jimmy and insurance."

"Just be careful and keep your phone with you at all times. Are you taking Molly and Sheyna?"

"Yes, and I'm going to ask if they can come inside with me too. If not, I will talk to the people on the porch so I can watch the car."

"Good idea," Josh smiled. "Call me if you have any trouble at all."

"I will sweetie," Olivia stood on tiptoe to kiss him goodnight. "Drive safe home."

She watched as he backed out and drove away, then she fed the girls and made herself some quinoa with veggies in it and sat at her computer to eat a quick dinner. There was nothing exciting in her email, so she dutifully entered all her purchases, listing which ones were for herself and which for clients, then listing the client purchases again, in each of their respective files. She went into the storage room and took the box with the crystals and brought them into the kitchen to go through. They needed a little cleaning up, but they almost all seemed to be in great shape. What a cool find. She planned to make a crystal curtain for her high windows in the living room that faced west. When the afternoon sun came in, it would turn the room into a glittering paradise, casting flickering rainbows across the whole room.

Before bed, she made herself a cup of decaf tea, let Molly go out, let her back in and re-checked all the doors and windows to make sure they were locked. Josh had installed new deadbolts on both downstairs doors and put safety bars at the bottom of her upstairs sliders, so she could secure them easily. She drew the drapes over the sliders in her bedroom after making sure the bar was in place and lay down to read with her tea. After a few minutes, Molly and Sheyna curled up on her bed for a snuggle, so she put the book down and turned out the light, cuddling them until they all fell asleep.

CHAPTER NINETEEN

Monday morning Olivia fed the girls and ate some oatmeal, then made herself a sandwich to take with her for lunch later. It was almost ten o'clock when she'd gotten the new crates set up in her SUV and loaded the girls in for the drive to Eastman's Grant.

She arrived at Mrs. Tanner's house to find Jimmy playing on a tire swing in the front yard. She waved and smiled at him and he waved back. Mrs. Tanner was on the porch watering her mums, which were showing signs that they hadn't enjoy the cold nights of last week.

"Hi Olivia, These poor mums have just about had it, I'm afraid. We had that one really cold spell and I forgot to bring them in, so I'm just gonna keep watering them until they're gone. No use in bringing them in now, they're already past saving," Mrs. Tanner was off to her usual garrulous start. "How've you been doing? Have you figured out who killed Mr. Ketterer yet?"

"Hi Mrs. Tanner. No, I wish we had it figured out, but so far, we're still not sure." Olivia managed to a sentence get in, so she tried a second, "Is it possible that Jimmy saw something out the window that day while he was playing by himself?"

"I doubt it dear, and there's not really any easy way to ask him. We can try. It's possible I guess. It's hard for me to ask about time, because I haven't figured out how to do it so he understands exactly when I mean unless it's bedtime or dinner time or something easy like that. "

"Mrs. Tanner, I wanted to ask you, was Jimmy ever evaluated to see if he'd be a good candidate for a cochlear implant?"

"When he was first diagnosed, the doctor sent him to a specialist, who suggested that for him, but our insurance doesn't cover it. Says it's excluded. We've just been making do without it, using our own type of sign language, but I really don't know what we're going to do when he's supposed to start school," Mrs. Tanner replied sadly. "He's a bright boy, but the odds are stacked against him, being deaf."

Olivia decided to try to find out if Jimmy had seen anything first if possible, before sharing her news about the Hearing For All Foundation, because she had a feeling Mrs. Tanner was going to be too excited to effectively communicate once she knew Jimmy would probably get his implant after all.

They walked over to the tire swing and Mrs. Tanner knelt in front of Jimmy, stopping the swing so he was facing her. She pointed toward the antique shop, then pointed to him and to her eyes, then motioned at her wrist watch, waving her hand to convey past, then made a questioning face and put her hands out in a questioning pose.

Jimmy glanced nervously at Olivia, then back to his Grandmother, then nodded. He pointed to himself, then the living room window, then his eyes and then over to the antique shop. He raised his hand high over his head, and made himself look like a tall man with his arms out like he had big muscles. His Grandma nodded, smiling encouragement and he continued. Jimmy pointed to Olivia's truck, then got up and ran over, pointing to the back window. He climbed up on the back bumper to point to Sheyna in her crate, then to the antique shop, then he jumped down and mimicked the muscular man again and making a mean face, he threw his hands out like he was going to grab Sheyna.

Olivia was astounded at how well Jimmy and his Grandmother communicated with each other. This kid was wicked smart. She smiled broadly and hugged Jimmy. He blushed and hugged her back smiling, then raced back to his swing.

"So, he saw a big guy trying to catch a cat, probably Sheyna?" Olivia asked, making sure she'd interpreted the charade the same way Mrs. Tanner did.

"That's what I think," Mrs. Tanner said. She crinkled her brow, "So that's what I heard that day. It was a cat yowling. I'd forgotten about that," she looked troubled. "I wish I had known he'd seen something. I wonder if he was scared all this time and didn't know how to tell me."

"Oh, I don't think so, he didn't know about the murder did he?"

Mrs. Tanner looked relieved, "You're right, I never told him about it so he only knew about someone chasing a cat, and that's not something that would scare him, since the cat got away safely."

They went up on the porch and sat in the rockers to chat and Olivia told her about her research into Jimmy's situation and that The Hearing For All Foundation would likely be able to help him get his cochlear implant. As she'd anticipated, Mrs. Tanner was ecstatic and cried with joy.

She offered Olivia something to drink and cookies, but Olivia declined politely, saying she wanted to go and visit Tiny and get back home before it got too late.

"Please say hello to him for me," Mrs. Tanner said, sobering. "I've been a little worried about him the last few days. I usually see him every day like clockwork, going to work on his motorcycle. He always waves at us when he rides past. I haven't seen a sign of him since Thursday afternoon when I saw him coming home around three PM."

Olivia was startled and suddenly knew why the voice on the answering machine she'd gotten when trying to return the missed call on her cell sounded so familiar. It had been Tiny's voice.

"Did you see or hear anything over there since you saw him?" she asked quickly. "Were there any cars or bicycles you didn't recognize, or anything unusual going on in the neighborhood?"

"I saw an old grey van at Tiny's place Thursday evening, just around dark. I don't know how long it was there or anything I just assumed it was a friend of his and I never looked out again, since it went dark pretty quickly after that," Mrs. Tanner looked even more worried now. "Do you think something has happened to him?"

"I don't know, Mrs. Tanner, but I'm going to call a State Police Detective I know and ask if he can meet me there." Olivia said worriedly, taking her cell phone from her pocket and speed dialing Josh's number.

"I hope he's okay," Mrs. Tanner said. "He's a really nice boy, for all that he looks like a hoodlum, with all those tattoos. He was so sweet to his mama and has kept the place up nice since she passed. He comes over once a month to make sure everything is alright with us and we don't need any help."

Olivia spoke quickly to Josh over the phone and hung up, putting the phone back in her pocket.

"Mrs. Tanner, I think it would be a good idea for you take Jimmy and stay inside until Josh gets here just in case anything has happened," she saw Mrs. Tanner's face pale. "Not that I think it has, but just in case. Hopefully Tiny is fine. I like him too," she added. "He is a really nice guy."

Mrs. Tanner motioned to Jimmy to come inside and he ran over to them.

Olivia thought for a moment, "Would it be okay for me to leave Molly and Sheyna in your house with you while Josh and I go over there? I don't want to leave them in the car alone. My old car was stolen recently and if they'd been in it..." her voice trailed off. "Well, thankfully they weren't."

"Of course dear, they are welcome to come in and stay with us for a while! Jimmy will be thrilled to have furry company."

"Thanks so much!" Olivia went to bring the girls into the house and locked her SUV carefully. She waited on the porch for Josh to pick her up. She'd insisted on going with him to check on Tiny, and he'd reluctantly agreed, provided she stayed in the car until he checked the place out.

It was about fifteen minutes before he arrived in his police car. She climbed in and he pulled out toward Tiny's place.

"When was the last time someone spoke to him? Tell me again about the call you received and tried to return."

"Mrs. Tanner saw him come home around three

o'clock on Thursday afternoon, then she saw the van around dark," Olivia paused. "My cell phone rang at about four o'clock, but I had my hands full and didn't get there in time to answer. Unfortunately, I was busy and didn't try to call back until I finished my project around dark, and it just went to the answering machine," Olivia's voice was strained. "I wish I'd known it was Tiny. If I'd answered, maybe he'd be okay now."

"Hey, stop beating yourself up," Josh admonished. "We don't even know for sure that he isn't okay. Just because Mrs. Tanner hasn't seen him and he doesn't answer the phone doesn't mean something bad has happened. He might be away visiting someone or on a drunken binge or have a lousy case of the flu and not feel like talking to people. Let's see what we find before you freak out, okay?" he squeezed her hand comfortingly, as he pulled into Tiny's driveway.

The first thing they noticed was that the front door was ajar. He quickly and quietly backed the car up away from the house and parked so they could still easily see the house but it would be easy to pull out fast if necessary.

"Stay here," Josh ordered tersely, instantly becoming all policeman. "Keep the doors locked and slide over behind the wheel as soon as I get out so you can drive out of here fast if you need to," he looked at her fiercely. "If I don't come out in five minutes and let you know it's safe, or if you see anything scary at all, you get out of here and call in for backup on the radio immediately, okay?" he waited until she nodded then got out of the car, drawing his gun and locking the door behind him.

Josh walked up to the house carefully and onto the

porch. Standing with his back to the house, gun drawn, he knocked on the semi open door and yelled "Police! Anybody home?" There was only silence. He yelled again and when he received no answer, he shoved the door fully open and went inside with his gun drawn and in front of him. He quickly searched the house, noting the overturned lamp and chair in the living room, but finding no sign of anyone still in the house. Josh checked around the back of the house and didn't see anything amiss, so he hurried outside to motion to Olivia to drive closer.

He met her in the driveway. Opening the car door, he withdrew a black bag, donned a pair of clear latex gloves, and called Headquarters to send people out. When he'd hung up he looked at Olivia. She was pale and looked worried.

"Is he dead?" she asked in a small voice.

"No, at least not that I know of. He isn't here. There are signs of a struggle, but no one is in the house or back yard. I'm thinking he was kidnapped." Josh sighed heavily. "Here, come on out and take these gloves. Once the guys get here, I want to bring you inside for a few minutes. Try not to touch anything, even gloved. I want to see if you notice anything that is different from when you were here before. I don't want to allow you in before they come because it wouldn't look good, but I trust your eye for detail. The only things I saw were a lamp and a chair that were turned over, but I've never been in the house before, so I wouldn't know if anything else was unusual unless it was obvious like that."

"Okay," she took the gloves and held them ready to put on. "Josh, I'm really worried about Tiny. He's a big guy and probably pretty tough too, so if someone took him forcibly, they must have either knocked him out and tied him up, or they had a gun, or both. I'm afraid for him."

"Yes, I'm afraid for him too. I'm pretty sure he didn't leave willingly." Josh sighed again. He held her until they heard a car coming up the road, then they stepped apart.

O'Brian and Hendricks were in the first car and shortly behind was Fallon and McNabb. Josh greeted them all, then asked if they remembered Miss McKenna, and told them how she came to be there and why he was allowing her to look around inside.

O'Brian had a slight smirk, which he quickly wiped off when he saw his boss' frown. The other cops, shook Olivia's hand and stepped aside for Josh and Olivia to enter the house first. Olivia slipped the gloves on quickly and followed Josh inside, taking care not to touch anything at all.

She saw the overturned lamp and chair and felt slightly ill with worry for Tiny. She looked carefully at everything as they walked through the house, paying special attention to the kitchen, where she'd spent the most time. It was back in the living room that she noticed her business card lying next to the phone, on the little side table by the window. She showed it to Josh sadly, looking out the window toward the antique shop with a mist of tears filming her eyes.

Josh pushed the play button on the answering machine and they heard Olivia's voice announcing that she was 'returning a call from this number'.

"You had no way of knowing Liv," Josh said quietly, so only she could hear him. "It could just as easily been a salesperson or campaign recording. Stop blaming yourself, Babes," he looked around and saw they were alone in the room, and quickly squeezed her hand. "It's not remotely your fault."

"Logically you're right, emotionally, from my gut...." Olivia shook herself and sighed. "We need to find him Josh. He could be lying somewhere hurt or dying and even minutes could make a difference."

"I know sweetheart. Right now, I need you to go and stay over at Mrs. Tanner's or get the girls and go home where it's safe. I'm going to put out an APB on the van first off, then as soon as we're done inside, I'm sending the guys to search the yard and talk to the other neighbors. We'll find him."

"Okay Josh, I'll go to Mrs. Tanner's for a while, then home if you don't have any news, but please let me know as soon as you know anything." She pleaded. "I know it may not be true, but I feel responsible, besides he's a nice guy and I genuinely like him, and would hate to have anything bad happen to him."

"I will Liv, and I know," he walked her to the door. "I'll call you later."

Olivia walked down the road to Mrs. Tanner's house, looking around carefully to see if she saw anything unusual. There was nothing she could find. Molly jumped up on her and gave her kisses when she arrived at Mrs. Tanner's.

She reported what they'd found and Mrs. Tanner made them both a cup of tea while she talked. Jimmy was in the living room playing with Sheyna, and Molly soon went back to play with them. Mrs. Tanner pulled a pan out of the oven, filling the kitchen with the heavenly aroma of gingerbread. She set the baking sheet full of cookies on a wire rack to cool, and joined Olivia at the table.

"Tiny was so broken up when his ma passed, but after a while he got on with life, fixing her place up even nicer than she'd had it. It used to be just like it is now, but when she started feeling poorly, she kinda let it go, and then once Tiny came, he had to take care of her, and didn't have time for everything else." She paused for a breath, "He made it beautiful again though once he'd gotten his wind back in him after losing her."

"Was Tiny ever married?" Olivia asked.

"No, he brought a woman around for a while and Gladys and me, that's his ma, Gladys, thought they might end up marrying, but she found somebody with more money and married him instead. Tiny didn't seem too upset about it though, so we figured it wasn't as serious as we'd thought. He had a few others around, but none of them seemed serious at all." She sniffed, "Tiny is a really good boy and I sure hope they find him okay." She wiped her eyes and got up to put the cookies on a plate and offered them to Olivia, who took two. Mrs. Tanner put a few cookies on a plate and took them in to Jimmy.

She was composed when she returned to the kitchen.

Olivia stood, setting her empty cup in the sink. "Thank you so much for all of your hospitality Mrs. Tanner. I'm going to take Molly and Sheyna home now. Please call me if you hear or see anything."

"I will child," Mrs. Tanner walked her to the door, and patted Molly on the head as Olivia carried Sheyna out.

Olivia waved at Jimmy from the door to the living room and he smiled and waved back.

"You drive safely and please come back any time.

You'll never know how thankful I am for what you've done to help Jimmy." She hugged Olivia, then closed the car door for her once she was behind the wheel.

Olivia drove home slowly, then almost slammed on the brakes as a sudden thought struck her hard. *Why had the murderer been after Sheyna? She'd been so focused on Jimmy and then on Tiny, that she hadn't really registered what they'd learned.* She resumed normal speed still deep in thought. Was there something special about Sheyna? Well, of course she was special, but that was because Olivia loved her, but something special that would make someone want to grab her? She couldn't see it. Maybe Sheyna had scratched the murderer and he was out for revenge. She shuddered, remembering Jimmy's reenactment and the evil face he'd made to show what the guy looked like when he tried to grab the cat.

No wonder she'd been all bristled up when she landed on Olivia's SUV. That meant the murderer had still been there when she went outside. He must have taken off as soon as she took Sheyna and went back in. Maybe if she'd scratched him, he thought she'd have his blood on her claws and the police could get his DNA. *Why hadn't they thought of that back then?* She chastised herself and Josh both mentally. *Okay, lay off Liv, you didn't know the cat and murderer had ever seen each other then.*

Suddenly it dawned on her that the shrieking sound she'd heard was Sheyna and the footsteps had been inside, because she heard them and the shriek before she heard the bells on the door, not after. That's what had been bugging her the whole time. She already knew she must have heard the murderer leaving, but hadn't realized that Sheyna had also been inside until that point. That's why she was always so good about not trying to go out when someone opened the door. She had been an indoor only cat. She'd probably witnessed the murder. Olivia really wished she could speak Cat.

It was already dark when Josh called Olivia from his car. "No luck yet sweetie," he said with a sigh. "We've talked to everyone around, searched the property, even the woods for a little ways, but didn't see any signs of someone being dragged. It was pretty dark in there and the captain said it was too dangerous, so we had to give up before we could go very far. But it seems more likely that they took him away in the van, and that's what he says we have to focus on now."

"You won't stop looking, will you?" Olivia asked. "No, of course you won't. I'm sorry honey, I'm just feeling helpless right now."

"It's okay, I know you are, and no, we're not going to stop looking. Just maybe change the direction of our search, or at least expand it. We yelled ourselves hoarse while we were out there searching, in case he was somewhere nearby and could hear us, but we didn't hear anything except each other."

"Thanks for letting me know Josh. Please call me if you learn anything new."

"You know I will," he said. "Try not to worry too much and please try not to think it's your fault, because it isn't."

After they'd hung up, promising to get together as soon as Josh could get a moment free from work, Olivia fixed herself a light dinner, fed the girls and tried to read, but she kept visualizing poor Tiny lying somewhere injured and the words just wouldn't make sense. After a while, she gave up and went to bed. Just before she turned off the light, the house phone rang. Her nerves twanged as she answered to dead silence again. She hung up the phone with a bang, made sure the baseball bat was still close by and turned off the light.

CHAPTER TWENTY

Olivia woke up the next morning feeling like she'd had evil dreams all night, but she couldn't remember any of them. She took a shower, dressed in jeans and a turtleneck sweater and went downstairs. Molly asked to be let out and Sheyna asked for breakfast. Olivia obliged them both, letting Molly out and mixing their food, so that when Molly came in, their food went down for them.

She made coffee, then checked her email and called Josh. He didn't have any news about Tiny yet, but they were working hard and were following up on a potential sighting of the van. The captain had them all working the van angle, with only a couple of troopers still searching around Tiny's yard for clues—he had firmly shut down the search in the woods. Josh also asked if they could do the dinner at his place later in the week, since last night had obviously not happened according to plan.

Olivia hung up and went to work on her sales feeling frustrated and worried. She had a feeling she was the one who'd gotten Tiny into this by piquing his interest in the murder, so no matter what anyone said, she felt responsible. She was going to have to do something to find him before it was too late.

Just after one PM, she called Annie to ask if Molly and Sheyna could stay with her for the day. Annie said she was happy to have them. Olivia hung up, put on hiking boots and took her backpack filled with warm clothes, a tent, a knife, some zippered baggies, a sleeping bag, her tiny alcohol stove, food, water and some other essentials for camping in the woods overnight, just in case, and loaded the girls into the car. She ran back inside and rummaged through her hall closet in the dark for a roll of flagging tape. She grabbed both rolls, flung them onto the kitchen table where she could see them, then chose the hot pink flagging tape, and left the orange one on the table.

"Hi Livvie, I'm so happy to have the girls over today. I was bored silly for some reason, so this will give me something fun to do." Annie hugged Molly, as Olivia carried Sheyna into the house.

"You have no idea how grateful I am to you, for always agreeing to watch them for me, at a moment's notice. I feel bad asking with no prior warning though, are you sure it's not a problem?"

"Never! I adore having them, always," She smiled. "As long as I am home, they . . . and you . . . are always welcome. So, where are you heading?" she glanced at her hiking boots, "off for a hike?"

"Yes, the weather is nice for it today," Olivia hated to deceive her friend, but a lie of omission didn't feel quite as bad as making something up would have, besides it was for a good cause. She knew her friends and Josh would never let her go off by herself searching for Tiny, and she had to find him.

Once she was on the road to Eastman's Grant, she thought hard about how to proceed. Josh had said that his men weren't able to go far into the woods because of the darkness, and shortly afterward they had started focusing more on the van. She had a feeling he was in those woods somewhere. Whether he was alive or not, she didn't know, but she was hoping for the best.

Olivia parked at the antique shop, on the side where her car was not so visible, as she could see a State Police car in Tiny's driveway. It wasn't Josh's car, but still…she knew they'd send her home if they saw her, whoever it was. She felt bad about not telling Josh what she was up to. He had been so good about including her in the case and teaching her things. He'd taught her some basic self defense moves, and quite a bit about how to escape should she ever be tied up with duct tape or handcuffs. She now always carried a couple simple hair barrettes for opening handcuffs.

She put on her backpack and headed into the woods behind the antique shop, walking parallel to the road until she was in a good position to cross the street without being seen from Tiny's house. Once she was on Tiny's property, she knew she had to be careful in case the troopers were actually searching the woods. Josh had said they were only checking around the house and yard, but it was possible they'd decided to venture into the woods against orders.

She checked to make sure she had cell phone coverage, then decided to hide her phone on her calf, in case whoever took Tiny happened to catch her too. She used a couple of little straps from her backpack to secure it, turning it off first, to keep it from ringing and giving her away to anyone who might be nearby, and to save the battery.

She listened carefully for any sounds that would indicate the presence of other people, as she looked for a path. She wasn't sure there would be a path, but it was pretty likely. Most people who lived on the edge of the woods and had kids, would have some sort of path, even a very rough one made by kids exploring.

She halted abruptly as she remembered Tiny talking about his ma helping him build a tree-house. He'd even said it was still there, standing strong like she did. Olivia knew she had to find that tree-house. It would have been the perfect place to hide someone. She tried to remember if he'd said anything else about it. Did he say it was deep in the woods? She thought he might have. Josh's people hadn't gotten to search that far, because it got dark and the Captain ordered them out.

Olivia kept walking in the direction she thought was right to find a path. She had to go around briar patches and climb over a few fallen trees, but she finally found a path. She checked her direction from where the sun was to make sure she wasn't headed toward Tiny's house, but away from it, then walked along the path, searching the trees carefully for any signs of a tree-house. She saw evidence that someone had been down the path recently—scuff marks in the dirt here and there, a few misplaced rocks with a hole where they'd been, and a fresh cigarette butt.

She knew Tiny and Josh didn't smoke and she was pretty sure about O'Brian and Hendricks too. She'd been in the room with all of them, and none smelled like tobacco. She didn't know about any other troopers who might have been searching, but it was more likely to have been from one of the kidnappers. She took her small camera out and took a picture of the cigarette butt, showing the area as best she could, then she used two small twigs to pick the butt up and put it in a zippered baggie in the side pocket of her backpack. She'd read enough Nancy Drew novels when she was a kid to know better than to touch any possible evidence with her hands. She left a piece of the flagging tape Josh had taught her about when he was telling her about investigation methods tied to a shrub next to where she'd found the cigarette butt.

As she clambered over some large boulders in the path, she saw that a smaller, barely noticeable path led off to the left and the main path kept going straight ahead. She saw a patch of uprooted moss on the small trail and knew someone had been down it recently, so she decided to try it. She tied a long dangly piece of hot pink tape to a bush at the start of the new path in case anyone needed to find her later. She tried to ignore that grim possibility, but it was better safe than sorry.

Farther along, she spotted another cigarette butt, this one a different brand. She got out the camera, opened a new baggie and repeated the steps she'd used for the last find, tying another piece of hot pink flagging tape to a shrub to mark the area. At least she was now sure someone had been here in the last day or so.

The path crossed through a boggy area, where Olivia had to rock hop to avoid stepping into either rank smelling mud or thick wet moss covering muddy water. She was very careful, since face planting into either one was not an option she wanted to consider. Molly would have loved wading through the muck. Olivia was so glad she was clean and safe at Annie's.

There were a few trees Olivia stopped to look at

more closely making sure they didn't harbor a tree-house, but so far, none had. She stopped briefly to take her pack off to relieve herself and eat a few bites of trail mix, then headed on. The small path wound around forming a circuitous maze-like course, switch-backing and looping several times. How ingenious Tiny's mom must have been, to design it in such a way that it would seem to be much farther away from the house to a small boy than it really was. He'd have felt as though he were deep in the forest, when he was probably less than a half mile from his house as the crow flies.

The small path looked a lot less disturbed than the first path had, which convinced Olivia that Josh's men hadn't been down this way—someone else had—and they'd been moving slowly and carefully, perhaps carrying something heavy, like an unconscious Tiny. She wanted to hurry, but was afraid she might miss the tree-house, so she walked as fast as she could, while still eyeing all the likely trees. It would have to be fairly large in order to accommodate Tiny, if in fact they'd hidden him there.

She stopped again to eat a few bites and to put on her light fleece gloves. Her body was warm from hiking, but her hands were getting chilly. She could tell the temperature was dropping and the light was fading a little too. She glanced at her watch, it was almost four o'clock. At this time of year, it would be dark in the woods within a few minutes. She took her headlamp out of the pack and put it on her head, but didn't turn it on yet. It was going to be colder tonight than it had been the past few nights, she could tell already. She needed to find Tiny within the next few hours or he could be in danger of hypothermia. She put on a fleece vest over her turtleneck. Just the brief stop had cooled her body down considerably.

She lugged the pack back on and continued down the path, watching carefully for a tree-house and for the path—getting lost was a very bad idea.

She'd gone probably another eighth of a mile, when she heard distant voices. She silently and quickly got off the path and hid behind a copse of trees where she could see, but not be seen. Her heart pounded so loudly she was afraid they'd be able to hear it as the voices came closer. She still couldn't see them, but they had to be just around the next bend in the path and headed her way.

"He's gotta know where it's at Nils," whined a woman's voice. "I'm tired of digging for nothing. You gotta make him tell us."

"Alright Elsa, we'll try again, but this is the last time I'm wasting water and food on him. If he doesn't tell us, he can lie there and rot." A man's gravelly voice stated.

"He'd better give it up, I want that money!"

"Yeah, and I need to get those fake coins before someone else finds them and we end up in prison for insurance fraud."

"Nils, you said we could never get caught. I am not going to prison!" The woman called Elsa yelled, "This is all your fault!"

"My fault?" he yelled back. "I did everything I was supposed to do. How is it my fault; you knew all about it from the get-go."

"Fine! Whatever! Let's just make him tell us where the stuff is and go get it." Elsa said, a little quieter.

"Alright, come on then."

Olivia could hear strange scraping noises, and guessed they were climbing some kind of ladder into the tree-house. It was so dark now that she could barely see without turning on the headlamp, and she didn't dare to do that. She decided to try to get closer to the noises and hopefully find the tree-house. She moved carefully through the dark, trying to feel her way along, back onto the path. She'd just reached it when she slipped on a wet rock and fell, banging her leg hard on another rock. She bit her lip to keep from screaming with the pain and frustration. Her leg hurt badly, and was probably already swelling and bleeding through her torn jeans.

When the pain subsided enough for her to breathe, she slowly sat up and took stock of her injury, wincing as she felt the large hematoma forming on her leg. She breathed in and out slowly and silently to calm herself and dull the pain, and used her hands to push herself up until she was standing. Her leg throbbed, but she could walk on it.

Slowly and carefully she felt her way down the path toward where she'd heard the voices and climbing noises. She hadn't gone too far before she heard the voices again, this time from much closer than before. She was even more careful to not make noise as she crept forward on the path, until she could hear the voices directly overhead and see faint light inside the tree-house. Elsa and Nils seemed to be trying to talk a little quieter now. Maybe they'd realized they weren't all that far away from the house and that sound travels well at night in the country.

Maybe she'd given them too much credit, because the voices rose in volume again immediately.

"Are you gonna tell us where the loot is buried?" Nils was asking in a threatening voice. "Give him some water, he can't talk."

"Yeah, yeah, I'm gettin' it, keep your shirt on Nils,"

Elsa's whiny nasal voice chimed in.

Olivia could hear raspy breathing and an even raspier cough. Tiny, she thought. He was still alive. Before they decided to kill him, she had to get him out of there somehow, since she knew he didn't have the answers they wanted. Tiny must be tied up and was probably very weak, maybe sick, so it was up to Olivia. Poor Tiny, his life depended on her and she was terrified, afraid to use her headlamp for fear of being spotted, and her leg throbbed so bad it made her teeth hurt.

"Okay you had your water, now tell us where he buried it and we'll give you more, and maybe some food too," Elsa said in a cajoling whine. "How'd you like some nice warm soup?"

"Stuff it Elsa!" Nils barked. "Dawson, if you don't tell us where he buried it, you're gonna *be* the food. We're gonna leave you here for the tree rats to eat. They say starving is a rough way to die. Now tell us what you know and we'll let you live."

"I . . . don't . . . know anything," Tiny rasped weakly. "Please . . . more water."

Olivia heard slurping noises.

"Well, why'd you give it to him when he didn't tell us anything?" Nils complained, whining as bad as Elsa. "If he doesn't talk, he doesn't get water or food, got it?"

"Well, he can't talk if he can't get his mouth to work, can he?"

"Whatever! So she gave you more water, now you'd better start talking or it'll be the last water you ever drink."

"Get . . . me . . . down and I'll . . . take you . . . there." Tiny got the words out painstakingly.

Olivia crept into the trees where she could still hear but wasn't visible in case they decided to bring Tiny down. She admired his ability to think under pressure.

"No, just tell us where it is. Once we find it, we'll come back and let you go." Nils said smoothly. "I'm not taking a chance on you getting away until we've got the goods, now talk!"

"How do I . . . know you'll come back, and not . . . just leave me to die?"

"Why would I kill you if I don't have to? If people cooperate with me, I don't kill them, but if they cross me…well, let's just say they won't do it again."

"Okay, I'll tell you," Tiny said weakly. "He buried it on my property over by . . . the shed," he paused for breath. "I caught him digging and he cut me in."

"Where, by the shed? We're not gonna be digging all around the thing?"

"Please, more water," Tiny begged.

"Give it to him Elsa."

Olivia heard the slurping sounds again.

"In the back, on the side by the house."

"Okay, thanks for the information, finally!" Nils said triumphantly. "I'm putting your gag back on so you'll stay nice and quiet."

Olivia heard sounds of a brief struggle.

"And now that you've told me, after refusing to all this time, I'll let you in on a secret," Nils' voice turned cold and sinister. "It doesn't really matter anymore if you lied or told me the truth. Either way you're going to die. If you lied, and I end up wasting my time digging, I might be angry enough to come back and put a bullet in your dumb biker brain, but then again, it might be more comforting for me to think of you slowing freezing to death", he paused. "I've always hated you stupid bikers in your pathetic black leather.

Come on Elsa, we're gonna knock all those steps off, so no one can see the tree-house and even if he gets loose, he won't make it down without breaking his legs," Nils laughed and motioned to Elsa to climb down. She turned on her headlamp and started down backward. He followed behind her with a crowbar.

Olivia watch the two blondes climbing down, being careful not to be seen. Nils used the crowbar to pry the boards they'd used as steps and handholds off the tree, as he descended, finally reaching the bottom and prying off the last one, then throwing them into the trees, coming very close to hitting Olivia in her hiding spot. She flinched.

"Do you think it's safe to go over there? You know the cops were there earlier," Elsa asked.

"If your brother-in-law is doing his part, it should be safe," Nils snarled. "Blasted idiot."

"Hilda's husband is not an idiot Nils. He's very smart."

"Whatever. Let's go before it gets any colder, my feet are freezing off," Nils pushed Elsa ahead of him, turning on his headlamp as they started up the path toward Tiny's house.

Olivia waited until their querulous voices had faded, then crept out of her hiding place and turned her headlamp on. Wincing from the pain in her leg, she reached down to unstrap her phone to call Josh and found that it wasn't there. The empty straps were dangling around the top of her boot. Her heart sank. How was she going to get Tiny down now?

After a long moment of sheer frustration, she sighed and started crawling around on the ground looking for the boards Nils had flung near her. When she had found all she could, she searched for a rock to hammer them back onto the tree. Luckily, they seemed to all still have their nails intact.

She was hesitant to make noise because unlike some people, she knew how well sound traveled at night in the woods. She dug through her backpack for an extra shirt and wrapped it around the rock. Experimentally she held the first board in place and banged one of the nails into the tree, it took several hits before the huge nail was in, but it was pretty quiet. She banged the next nail in. So far, so good, she thought. At this rate, she might be able to get to Tiny and get the sleeping bag around him in time to keep him from dying of hypothermia, as long as the rock and the nails cooperated and Nils and Elsa didn't hear her pounding and come back.

CHAPTER TWENTY-ONE

It was six-thirty when Josh received the call from Abby. His office had patched it through because she said it was an emergency. His heart faltered when he heard what she had to say. Annie had called her because Olivia had failed to show up from her hike to pick up Molly and Sheyna and it was long past dark. They didn't know where she'd been planning to hike and were worried sick that she'd fallen or something.

Josh hung up and pulled onto the side of the road, because for a minute he literally couldn't see. The past rose up and threatened to crush him under its enormous weight. He relived the call, telling him of Susan's death, and the coroner's report of their unborn child who'd died with her, that they hadn't even known about yet. It couldn't be happening again. Slowly the weight eased off like a slimy monster sinking back into the bog and he could breathe again. He wasn't going to let it happen.

He spun the car around and headed for Olivia's house to see if he could figure out where she'd gone, from what she'd left behind. He still had the key, so he let himself in and looked around desperately trying to read her mind somehow. The living room didn't tell him anything. He went upstairs to her bedroom and saw a cacophony of clothes strewn across the bed, which looked like she'd been trying to pack quickly. Back downstairs, he headed for the kitchen and the roll of Blaze Orange flagging tape told him what he hadn't wanted to know.

He'd been the one to teach her about using flagging tape to mark evidence and they'd discussed using it to mark your path if you were lost or were afraid you might become so. The drawer for the baggies was ajar also—another thing he'd taught her to have on hand if you were looking for evidence. She was off trying to solve Tiny's disappearance, and he had a bad feeling she might have bitten off more than she could chew.

He radioed in to let the captain know about Olivia's disappearance and that he suspected she was investigating, and asked him to send O'Brian and Hendricks for backup; he was on his way out to Tiny's place to look for her.

The captain said he needed to come by Headquarters first because he had something important to show him regarding the case that might help in finding her. Josh hated to waste a minute of the time he could be looking for Olivia, but the captain gave him a direct order and it was on the way, so he agreed and rushed to Headquarters.

As soon as he walked in the door, Captain Corwin, ushered him into his office and shut the door. O'Brian didn't meet his eyes as he walked past him.

"Abrams, it's come to my attention that you've got a special interest in Olivia McKenna, besides a professional one, as a suspect in a murder case. That's grounds for me to fire you, and maybe even somethin' worse," the captain paused, as Josh's expression darkened. "We think she may be involved in Dawson's kidnappin'. Her fingerprints were found on the lamp that was layin' on the floor at his house. Can you explain that?"

"What?" Josh said in angry astonishment. "You called me in here to accuse her of something, instead of helping to find her. She didn't have anything to do with the kidnapping. She's the one who's in danger right now, and we need to be out there looking for her."

"I've been wondering for a while if you were possibly involved in all this with her. You've just given me my answer, Abrams," he pressed a button on his phone. "Send them in."

Looking like they'd rather be anywhere else, O'Brian and Hendricks entered the room.

Josh's mouth dropped open, "You seriously think I'm involved in this? I just got a lead that there might be something fishy about Olander and was about to follow it up, when I got a call that Ms. McKenna was missing after a hike. I want to go find her and you decide she's a murderer and I'm in on it?"

"Arrest him, O'Brian," Corwin said smugly. "You saw the fingerprint results.

I always thought there was something not right about you Abrams."

"No!" Josh yelled. "Olivia is missing out there and we need to find her! There is no way she's involved in any of this except in trying to find Dawson."

O'Brian was torn. He was positive Josh was innocent and pretty sure Olivia was too, but the fingerprint was a perfect match, and he'd been given a direct order from his captain.

"Sorry Josh," he said quietly. "I don't want to do

this, but I don't have a choice."

Josh drew in a shuddering breath—and charged through the door and out to his car, roaring out of the parking lot in the direction of Tiny's house.

"Go get him!" the captain yelled at Hendricks. "You," he said to O'Brian, put out an APB on his car and try to get him on the radio and make him come back. I know you're friends with him, maybe you can keep him from getting himself killed."

Hendricks ran to his car. Corwin was so mad his hands were trembling. He took some aspirin and called Hendricks on the radio, "Get Fallon and McNabb out there to back you up. Remember, he's a dirty cop. He may be a murderer and a kidnapper. He's on the run and he's armed and dangerous. Get him before he kills someone else!"

O'Brian shut the captain's door, stunned. The whole thing was crazy. He'd known Josh way too long to believe he was capable of something like this, and Olivia really didn't strike him as a murderer either. He hadn't checked it closely, because the captain hadn't given him time to, but before he put out the APB, he was going to make sure that fingerprint was Olivia's.

~~~

Olivia worked as fast as she could, hammering the boards back in place with the shirt covered rock, stopping a few times to straighten a nail that had gone crooked. It was slow tedious work. She had to climb up on each board after she nailed it in, carrying another board and the rock in order to nail the next one, then climb back down to get another board. She'd tried taking two at a time, but couldn't hold onto the tree, the board she was nailing, the rock and the extra board. It was hard enough without the extra board, and she'd fallen off the second step a couple times before she figured out the best way to do it.

When it had been long enough that she felt it safe, she called out to Tiny softly, telling him to hang on, she was going to get him out of there. She heard him thump the floor of the tree-house in response. They'd left the door to the tiny house open, so the cold could come in quicker, and as Olivia had already had to stop work to put on heavier gloves and her down jacket, because the temperature was falling rapidly, she knew she had a limited amount of time before Tiny would be in big trouble.

She yelped as she felt a splinter jab into her thumb from the board. Luckily it was a large one so she was able to pull it out easily and keep on working, and no one but Tiny heard the rather un-nice words she muttered. There was a nail missing on the next board and she was worried about how she'd manage to stand on it to nail the following one. She wasn't even going to think about trying to get Tiny down on the now-not-so-secure ladder. She was almost halfway up now. Why did Tiny's mom have to pick such a tall tree? Well, at least she'd found him; without the tree-house, who knows what Nils and Elsa would have done with him.

~~~

Josh started toward Tiny's house, then abruptly swerved and headed to Annie's to pick up Molly. She'd be likelier than anyone to be able to track Olivia in the woods at night. She loaded her into his car and told Annie to take Sheyna and go stay with Abby just in case, since someone might have been watching her house too.

He drove as fast as he dared on the back roads to the antique shop, where he spotted Olivia's car on the side. He parked next to her, unloaded Molly and peered into Olivia's car. There was nothing to tell him anything. He took her scarf from the backseat and put it in his pocket. He then donned his emergency backpack from the trunk of his car, which thankfully, he'd remembered to put back, put his headlamp on and quietly closed the trunk. Like Olivia, he decided it was best to take to the woods behind the shop and walk parallel with the road until he was out of sight of Tiny's house. Once he'd gotten into the woods, he showed Molly the scarf, let her smell it and asked her to find Olivia.

She pulled him along, around brambles and bushes until she turned and strained to pull him into the road. Josh carefully held her back, looking first to make sure they were in a good spot to not be seen. They were, so he figured Molly knew where she was going and he followed her across the road. She led him in a fairly straight path for a while, avoiding stickers and large brush, then there was suddenly an actual trail ahead of them.

"Good girl Molly!" Josh said quietly, hugging her. "Okay, let's find Olivia," he let her smell the scarf again and she headed down the path pulling him behind her. It was slow going in the dark, even with a headlamp. Unlike what many people believe, dogs do not have wonderful night vision, so Molly was relying on her nose and couldn't go very fast without tripping over the many rocks and tree roots in the path, nor could Josh. He had to help her a little when they crossed over a large boulderfall. It was harder for her to manage in the dark. Back on smoother terrain, she tried to pick up the pace.

Molly dead-stopped so suddenly that Josh almost fell over her.

"What's the matter girl?" he asked trying to maintain his balance. "What is it?"

Molly sniffed the ground then turned back for a little ways, then turned left and sniffed along the side of the path. Josh looked around and spotted the hot pink flagging tape dangling from a tree by the little offshoot path.

"You're the dog!" he said grinning and thumping Molly's back appreciatively. "Okay, let's go find her."

Josh followed Molly down the narrow path with renewed hope and energy.

~~~

Earl Hendricks disconnected from the radio call with Fallon, and continued driving toward the Dawson property. Never in his wildest imaginings had he ever thought Josh Abrams would end up being a dirty cop, much less a murderer. The captain had been sure though. *Well,* he thought, scratching his head, *it just goes to show you....*

He hoped he'd be able to collar Abrams without killing him. Not that he really either liked him or disliked him, but he'd hate to kill a fellow cop, even a bad one. He thought about everything Captain Corwin had said— *Lieutenant Hendricks,* he thought—*that had a really nice ring to it.*

Fallon and McNabb were waiting in the driveway when he pulled in with a screech of tires.

"Evening guys, the capt'n said Abrams is to be considered armed and dangerous. He's sure he's guilty, and the way he ran out of the HQ, I guess he's right. You don't run if you're innocent do you?" Hendricks sounded like he was trying to convince himself.

"Sarge, are you sure about this? I mean he's one of us and I've always admired him." Fallon said in bewilderment. "I'd a sworn he was a straight arrow."

"Me too," McNabb said fervently. "I can't believe he's a bad cop."

"Well, I guess we'd better start believing it, because the captain said Abrams was off the deep end and would kill us rather than go to prison if we didn't either disarm him, or kill him first. He's a crack shot too, you know." Hendricks was taking charge. "McNabb, you stay here in the yard and watch for his car. Don't take any chances. If you think he's gonna shoot you, shoot him first. Fallon, come with me. We're gonna check out that path in the woods back there and see if he's in there hiding. The captain said he'd be back there somewhere for sure."

McNabb shook his head and walked off toward the house.

Fallon followed Hendricks into the woods along the path. Hendricks had taken his big flashlight from the car and it illuminated the path fairly well. Fallon stumbled along behind him with the smaller one from his belt, still trying to wrap his head around the idea of Josh Abrams being a murderer and a dirty cop. He hadn't known him well, as Josh was his superior by more than one rank, but he thought he'd known him well enough to have spotted something that off.

~~~

Olivia's leg throbbed and burned from her fall, she had one thumb that burned from the splinter she'd pulled out, both hands had massive blisters even through her gloves from hanging onto the rough boards and pounding nails with the rock, and her feet were freezing in her summer hiking boots. Why hadn't she thought to wear the winter ones? She heaved her body up another rung of the partially reconstructed ladder, dragging a board and her rock. Only about five more rungs to go before she could reach the doorway and get to Tiny. She'd have to put her pack back on before she went up that time. As tired as she was, it wouldn't be easy to climb with that heavy pack, but she needed the things inside it to help him.

She lost her grip on the board and dropped it to the ground below as she started to pound the first nail into the tree. She almost threw the rock in frustration. *Take a deep breath Olivia,* she admonished herself sternly, wanting to weep instead. Doggedly, she climbed back down to retrieve the board.

Only five more to go. She grabbed the recalcitrant board and arduously climbed back up to where she'd just been. She hammered the first nail in, shifted her weight and grip to the other hand and foot, to hammer the second one, lost her balance for a minute and hung precariously by one hand and one foot, then regained her balance by dropping the rock to grab the tree with the other hand. She screamed in frustration, clinging to the tree with her arms around it. She screamed until tears poured down her face.

She heard Tiny thrashing about above her, and got a grip on herself immediately.

"It's okay Tiny, I'm getting there. Just having trouble dropping things and I got mad. Hang in there."

Wearily, she climbed down, retrieved the rock and another board and climbed back up. She drove the second nail into the board and climbed up onto it to start on the next one. *You can do it Liv,* she told herself. *Only four more to go.*

~~~

Josh pulled Molly to a stop and stood still listening. The hair stood up on the back of his neck as he heard the distant screaming. He had to get there now. He started running down the path blindly, in full blown panic mode to get to her. Molly was behind him, being pulled along in his wake. He ran all out until he hit a root with the toe of his boot and fell face down in the dirt. Hard. The jolt brought him back to his senses and he realized how stupid that had been. He wouldn't do her any good by knocking himself out or getting lost in the woods in the dark. Molly could find her, if he let her go in front like he'd been doing. They just had to get there as fast as they could. He petted Molly's head and let her go ahead. She seemed to sense the urgency and went down the path as quickly as she could, with Josh following on her heels.

It was rough going, as the path switch-backed and twisted constantly. Josh's foot sank into thick slimy mud and a fetid stench rose from the ground, almost making him gag. Molly slogged through the muck as though she liked the feel of it. Josh gritted his teeth against the smell and followed her carefully, trying not to slip and fall. Once back on solid ground, the pair made a little better progress but the going was still slower than Josh would have liked.

~~~

Joe McNabb walked around to the back of Tiny's property, checking to see if he could catch sight of Hendricks and Fallon. There was nothing. He wished Hendricks hadn't ordered him to stay behind like this. If

Abrams really was bad and was looking to kill his fellow troopers, he didn't want to be separated from his partner. They were supposed to have each others' backs. Not that he didn't trust Hendricks to cover his partner exactly but Fallon was too new and too excitable. He shoulda been the one with him, not Hendricks, if it came to a standoff.

He heard a clunking noise and started around to the other side of the house. His head exploded in pain and everything faded to black.

~~~

Olivia steadied her trembling legs by holding onto the tree with her arms in a giant hug for a moment to relax her cramping feet. Once she could move without her feet cramping again, she carefully descended to grab the last board and begin the long climb back up to nail it in. Before she started back up she sat for a few seconds stretching her feet, legs, hand and arms. Everything was trying to cramp up now, but she was almost there.

Come on Liv, she coaxed herself as she climbed, *one more and you're there.* Finally she was in place and painfully hammered the last two nails into the tree.

"Hang on Tiny, I'm getting my backpack and I'll be right there." She called up to him. She slipped and scared herself silly for a second, then once more climbed to the ground. After taking a long sip of water, she heaved the pack onto her back and began the rough climb up. She held her breath as she climbed over the board with only one nail, but miraculously, it held her weight, even with the heavy pack.

She reached up to pull herself through the doorway and into the tiny tree top cabin. Tiny was lying on the floor, trussed up like a calf in a rodeo. She took off her pack, pulled her large knife out of it and quickly cut through the cloth gag, then the ropes that were binding his hands and arms, then finally freed his feet. He was so weak, he could barely move. She knew he must be getting hypothermic as well, so she hurriedly took the down sleeping bag out of her pack and eased his feet into it, then rolled his body into the rest of it and zipped it up, pulling the hood up over the top of his head. She opened the water bottle she'd brought inside the pack, wrapped in clothes to insulate it, wishing it was warmer, and held it to his mouth so he could drink a little bit.

He tried to speak, but she shushed him, patting his face gently, lifting him into a sitting position with his knees against his chest to help keep his core warm. She pushed her pack up against his back to help him hold himself up.

"Just rest Tiny. We're going to get you out of here soon. For now, just rest. I'm going to warm up some soup for you to help bring your body temperature up and to give you some strength back."

Olivia took her tiny alcohol stove over by the open door, poured a small amount of denatured alcohol into the bottom, lit it and put her titanium cup filled with water on it to boil. Tiny watched weakly as she opened the top of a silver packet and poured the boiling water into it. A wonderful aroma arose from the packet into the frigid air. Tears leaked down Tiny's cheeks as he seemed to realize that he might make it out of there alive after all.

Olivia let the rich vegetable soup cool a little, then fed it to Tiny in small spoonfuls, a little at a time. The first couple of bites dribbled from his mouth as he was having a hard time getting his lips to work right, but pretty soon, he was being able to swallow every drop and was starting to look a little better. Olivia warmed some of the water from the bottle slightly on her stove, then wiped Tiny's mouth and gave him some of the warm water.

Tiny drew a shuddering breath and groaned. Olivia saw the look of pain on his face and knew his circulation must be coming back painfully into his numbed armed and legs. It was going to hurt. A lot. And there was nothing she could do to help him with that, because he'd come too close to hypothermia and might also have frostbite and she didn't dare rub his limbs, for fear of causing more harm than good.

"I'm sorry Tiny, I know it hurts. It'll get better soon; just hang in there." She sat next to him and put her arms around him to try to ease his pain with a comforting hug and warm him with her body heat."

"Thanks Miss Olivia," he whispered hoarsely, shaking from cold and pain.

"Don't try to talk yet Tiny. Save your strength for getting through the pain. It's going to hurt for a little while, but it will get better soon and you're going to be alright." She gave him more of the warm water and sat to hold him until he was warm and over the worst of the pain.

CHAPTER TWENTY-TWO

Sergeant Hendricks and Trooper Fallon were struggling along the path, and had been going up steadily for a while now over huge rocks and slippery scree. Hendricks' quads were screaming at the unaccustomed exercise.

"How far is it supposed to be to wherever the captain said we'd find Abrams?" Fallon asked when Hendricks abruptly stopped and sat on a large boulder.

"He didn't say how far. He just said he'd be out here somewhere and something about a tree-house." Hendricks was getting disgusted. Much as he wanted a promotion to Lieu, he wasn't sure it was worth freezing his tush off in the dark on the side of a blasted mountain.

"A tree-house? You're kidding, right? No way anyone could find a tree-house in the middle of a wooded mountain at night." Fallon was incredulous. "We're going to end up on the top of some unknown mountain in the freezing wind and die of frostbite and hypothermia looking for a tree-house?"

Hendricks rose to his feet and spat, "Yeah, you're right, let's get outta here, this is nuts."

They turned around and headed down the mountain, Hendricks muttering under his breath about crazy fool dreams and idiots.

Fallon stopped with an involuntary and quickly stifled shriek. He jumped back like something had bitten him.

"What on earth's gotten into you, Fallon?" Hendricks jerked in surprise.

Fallon held up a long hot pink plastic streamer that had wrapped itself around his face as he walked into it.

"Flagging tape. And it looks brand new, not faded at all." Fallon said, "Darn near scared the pants off me grabbing my face like that."

They shone their lights around and saw the little path going off to the side.

"Well, looky here, Looks like someone wanted to make sure he could find his way back, doesn't it?" Hendricks regained his ambition quickly. "You stay behind me, but be ready for action."

Fallon rolled his eyes, bit his tongue and followed his superior officer.

~~~

Josh and Molly were steadily making their way down the path, going as fast as Josh dared. He stopped for a minute to relieve himself of the pack and eat a quick bite. As he was putting the pack back on he heard a voice in the distance behind him. It was too far away for him to make out the words, but he knew the voice—Hendricks. He fastened the pack quickly and told Molly to come and they headed onward as quickly as possible.

He hadn't gone very far when he noticed a light somewhere ahead. He stopped in confusion. Who could that be? Maybe Olivia, maybe the kidnappers, or it could be more State Troopers out to catch him. How could the captain believe he was dirty? If only he knew that Josh hadn't kept a cent of the money he'd earned over the years as a cop, he'd know better. Josh couldn't have told him or he'd never be able to work in the department again, with everyone knowing. They'd treat him differently. But most importantly, he wouldn't have had time to make him believe him and still gotten to look for Olivia in time. He hoped he was in time. That despairing scream still echoed in his head.

He had to decide what to do, which way to go. Hendricks would catch up with him and he'd be standing in the middle of the path like an idiot waiting to be hauled off to jail.

"Come on Molly," he patted her head and they continued warily toward the light. After a few hundred feet it became apparent that the light was coming from a tree-house. Josh dimmed his headlamp to the lowest setting then led Molly close toward a small copse of trees near the bottom of the big tree. Before they reached the trees to hide, Molly barked and tried to pull Josh toward the tree.

Josh froze as Hendricks came running up with Fallon behind him and yelled.

"Hit the ground Abrams!"

Josh sank to his knees quickly, seeing Hendricks' gun pointed at him.

"Flat on the ground with your hands behind your head! Now!" Hendricks barked.

"What on earth are you doing?" Olivia yelled from the doorway of the tree-house. "Josh? Molly? Are you there? Officer Fallon? What is going on?" She climbed down onto the top rung.

"Stay where you are ma'am." Hendricks ordered. "He's under arrest for murder and kidnapping, and so are you . . . Fallon, hold your gun on her so she doesn't try anything."

"Who did we kidnap?" Olivia asked in confusion.

"You know who, a man named Dawson. Now stay up there and don't move until I get him cuffed."

Tiny managed to crawl to the doorway and stick his head out. "Hey officers, I'm Tiny Dawson. They didn't kidnap me, Miss Olivia just saved me, and I think he was probably coming to save both of us."

Fallon put his gun in his holster in disgust. He'd known Abrams was a good cop. Hendricks was a nut job. Maybe the captain hadn't even sent him out here. Maybe Hendricks had made up the whole thing 'cause he was loony tunes.

"How do we know you're really Dawson?" Hendricks asked, starting to deflate a little. "You could be in on it too."

"I never figured you for a conspiracy theorist Hendricks, but it's starting to sound like you are," Josh said from the ground. "Olivia, Tiny, are you both okay?"

"Yes Josh, we are now," Olivia's voice was raw with emotion. "Please let him up," she said to Hendricks. "It's freezing on the ground." She climbed back up into the doorway to help Tiny sit back, as he was looking dizzy from leaning down.

"Yeah, yeah alright, you can get up Abrams," Hendricks suddenly lost all his bluster. He looked up at Tiny. "Yeah, I recognize you from the picture they gave us when you were kidnapped. I guess the Captain had some bad intel."

Josh told Molly to stay, then rushed up the makeshift ladder, feeling a slight give on one of the rungs, but arriving safely in Olivia's arms in the tree-house. They clung to each other tightly.

"Are you sure you're okay?" Josh asked, looking at her closely. He looked questioningly at Tiny.

"We're both going to be fine. I'm already fine, poor Tiny has a ways to go, but he'll be okay." Olivia buried her face in his chest. "Why did they think we kidnapped Tiny?"

"It seems someone gave the captain bad information. It showed your fingerprint on the lamp that was knocked over at Tiny's house, so it looked like you were in on the kidnapping. It wasn't a giant leap to assume I was in on it with you, since he'd figured out I was interested in you romantically."

"So, someone is trying to frame us? Any idea who?"

"Not yet, but I'm going to find out," Josh's voice was determined. "Let's get you both down from here and get Tiny to a hospital to be treated."

"There's a rung that's only got one nail about halfway down," Olivia said. "It's going to be tough getting him down that."

"I can make it," Tiny said gamely. "The pain is already much better. I saw the blood all over your leg and hands, so if you could go up and down that ladder, doing all you did for me tonight, I can definitely make it down once."

Josh sighed and looked at Olivia's bloody, blistered hands, and the dried blood on her pants leg.

"You're okay, huh? I shoulda figured how okay you were," he hugged her again. "Little—fierce—Shakespeare severely understated it in your case, Tiger."

Olivia grinned up at him and kissed him furtively, casting a sidelong glance at the men below.

He hugged her back, and looking at the men below, he kissed her properly, evoking a cheer from Fallon and a resigned look from Hendricks. Tiny grinned broadly through his pain.

Olivia and Josh helped Tiny get out of the sleeping bag, and Josh used Olivia's knife to cut it so he could wear it as a jacket for the trip down the tree and out to the cars. He still needed the warmth it provided. Olivia repacked her backpack.

With the paracord in Olivia's pack, they tied Tiny off to the rope belaying system he showed them. Olivia had been thrilled to see that, as she'd anticipated a torturous descent with her and Josh trying to climb holding onto Tiny somehow on the rickety stairs. She descended the ladder, using one hand periodically to guide Tiny on the rope so he wasn't bouncing off the tree too much or getting caught in branches. Josh belayed him from the top. Then he pulled the rope back up and sent Olivia's backpack down to her. He closed the door and climbed down. Olivia was hugging Molly and praising her.

"Tiny, are you going to be able to walk, or should we make a stretcher out of branches to carry you?" Josh asked.

"I can walk," Tiny said. I may need to lean on someone once in a while, but I'm doing better," he paused. "Listen, Nils said he might come back and shoot me if I'd lied to him about where Jamison's loot was buried, and since I had no idea, I lied. I told him it was behind the shed on my place. Maybe you should open the door, like he'd left it and someone with a gun stay here in hiding in case they come back."

"Tiny, I think you and Olivia both need to be in my

unit." He grinned and slapped his forehead. "Nils Olander! I'll be . . .. Hendricks, can you and Fallon get Tiny and Olivia out to the hospital? I'll stay here and see if they show up. It was Nils Olander, the last homeowner robbed by Larsson and Jamison."

"I am not leaving you here," Olivia said. "I don't need to go to the hospital for a few blisters and bruises, and I won't risk losing you."

Josh shook his head, "No. Absolutely not!"

"Josh, I am not going without you."

"I can get Dawson out, and Hendricks can stay with you two," Fallon chimed in. "If that's okay with you, sir?"

Josh shook his head again, chuckling ruefully, "I guess I don't have a choice. Liv, are you sure I can't get you to go with them?"

"Positive."

"Wait, you said you sent the kidnappers to your place? McNabb's there by himself," Hendricks blew out a breath sharply.

"Alright, Fallon, you and Tiny had best get moving; McNabb may need backup. Hendricks and I can handle it here and Olivia can hide in the bushes if anyone shows up," Josh took charge.

Josh climbed back up and opened the door to the tree-house, and Fallon and Tiny moved off up the path toward Tiny's house.

"What about the steps being back on," Olivia asked. "Nils took them all off with a crowbar, won't they notice?"

"I am hoping they will be so ticked off, that they won't notice it. They expect everything to be the way they left it, so unless it's glaringly different, they may not see it right away. They are used to the steps being there from before," he paused. "Okay, clue me in, I heard the name Nils, so I've been assuming you're talking about Nils Olander. Am I right? Who is the 'we'?" Josh queried."

"His wife, I think. Her name is Elsa, and they are quite the lovely pair," Olivia said wryly. "I'm rather surprised they haven't shot each other by now."

Josh chuckled, "It would save us some work, but I doubt we'll get that lucky."

"Alright, let's go behind the trees over there where we can watch the path without being visible. Hendricks, you okay?" Josh asked.

"Yeah Lieu, I'm good. I'm sorry for trying to arrest you, but I had orders and bad information."

"Yeah, no harm, we're cool man." Josh thumped him on the back. "The captain has a way of being pretty persuasive when he throws orders at you, if you want to stay on the payroll anyway. He was just dead wrong on this one."

Olivia passed around the last of the now tepid soup she'd made that Tiny hadn't finished. Tepid or not, it felt welcome going down, in the cold night air. Between the three of them it didn't last long. They stamped their feet and walked around in the shadow of the trees as quietly as they could to keep warm.

~~~

Fallon and Tiny made the trip back through the woods fairly fast considering Tiny's physical state. They didn't see any sign of McNabb in the yard and Fallon checked the front door, but it was locked up tight.

"McNabb! Joe!" he yelled loudly. There was no

response.

"Dawson, I need you to stay right with me to look for McNabb. It's safer if we stay together."

"Okay, just don't go too fast," Tiny said, only half joking. "I'm about done in from that hike out."

They rounded the house to the area of the shed and could hear someone moving fast through the bushes, heading for the path. Before Fallon could decide whether or not to give chase, he heard a groan from inside the shed. They hurried to open the door and free McNabb, who was just coming to.

"Hey Joe, take it easy." Fallon said. "What happened?"

Joe McNabb sat up, gingerly feeling the back of his head, "Oh man Abrams musta snuck up on me from behind. I never saw anything."

"It wasn't Abrams, Joe, He's not bad after all. It's Olander, Abrams said he was one of the robbery victims," Fallon filled him in.

"His wife, Elsa is with him too. He killed the guy who murdered the antique dealer," Tiny threw in. "I heard Elsa complaining that he should have made real sure he wasn't lying before he killed him. She thought he knew where the stuff was buried."

Fallon helped his partner up, steadying him until he had his balance.

"You okay to ride in the car yet Joe? I know being hit in the head can make you nauseated."

"Yeah, I'll be fine, just a little dizzy still and my head hurts. I'm not gonna be sick."

"I don't like leaving when the Olanders seem to be heading back out to where Abrams, Hendricks and Miss McKenna are, but I'm under orders to get Dawson to a hospital, and you have to go get seen too McNabb," Fallon said, leading the way to his car.

~~~

Josh threw his hands out to gesture for silence. In the distance, they could hear angry, voices heading their way.

"Okay, here they come. Liv, I need you to keep Molly quiet and both of you stay behind the trees—this is not negotiable." Josh looked at her sternly.

Olivia nodded her head.

"Hendricks, let see if they start to climb the ladder. If they do, we can get them once they are part way up, because they won't be able to hold on to the tree and draw guns very easily. I'll count with my fingers, on three we come out. Got it?"

Hendricks nodded his comprehension.

Olivia startled, patting Josh's arm as she remembered where she'd heard the name Hilda before. The last piece of the puzzle dropped into place.

Josh put his finger to his lips for quiet and she subsided.

The three humans and Molly waited in silence as the petulant voices grew louder and closer.

"All that digging, I'm gonna let him hang off the tree by his toes!" Nils growled.

"You gotta make him talk Nils, I want the money we'll get for that stuff, and I am not going to prison."

"Yeah Elsa, I want the money too, and if I go to prison, you can be sure you're going with me."

Elsa jumped in front of Nils as they reached the ladder, "Ladies first Mr. 'I'm such a Gentleman'," she whined sarcastically, and started climbing ahead of him.

Nils rolled his eyes and followed behind her up the

ladder.

They'd gotten almost halfway up, when Josh did the countdown on his fingers, one . . . two . . . three. Josh and Hendricks quickly ran out from behind the trees with their guns drawn.

"Police! Hold it right there!" Josh called loudly. "You're both under arrest."

Elsa Olander screamed, and flailed her arms wildly as the board she'd been standing on teetered and gave way. She fell back onto her husband sending them both crashing to the ground below.

Josh and Hendricks rushed to grab Nils as he drew his gun and tried to crawl away, scrambling to his feet to run, just as Josh tackled him from behind. Hendricks grabbed the gun as Olander dropped it, screaming curses in Swedish.

Behind them, Elsa had managed to get to her feet and ran wildly down the path.

"Tackle, Molly!" Olivia yelled, sending Molly after the fleeing woman.

Molly flew down the path and bowled Elsa over at the knees, then sat on her and waited until Hendricks ran up to relieve her of her loudly screeching prisoner.

Olivia raced up and hugged Molly, telling her how wonderful she was, as Hendricks handcuffed Elsa and led her over to where Josh was holding her husband in a matching pair of handcuffs.

"I thought you were going to hold Molly and wait behind the trees," Josh raised his eyebrows at Olivia, an irrepressible grin tickling the corner of his mouth. He burst out laughing, and Olivia and Hendricks joined him.

"Yay Molly! Even littler but every bit as fierce as her mom." Josh shouted jubilantly. "Alright, let's get these two fine upstanding citizens back to civilization where they can spend some quality time in a nice warm cell."

"Josh, wait, there is something you need to know," Olivia said quietly.

~~~

Bob O'Brian looked carefully through the magnifying glass again, to be sure he was seeing what he thought he was seeing. Looking around hastily, he headed to the fingerprint lab to talk to Sally Baker. If he was reading it right, there was no way this was an error.

~~~

Fallon hung up his cell phone looking stunned. He walked back into the ER to talk to McNabb. The doctor on duty had already decided to admit McNabb for the night for observation, since he had been unconscious for an extended period of time and might have concussion. She was now checking Tiny out, and decided he should also stay at least overnight, maybe longer, as he was dehydrated, his body temperature could still be a tad bit higher for her liking, he had the beginnings of frostbite in one toe and two fingers, and he just didn't look healthy enough overall to go home.

Fallon talked for a moment in a low voice to McNabb, so Tiny and the doctor couldn't hear him.

"Alright buddy, you rest up and don't bite any cute doctors now," he joked to McNabb, earning himself a look of feigned reproach from the cute doctor. "Dawson, you too. Take it easy for a day or two. I'll check in on you tomorrow."

He walked swiftly out the door, jumped in his car and sped away.

~~~

Josh, Olivia, Hendricks and their prisoners arrived at Headquarters a few seconds before Fallon pulled in.

"Hendricks, you stay and keep our sweet couple company for a few minutes and Fallon and I will go in and get their accommodations ready. Liv, maybe you should wait here too," Josh smiled at her. "We shouldn't be long." He stepped away and made a quick call on his cell.

"Alright Trooper Fallon, let's get this show on the road." The two men walked into Headquarters together.

Josh pushed in the code to the second door and they entered, looking around to see who was in sight. The captain came out of his office with a shocked look on his face.

"Abrams. What are you doing here? How did you get back here? Fallon, arrest him! He's a murderer and a kidnapper." Captain Corwin's face reddened in agitation. "Where is Hendricks? Come on Fallon, arrest him now before he gets away again!"

Josh stepped forward slightly, with his hands open, palms up. "Captain Corwin, I am not a murderer or a kidnapper, and you know this. I also am not a dirty cop—but you are. You've been taking bribes from your brother-in-law, Nils Olander, and covering for him and his wife, Elsa, your wife's sister. They are the murderers, and the kidnappers, and you are guilty as an accomplice, as is perhaps, your wife Hilda."

"That's a lie, all of it! He's the one who's guilty, Fallon! Arrest him!" Corwin shouted, reaching for his gun, to find his hands being cuffed from behind.

"Frank Corwin, You're under arrest for Accessory to Murder, Conspiracy to Commit Murder, Accessory to Kidnapping, Conspiracy to Commit Kidnapping, False

Imprisonment, and I am sure there will be more charges to follow, but that'll work for now," Bob O'Brian said, snapping the cuffs closed. "You have the right to remain silent . . .."

CHAPTER TWENTY-THREE

Josh carried Sheyna and Olivia led Molly as they walked into the little jewelry store to chose their wedding rings. They'd finally set a date, well, at least a month, sort of. They were tentatively planning on June, as they wanted to have their wedding outdoors and June would be a beautiful time to have it. There'd be spring flowers all over and the snow melt should be all gone by then.

The owner of the store, Max Levy was a fellow animal lover, and an old friend of Josh's parents. Animals were always welcome in his store.

He came around the counter to pet Molly and Sheyna, shake hands with Josh and hug Olivia.

Josh set Sheyna down on the counter and after exchanging news and pleasantries, Josh and Olivia started looking under the glass to see what struck their fancy. There were so many gorgeous bands in various precious metals and combinations, some with stones, and some without.

It took some time, but they finally found the perfect bands. Max checked their sizes and wrote up the order. They gave him a deposit and were browsing happily while he was writing. Once he'd finished, he handed Josh a copy of the order, then patted Sheyna again, and admired her collar.

He put on his loupe and looked at the collar closely. Sheyna loved the attention and purred loudly.

"Joshua, are you crazy? You are allowing your cat to wear a king's ransom in diamonds? In plain sight? Even I wouldn't put diamonds like this in my window, with all my alarms and the fine police force we have."

Josh and Olivia looked at each other in momentary shock, then burst out laughing. Olivia put her face in her palm.

"And we never saw it!" Josh roared with laughter. "Fine detectives we're going to make."

"No wonder Larsson tried to grab her that day, and that's why they were stalking me all along! But it wasn't me they wanted, it was Sheyna." Olivia shook her head in amazement.

"Joshua, please let an old man in on the joke," Max looked from Josh to Olivia in confusion. "I'm not as good at getting the punch lines as I used to be, I think."

Josh put his arm around Max and once they'd stopped laughing, they explained the whole thing. Max was amazed at what they'd found out, and amazed at Olivia's courage and her sense of honor.

"She's a keeper Joshua. You're lucky enough to find one like her, you hold on tight and you never let go." The old man smiled fondly at them.

~~~

Olivia and Josh backed out of Tiny's driveway, waving goodbye to him as they pulled into the road.

"He's doing fine now, isn't he? I know the doctor was a little worried about that one toe, but it seems to have come out fine, though he should always be more careful of it as well as the two fingers that were also affected by frostbite. They will be more susceptible from now on." Olivia leaned back serenely, as Josh drove. "I was so afraid I wouldn't get to him in time, but it all turned out fine."

"Yes it did Liv. You have no idea how scared I was when I found out that you were missing, and when I figured out where you'd gone," Josh sighed. "You're always going to charge in and do what needs to be done in situations like that aren't you, whatever the risk to yourself?"

"Josh, it was because of me that he was involved, so yes, if I put someone in harm's way, then I'll do what I have to do to get them out of it. I know you would do the same, so don't lecture me." Olivia bristled a little.

"I wasn't going to lecture sweetheart. I was going to suggest enrolling yourself in a really good martial arts class that will teach you a myriad of self defense maneuvers that will greatly reduce my stress levels and potential grey hairs."

"Oh," Olivia said in a considerably calmer voice, "I think I'd like that." She glanced at Josh out of the corner of her eye and saw him glancing at her and they both burst out laughing.

"So are you going to try to go back to work as usual, now that Corwin is gone and everyone knows you don't need the job?" Olivia patted his leg in sympathy. "I know how hard you tried to keep them from finding out that you have money."

Josh blew out a hard breath, "No, I think that train has gone. It wouldn't be the same, because I wouldn't be treated like just one of the guys anymore; I'd be the rich guy who doesn't belong there." He was silent for a moment, "What would you think if I said I'd like for us to start that detective agency we talked about once upon a time, before we even knew each other well?"

Olivia yipped and jumped up and down in her seat in excitement, causing Molly to bark and Sheyna to yowl in protest from her crate.

"Yes! That would be wicked perfect Josh! We'll make a great team, you know," she said happily, hugging him around the waist as he drove.

"As long as we don't have a wreck on the way back to town," Josh laughed, trying not to swerve all over the empty road. "We'll need to look into getting our licenses and figure out all the ins and outs of the actual business end of it too, but I think it will be something we can do together to make a difference and I think we'll be good at it. If we solved this convoluted case, we can solve anything," he laughed.

"I know, right?" Olivia laughed. "Let's see if I have it all straight in my head.

Larsson, Jamison and the Olanders were all in on the Olander robbery. Olander was also cheating the insurance company by selling off the original coins he'd insured, then claiming them as stolen. That was his cut in the deal.

Larsson and Jamison were supposed to split the rest of the loot, but when Larsson got caught, Jamison took it all and went underground, changing his name to an alias and trying to hide from everyone who'd known him before, so he could keep it all," she paused to breathe.

"When Larsson got off parole, he went looking for Jamison and tried to make him give him his half, but he refused and Larsson killed him. I was there, so he couldn't search the shop then, so he broke into the shop later after things settled down a little and found some of the stash, including a case of the fake coins. He took those with him on his bicycle, but couldn't carry more. When he realized they were the fake coins, and he couldn't get access to the rest of the loot in the shop, because the police had removed it, he decided to try blackmailing Olander over the fake coins.

That was a big mistake, because Olander is not a nice man, and he doesn't like anyone to cross him. Olander threatened to kill him, stole the fake coins back from him at gunpoint, and forced him to help him and Elsa break into the shop again and then to steal my Suburban, and after all that he killed him anyway just because he'd crossed him once." Olivia stopped for breath.

"So it was Larsson who tried to break in to your house, grab you from the Suburban that time, and finally did break in, but Olander who tried to grab your purse at the yard sale, killed Larsson and kidnapped Tiny." Josh said, breaking in. "If you hadn't gone looking for antiques at Jamison's shop that day, you'd never have been involved in all of this, and we would probably never gotten it solved, especially since the former captain was in on it."

"So much greed," Olivia said sadly. They had gotten away with so much money already, but they all wanted more. Avarice is not a pretty vice."

"Hmm—antiques and avarice—sounds like a title for a book, doesn't it?" Josh put his arm around Olivia and she leaned against him contentedly.

Made in the USA
Lexington, KY
10 January 2017